"Valentine can handle the situation," Amelia said softly. The amusement in her pale blue eyes was unmistakable. "She needs no back-up from your people."

Sergeant Gerry didn't know what to do. Or say. It was as if the challenge and the gesture of support had gone unnoticed. Or had been waved — or laughed — away.

To her surprise, Amelia continued. "There are nineteen individuals in the house. Plus the President's son. A quarter of these are most likely staff members for the house, or personal servants. Eight are fugitives, all on the Commission's Most Wanted List of Undesirables. Four are androids and two are aliens."

"How many people does your — Valentine . . . have?" The question came out breathlessly. *Aliens? Robots and aliens?*

"Half that number." Amelia was clearly not worried. "Why don't you tell the President that if all goes well, the matter should be resolved within . . . minutes."

PRIORITIES

THE CONTROLLERS SERIES

BY LYNDA LYONS

PRIORITIES

THE CONTROLLERS SERIES

BY LYNDA LYONS

The Naiad Press, Inc.
1990

Printed in the United States of America
First Edition

Edited by Katherine V. Forrest
Cover design by Pat Tong and Bonnie Liss
   (Phoenix Graphics)
Typeset by Sandi Stancil

Library of Congress Cataloging-in-Publication Data

Lyons, Lynda, 1949—
   Priorities / by Lynda Lyons.
        p.   cm.
   ISBN 0-941483-66-5
   I. Title.
PS3562.Y4485P73   1990
813'.54--dc20   89-48963
                                                            CIP

To Boots

whose Tara inspired Valentine
. . . and me.

About the Author

Lynda Lyons, according to a friend, is "the kind of person everyone wishes they knew — a true original." Although she was born in the heart of the midwest, Linda brings to mind a Renaissance persona more comfortable in the salons of Europe than the Bible Belt. "She is a multi-talented mystery," a friend says, "who seeks honesty in the world around her — and is scrupulously fair. She relishes the opportunity to challenge the assumptions we live with." Ms. Lyons uses the power of fiction to breathe life into new worlds — and new people. A firm believer that unconventional characters drive unpredictable story lines, she wrote *Priorities* as future fiction "because the characters demanded a change in venue."

Prologue

I am in love with Amelia.

(To know this gives me a thrill . . . but what does it mean? Is it . . . could it be as true as it feels? Yet it seems to have no sexuality! Sensuality, yes . . . but to link "erotic" with Amelia somehow seems unkind. Eventually you'll see what I mean.)

She's never what anyone expects — because they see Valentine first.

Valentine looks like the winning contestant in the beauty pageants they still have in those little rural towns. She's nearly six feet tall, slender and shapely, with hair the color of golden-tipped flame, skin so pale it looks translucent and eyes the color of . . . well, blue. The sky or the ocean. Round, intelligent and intense like they're trying to outdo the fragility of her features or the plushness of her mouth.

Bear with me here. I can think words like "plush" about Valentine, you see, because I can't use even one of them with Amelia.

I'd heard about Valentine before I ever got there. Two months out of school, I got a job in Input at the International Control and Registry Center — government-owned, which meant lower pay, but opportunities galore. Working at the ICRC was also lots more interesting than sitting in some human data processing warehouse for a few more dollars an hour.

Valentine was well known; her reputation from the Academy had made it to the ICRC before she did. She had graduated first in her class and was the first woman to become a second- and then first-grade squadron leader within months of her original assignment. But she'd have been singled out even if she'd been a nondecorated paper-pusher. She looked like an updated version of one of those characters from a priceless old Action comic book — all bust, legs and statuesque posture, red hair flowing, her tall shapely body doing the most astonishing things to that otherwise drab uniform the Controllers wear — dark green trim on drab green jumpsuits with brown government-issued holsters for weapons, and narrow belts with all sorts of strange scary looking things hanging off it. Weapons, I'd heard. Bondian gadgets they used in the field.

The ICRC's Input Division, like most others, looked out on the main bank of glass 'vators, onto the traffic coming and going to the executive offices upstairs and the labs and ports downstairs. Since everybody used those 'vators, we never lost interest in seeing who was on them — especially with the possibility of seeing a captured android. Sometimes they were brought up still functional (though they weren't supposed to be — either brought up in the main 'vators or still functional inside the building, I mean) and we'd all hold our breath to see if it was a true renegade, with an arm missing or black patches blasted through it, or acting erratically (stomping, head twisting or unnaturally cocked . . . benign behavior actually, but pretty exciting for those of us who had never seen a defective droid.)

The captured androids — and Valentine — these were the draws. The first time she came up on the 'vator, she was pointed out to me immediately. Not that she needed to be. If she was aware of twenty pairs of eyes straining to get a look at her, she didn't show it. She didn't even look in our direction. She was with a subordinate who stood slightly behind her. He saw us; there was a smug, if well-checked, grin on his face. She didn't seem to be focusing on anything in particular — just stood there, with that strikingly rigid posture. She even looked a little bored.

I was impressed; and I wasn't the only one. Aside from her looks, there was something about Valentine. She transcended her womanliness in that familiar uniform with the understated stitching above her right breast pocket that signified her position. She carried herself in a very special way. If I could identify it, I guess it would be similar to those old-time movies where beautiful woman come gliding down long, curving staircases, back stiff, head up, knowing their femininity, their beauty, the appeal of their self-confidence.

Valentine exuded self-confidence, all right. It didn't seem to have much to do with how she looked, though; but I wasn't sure. At eighteen, I didn't have a whole lot of self-confidence in my analysis of people — particularly a person that unique — but Valentine was a highlight that first summer.

The ICRC level on which I had entered was a transient one; while we inputed data from the files from other departments, our machines were also analyzing us. Speed, accuracy, comprehension and condensation abilities of each Inputer were registered and when the postings for new positions would go up, those facts were taken into consideration along with the other, usual stuff like absence, tardiness, cooperation — that sort of thing.

I was reasonably fast, very accurate, and had a knack for editing some of the more windy, overly formalized or hastily scrawled notes. When a position opened up in Decoding, I requested and got it without too much trouble. I liked it so much I thought I might just want to work there right up through pension. Of course, this was partly because it was my first taste of what it felt like to get closer to the heart of the organization.

In Decoding, I met my first agent, my first working (non-domestic or entertainment) android, my first spy (not that he introduced himself as such!), a couple of Controllers and . . . I met Valentine herself.

4

Well — not exactly met. No one said "I'd like you to meet Jann, Valentine . . . Valentine, Jann." What actually happened was, I was nearest the door when she walked in, disc in hand, an urgent look on her face — and she handed it to me and ordered, "Do this one."

I'd only been there a few weeks but I knew damned well I wasn't authorized to do sensitive decoding. The rule was, you did the garbage until your supervisor decided you were ready; and then you were fed small chances here and there until they felt you were ready for Classification. It could take six months or two years, depending upon the benevolence or aspirations of the individual supervisor, if you know what I mean.

My supervisor, Marjorie, was as unthreatened by the new people in the department as she was by the most complicated codes. Without hesitation she flipped the override button on my machine — I'd not even known it had that capability — to cancel out what I'd been working on, and said, "Priority, Jann."

I took the disc Valentine held out — trying hard not to look up into her face — and turned back to my machine, my heart thumping. Sudden fears became little tornados whirling around inside my head. What she had given me was probably incredibly important — what if I screwed up? I could feel (or thought I could) Valentine's impatient breath warming my neck. She was a one-shot woman — that much I could safely guess. The consequences of a foul-up seemed astronomical. It didn't occur to me that Marjorie wasn't about to let something like that happen; I was punching the buttons on the keyboard

5

with the chilled fingers of someone who's absolutely sure the fate of the world rests on her head and her head alone.

The message was simple and unsensational. A brief reminder of a meeting; the longitude and latitude; a date four days in the future. I didn't even have to go into the Q file for assistance, as the coding wasn't what I'd thought it would be: android to android (serious stuff). Still, it was a meeting between someone and someone — or someone and something — and I'd cracked and analyzed it fast without having to reroute once.

While the decoded words hung on my screen, I could feel her lean down to read it with me. I took a tiny, almost unconscious whiff of the air, curious about what kind of perfume she would wear. Nothing. A little bit of leather, maybe, but I might have been influenced by hearing the holster crackle as she leaned in.

I saw Valentine quite a few times after that. She always said the same thing: "Priority, Jann." I think her business-like attitude helped me bypass what might otherwise have been an infatuation based strictly on her beauty.

I'm not saying the woman had no personality; I have no doubt I was introduced only to her "work" side — the unwavering professionalism of a tunnel-visioned career officer who neither seemed especially disturbed by or responsive to my gropings at familiarity with her. ("Hi, Valentine. Pretty hot out there today, isn't it?" She might nod or she might not.)

I quickly grasped how inconsequential I was to her. And the snobbery was not due to position but rather my irrelevance as a source. I was a means to information, nothing more. If I wasn't there when she entered the department — always with that same urgency — she did not hesitate to approach someone else, and always with the same words: "Do this one." If by chance she heard the Decoder's name, she would remember and use it the next time — but there was nothing personal about it.

It didn't take hearing more of the endless stream of stories about her for me to believe that Valentine was every inch the shrewd, heroic, clever and patriotic soldier they said she was. That she confronted the most unpredictable of droids with a bravery that almost always went hand-in-hand with danger. That in the field she was imaginative to the point of recklessness. That her accomplishments had far surpassed all those before her and probably would those behind her, for a long time.

This is what I mean when I say people see Valentine first. But I also realized quickly that she had other limitations. As a human being, she was a closed door. The ultimate Controller with an image that had come to represent the entire Division. Being a Controller was no longer just a job and a dangerous one at that. No longer merely a patriotic position. It was a doorway into Romance. I hear the Academies are filled with as many ambitious, talented young women as muscular, adventurous young men these days . . . largely through her influence. But if the words "Valentine" and "Romance" had become synonymous, the reality in her case was a far different truth.

As for me, I liked being a Decoder, especially the challenge. The money was good, and as I mentioned earlier, the opportunities were there. You could even do field duty as an on-line translator. Or really "travel to distant lands and planets — meet exciting people and work with ambassadors in the most exotic of cultures," as the government ads claimed. By the time I turned nineteen, I had the prestige of a Senior Decoder, because of my luck in being classified early — due to that encounter with Valentine — and I'd made quite a few friends by then. I was comfortable.

And then I met Amelia.

I really shouldn't say "met," because it sounds like she was new. She wasn't. She'd been there for about four years — before me and before Valentine. Amelia was Valentine's boss.

She was also an android. Maybe. She sure wasn't supposed to be.

It was about the biggest debate you could get into around the place and had been since she'd been appointed as Director.

Since the whole point of the Controllers Division was to bring down renegade androids, the public had been pretty outraged at that appointment. How could you possibly have a suspected droid — no matter how sophisticated — spearheading the operation? There were stories about her being a human-turned-lab-concoction after sustaining a lethal injury in the field, stories that had her being artificial this or that, stories of a here-and-there replacement job — too many stories. It was interesting both that there were so *many* rumors, and that there was no official background on Amelia — no top-level leaks or public statements despite the fact that the ICRC Directorship had long been a source of heated controversy because of its importance. The Director was appointed jointly by the President and the Committee, and the power and responsibility of the position had grown as quickly as the android industry itself.

Moral and ethical questions regarding limb and organ replacements — artificial, as opposed to cellular — had grown more complex over the years; the courts had become clogged with related cases. Who, for example, was responsible for serious damage done during an assault on an officer when the five-foot-two-inch-tall perpetrator had two artificial limbs, the equivalent — the police argued — of carrying two concealed weapons? The defense attorney argued that computer analyses from the medical supplier showed the proper strength allotted the man for size and weight in the first place — and tests following his arrest didn't match them.

My favorite part of this particular story was that the guy's lawyer not only got the charges dropped, he ended up successfully suing MedLimb for breach of contract, negligence, and undue mental stress.

What does all this have to do with Amelia? Over the years, the courts started using figures — percentages of artificiality — to identify legal responsibility. That's not how we looked at it when we were kids. Who hasn't gone to school with a poor kid everyone called a droid because he'd had one too many operations? Like one in my class who'd been in a bad accident. Instead of repeated cloning surgeries as he grew, his family had gone for less expensive materials — visible temporary replacements. It may have saved them thousands of dollars, but it made his life hell. Of course, he fell well within the parameters the government used to determine humanity; that was never the point, though. Like everybody else, I've heard stories about people who got accidentally turned into androids — they'd had so many replacements and eventually went psychotic but couldn't be destroyed because of their families — but, who knows if you can really believe such a thing. People don't become androids, no matter how many parts are replaced. It's just the kind of stuff people always "hear" about, even if there's no truth to it.

But stories like this added to the mystique of Amelia. It didn't help when a reporter had come right out at the press conference when Amelia was appointed and asked point-blank, "What exactly is Amelia, statistically speaking?" The President had hesitated — you have to remember that this man has a tendency to be so direct, he's actually a little hard to decipher at times, especially when he answers in that sarcastic tone of his. He looked right into the lens and said, "You might as well call her an android and get it over with." That "say-everything-but-nothing" statement shut everybody up for a minute . . . and then he closed the conference, and that was that. The President wouldn't even respond to those kinds of questions after that. It didn't stop the reporters from asking but the only statistics he ever refers to is the ICRC's dramatic success rate for capturing renegades and defectives and the black-marketeers who make a career of selling them.

Working at the ICRC had increased my curiosity about Amelia. I could never uncover how the question about her had come up in the first place. To encounter the impressive Valentine and know that not only was she second in command — but almost fanatical in her loyalty to her boss . . . well, what did that tell you? Could such a well-known robot-killer (I know, childish slang; okay, "dedicated professional") be that loyal to a person who was herself primarily a droid? It didn't seem likely.

Most of the people I worked with — and I — didn't believe an actual android could run an operation like the ICRC. It was too complex, too incredibly well organized. People's lives depended upon the smallest decisions and too many of those decisions could not be data-based; they were judgment calls, decisions that required the sensitivity and humanity and even the political awareness of a human.

So my curiosity had pretty much dwindled into a cornerstone summed up by the question, *"What the hell would Valentine's boss be like?"*

I may be giving the impression my workdays were spent star-gazing and gossiping, which is not the case at all. The Controllers — certainly the center of excitement around the place — were often all out in the field. You could feel the difference in the whole building then. The ports downstairs were quiet, decoding was routine, sent in from field vehicles and returned the same way. Even the cafeteria seemed quieter, emptier, most of us sitting around in small groups talking about last night's date, a new game room, an idiot promoted internally who was now causing us grief.

The higher (mostly desk-bound) staff wore uniforms, so it wasn't unusual to see the green jumpsuit on someone, even when the troops, as we called them, were out of the building. But it had never occurred to me that Amelia would wear one, too.

I noticed her because she wasn't wearing a holster. Staffers wore one (empty, I don't know why). But the woman in front of me in the food line, on a slow Tuesday afternoon, didn't wear one at all. She wore regulation boots, not as spit-shined as most I'd seen, no jewelry, no watch. I don't know why I noticed these particular things about her. They seemed out of context, somehow. She seemed out of context.

I'll tell you what she looked like: she was short. Shorter than me, anyway, and I'm five-foot-eight. Her shoulder-length hair was light brown and kind of frizzy on the ends, a little flyaway and drab, like hair gets when it's dry or you've spent too much time in the sun.

She was built perfectly — and I know that word is misleading. Remember I said I couldn't use words like plush? Amelia was . . . symmetrical. Shoulders, breasts, stomach, hips, legs, arms — if I had not focused on these parts, I wouldn't have seen them individually. That's how perfect she was.

I found myself leaning against the counter on which I'd been sliding my tray, trying to see her face. Her profile came around and it was just as symmetrical: non-denominational nose, a mouth without fullness, a chin of perfect structure and no personality.

Looking at her gave me the chills. They weren't bad chills; it was like when you're just going along and you come up on something totally unexpected . . .

so that you feel yourself react but it doesn't make sense. Your body knows something and your mind knows something, but neither of them are bringing their knowledge together into a concrete form. Adrenaline went straight to my thighs and turned my lower legs to mush; I wrapped my hands around the bars on each side of my tray for support.

She turned and looked at me. Her eyes were blue like Valentine's, but a real shock in her face. They were light blue — not that ocean blue that's soft, not an intense blue that strikes you as sexy or eerie, depending on the person; just blue. Like a color that didn't belong. Her skin was the same colorless pale flesh as the palm of my hand. She had small lines at the edge of her eyes and her mouth — lines I hadn't seen from her profile. Her cheekbones were sharp. Not an extra ounce of weight on this woman.

I don't know how I knew she was Amelia. But I knew. Somehow, I croaked "Hi" and then — for the first and only time around Amelia — I was scared.

I've thought about why a lot since that day. She was the top-ranked superior in a quasi-military government organization, which is certainly a reason for nervousness. Or maybe because, standing there, I did think, "She's a droid!" My mind just couldn't correlate all the information it was trying to receive. What was she, to be both android and the director of an organization specializing in destroying androids? The super creation of fiction, come to life and blocking my path, aimed right at me?

That adrenaline went from my thighs right up through my body. I felt the sweat break out on the back of my neck. You understand, I'm not saying any of this was justified. All she did was look at me. And then she said "Hi" and she smiled. The lines beside her mouth creased right into laugh lines and drew her mouth into a completely unsuspicious-looking smile.

"Jann," I said. "Decoding" — and jammed my hand toward her.

She took it. Her hand was small. And warm. And just the slightest bit moist. "Amelia," said she.

She turned away and moved on.

I hustled up beside her again, foregoing butter for my roll. "Hot out today, isn't it?" I asked with all the urgency of someone who desperately needed an answer. I felt as if something I couldn't get a grip on was pulling all this out of me. I was reacting to her like she was a magnet. I didn't miss the irony.

"Very," the possible android said. "I'm looking forward to autumn." She took a steaming cup of tea from the dispenser, offered me a piece of the earlier smile, and again moved on.

I watched her hold her security I.D. card up for the woman at the register. The woman did not look at it. Or at Amelia. Her eyes anxiously sought out the next person in line. Me. I wondered how often this happened to Amelia. Guilt by gossip. I hurried up, scrambling for my card as Amelia, tea in hand, moved away.

She sat at a table near the window and I followed her. Somewhere there are rules about fraternizing — unwritten and unspoken. There are lines you don't cross in companies, mine or any other. I don't know whether I was propelled by rebellion or something else entirely. But I found myself next to her table, maybe afraid to come right out and ask, but I was waiting and she looked up quickly enough.

"Would you like to sit down?"

I sat. My hands hovered over my tray, moving, touching, shifting fork and spoon, busying themselves while my full concentration was on her.

Her face was turned toward the window. Her elbows rested on the table. She held the cup up with one hand, cradling it with the other — the cup in line with her chin. She sipped. Steam curled hotly before her face. She did not flinch or squint or attempt to protect her lips from the hot liquid in any way. She sipped again and then drank deeply.

I knew I was staring at her, that my hands had even stopped their cover of movements over my tray and now lay on each side of it, as contemplative and silenced as I felt. She slowly brought her attention from the tea to me and met my bold stare with her own quiet gaze.

And then she said the most bizarre thing anyone had ever said to me. "That is a very charming angle of tooth," she said. Her head dipped slightly toward it.

I don't know if you're going to understand this, but I'm going to try and explain . . . what she was referring to, and how it affected me. See, I have a front tooth that overlaps the other. My mother does, too. Ever since I was little, there's been a silly family joke over it. My mom wanted to get me restructuring; my father said no. He said it was cute — just like my mom's — and he always teased her that that's why he'd fallen in love with her; it made her special. And that someday, somebody would fall in love with

15

me and they'd find it just as endearing as he did on my mom. A dumb little thing between them, really. What did I care when I was a kid?

Eventually, I did kind of wish my teeth were straight like my friends' all were — it was one of those things I meant to get around to — getting it fixed, I mean. It wasn't the kind of thing a regular person would mention though. Personality, hair, eyes — okay; but "You got a cute crooked tooth there"?

Do you understand why this made me feel strange? I've been around android domestics and teachers and clerks lots of times in my life. They don't say things like that . . . personal things. I mean you have to work at the wording to even get an android to comment on whether or not your personal appearance is satisfactory . . . let alone hearing one say something unsolicited and imaginative. Even thoughtful . . .

The chill was revived. It definitely wasn't bad this time. I felt excited. That adrenaline wasn't letting go. I was trying to suppress a desire to barrage her with questions, like you could with an android, while reminding myself that she was the Director, for God's sake.

Amelia interrupted this vivid internal reaction by setting down her empty cup and standing up. "It was nice meeting you, Jann."

It caught me off guard. Her leaving so soon. I immediately felt like I'd lost my big chance though I didn't know for what . . .

I was left to watch her walk away.

* * * * *

I found myself looking for her everywhere. And I didn't go to lunch at a time other than the time I'd seen her — but I never saw her in the lunchroom again.

The "debates" that were always arising over her started to freeze me up. I didn't argue, I didn't rail . . . because I didn't have anything to rail out with. But inside I felt anger and . . . hurt. A hell of a lot of confusion.

I couldn't put it into perspective, but I had this . . . protective feeling about her. I started to think of her as very special — and it had something to do with Valentine. As if my mind could only draw a comparison between the two unique females I had met in my life. Just those two.

Doesn't make sense, does it? I wouldn't argue with a soul about the plainness of Amelia next to her second-in-command. Amelia is plain — next to any woman. Valentine is a glaring spotlight on the fact. Or so you would think. Because I finally saw them together. And that's the night the confusion turned the corner to the something else I feel.

It was actually a very unspectacular event, like so many monumental things are.

They came into the decoding room together. Even I didn't see Amelia at first, which makes me wonder about other times when I thought Valentine was alone. I was in a corner, running finished precodes through the shredder, when I heard Valentine come in. See, the noise level changes when she comes in.

17

Chairs scrape, people shut up. You can almost hear the heads turning. Valentine handed the disc to be decoded to the man at the nearest machine. She looked exceptional that day. The fiery hair flowed around her face, making those features stand out even from where I was twenty feet away.

I saw the inputer nervously take the disc and Marjorie's predictable approach. And then I saw Amelia. She stood just behind and to the side of Valentine. She should have been dwarfed and erased; she wasn't; not to me, anyway. She stood quietly and her hands rested loosely in the hip pockets of her jumpsuit . . . casual and inappropriate, as if she were in disguise.

Valentine stood as she always did, arms as stiff as her spine, eyes glittering with impatience, her entire attention riveted on the decoder's screen.

I could see Marjorie's sudden, unusual hesitation as she saw that Valentine was not alone. A look crossed her face; I've wondered since if it was the way I looked the first time I'd encountered Amelia. Marjorie made small polite talk with Valentine as respect dictated . . . but to Amelia, she said nothing. Valentine nodded curtly back at whatever was said or asked.

And then Amelia saw me. The smile moved into her face. "Hello, Jann," she said, and I knew her voice was covering the twenty feet between us without rising, without effort. "It's finally here, isn't it?" she asked. "Autumn."

Valentine's head snapped up sharply from her concentration on the Decoder, her attention following

18

Amelia's voice. Her look was both abrasive and shrewd. Now *that* was a real chill . . . those sky-blue iridescent eyes raking me over. Looking at me for the first time. I found myself wondering if the human-made beings who had run amok "out there" experience anything like my reaction when they encounter her head-on.

"Yes." My voice came out a lot stronger than I expected it to. My eyes found Amelia's — I ignored Valentine. "I was really looking forward to it, too."

I smiled. She grinned at the same moment. It was definitely a grin — which is a lot different than a smile — and I'm not going to even try to explain that. She glanced down at the floor afterward and I knew her small hands were curling tightly inside her pockets. From shyness.

That was it. A couple of minutes later, she was gone. They both were.

Valentine always comes to me for decoding now. Asks for me by name. And when I say something to her, she answers in more than one word. Know why? Curiosity. She is *curious* about me now.

I know how crazy that sounds . . . but I figure if I see the two of them together even one more time — and Amelia initiates another shy dialogue with me, no matter how small — Valentine will go even further. She may even ask me out socially . . . just because Amelia has noticed me.

I'm sure I'll go. I'd be crazy not to.

Amelia is special. And I'll tell you this: I'm not the only one who thinks so. I know that now. I just haven't quite figured out yet . . . what it means.

—1—

The visual was perfect. Middle-aged female, hands
in lap. Young male, white coated, Instaplabak recorder
visible in the palm of his hand. When the woman
spoke, her voice was eager. She was enjoying the
interview. She wanted to talk.

*"I have these dreams. Romantic dreams. The . . .
other person is someone I know . . . not well. An
acquaintance. But in the dream I really care about
them. And they care about me."* Hands in lap
twisting, fingers intertwining. Lens not focusing on
the display.

"Males? Females?

"Men."

"But in the dream?" He'd missed it. The silent and quick "of course" hidden behind the word "men" . . . A predictable and important rule for an android. Opposite gender. Procreation. To a program attempting to grasp the concept of Life, this would be the cornerstone of Its fantasy. The precedent was set. The research tech would not be catching any of it.

"In the dream, I don't feel as they do. They're focused on me . . . but it doesn't matter. It's just as romantic."

"Even if it's one-sided? His analysis was somewhere else entirely.

"Yes. It's an adventure."

"An adventure?"

"It seems like that. It feels different . . . not just in the way dreams feel differently because they're dreams. It has a different level of . . . excitement. I feel excited all during the dream. The me in the dream does."

"Sexually? His voice was appallingly calm. The voice of a novice. Of ignorance.

"A little. Some." She obviously felt safe. Her wording was careful. But the desire to talk, to share, to boast, overrode caution. *"They're very attractive to me in this dream, whether the emotional feelings are reciprocated on my part or not. That's the excitement. The chemistry."*

"Do you become involved with them sexually?"

"Never." Her mouth said one thing. Her eyes, another.

"Do you experience regret at having left the dream?"

"I feel loss, yes. I miss them . . . only it becomes less specific. Because I know immediately that the object of my feelings in the dream . . . isn't someone that I will feel that way about the next time I see him. I know it's not an . . ." The hesitation was there but not long enough. She wanted desperately to use the word in connection to herself. *". . . unconscious attraction to him. So my reaction to the dream takes on a different shape. I miss what I . . ."* quick glance at the camera *". . . felt. Should I be telling you all this?"*

Amelia Roberts' index finger brushed the keyboard and the images faded until the screen was white. She remained sitting, her attention seemingly still on the screen, her thoughts far from the empty square. It was not the first time she had seen the interview.

Her fingers played over the panel, fingertips not quite coming to rest on the keys. She had already replayed the tech's test evaluation, had listened to the GEMCOM analysis. Neither interpretation disagreed with what she had heard, but both were irrelevant to what she had seen. More decisively she touched one button, tapped another, and allowed the side of her hand to come to rest on the bar on the far right of the keyboard.

A young and eager voice shot out of the speaker: "Did you call me?"

"Please," Amelia answered, unable to avoid seeing in her mind's eye the hesitation of the girl in the other room as she deciphered what the "please" meant, seeing her straighten abruptly, rolling back her chair, glancing at her recorder, considering it, dismissing it, and then moving more quickly — finally confident of what was wanted of her, but doubly

expression in them could become. It would state her height and weight but would say nothing about the way her body moved, how graceful and well-functioning her form was . . . or why it suddenly came to odds with her legs and feet . . . No explanation at all of why Amelia's office, Amelia's presence, caused the phenomenon to occur more times than not.

The file would not explain why the light skin on Jennifer's arms was covered with a fine mist of delicate hairs or how the skin of the face was flawless. How small and female was the nose. How the mouth, almost always slightly open, lips parted, conveying a certain breathless quality — continually caused Amelia concern that more oxygen than normal was perhaps mysteriously required by this one at times. Nor would the file impart any information as to how Jennifer subtly transferred this breathlessness to Amelia when in her presence.

Jennifer was waiting, caught in the silence of Amelia's study.

Amelia could see the look of renewed confidence begin to dissolve. Confusion brought Jennifer's lashes down, and the faint pink tinge up into her cheeks.

"That's all," Amelia said.

"That's all?" Jennifer echoed.

Amelia nodded.

Jennifer rose, the movement awkward, as if in belated response to an intention to do so a split second before. She half turned, laid the pad down on the edge of the desk and then picked it up. Her mouth opened to question and then closed firmly. She tore off the page on which she had written and laid the pad back down. Turning again, she moved and then reeled back, thrusting the pen down on the pad, her glance at Amelia apologetic, one edge of her mouth trying to tug her lips into a matching smile.

Again Jennifer moved, wheeling away with more determination. Again she turned toward the woman sitting quietly on the other side of the desk, and placed her hand firmly on the pad. "Thank you." She pushed the pad across the surface of the desk toward Amelia.

Amelia had been watching the mouth, watching the separation between the lips. The white teeth. The small tip of tongue dancing to the edge of the teeth and disappearing again. The breath held or taken or given — Amelia could not be sure — the twists and turns of her body in actions performed separately. As individual thoughts. Your pad. Your pen. *Your* pad . . . *here.* (I-will-be-brave-and-I-will-be-kind-and-I-will-hand-it-to-you.)

Brave.

Amelia leaned forward, breaking Jennifer's routine by reclaiming the pad with her fingertips. Jennifer left quickly then. Without another word, another glance, another display of uncertainty.

Amelia still leaned forward. Her hand still touched the edge of the pad. Slowly, very gently, she pressed her fingertips against the paper. A faint current could be felt as warmth against her fingers. It tickled her palm. Danced feather-light across her flesh. Breathed from the paper to her skin more hotly and then evaporated.

Abruptly she withdrew her hand. She tossed the pad into her desk drawer, her actions snapping back to the flatscreen and the business at hand.

"Oh no, you can't bother Amelia with *that!*" Jennifer's voice contained the shock she felt at the caller's question. "If you're having problems in your department, you'll have to go to your supervisor. Amelia is the *Director*. She's *much* too busy for things like that!" She disconnected and returned her attention to the files.

The C-shaped desk which curved around her was covered with information connected to the Doctor. Classified documents had been removed from their seals and were stacked by year and then by crime. It wasn't easy to find the one Amelia wanted.

Look at the file, Amelia had said. Even hours later, it was still hard to believe she had been given permission to do such a thing — and so casually!

Jennifer bit her lip happily, staring at the organized stacks — not knowing where to start, delighted at the opportunity and the honor she perceived it to be. That honor far outweighed her interest in what was actually in the files, though she savored the fact that they were all here, open and available to her, reminding her all over again of how lucky she was to be working for Amelia . . . to be sitting in this office between Amelia and the world . . . to be *helping* Amelia. Schooled but limited, she had no illusions about her talents. Neither had the Commission people when she'd started work here.

Her family had been as excited as she when she'd gotten the job in Records. Inputing, they called it, when all it really was was shifting storage copy to deeper storage. Not even the originals.

The handset chimed and Jennifer picked it up, unable to get out a greeting before the words bit into her ear: "You've been looking for me." It sounded dangerously close to an accusation and Jennifer's throat tightened immediately at the sound of Valentine's voice.

"Yes, I . . . Amelia . . . she . . ." Jennifer struggled to swallow the nervousness the other woman never failed to trigger in her.

"She wants to see me?"

Jennifer imagined Valentine already dumping files, or turning a ship around — sending subordinates to make the jump back from out there. "Oh no no no . . ." Jennifer's words tumbled all over themselves in her eagerness to divert Valentine from leaping too far toward a wrong conclusion. "She doesn't . . . I mean, she does . . . but not now . . . I mean . . . now . . . as soon as possible . . . but not until . . ." She pulled in a breath, trying to calm herself. "I have to look over these first. And — and brief you," she finished weakly, instantly overcome with a hot flush of embarrassment. Brief *Valentine*? She heard a soft snort of disgust in her ear.

"I'm coming in," Valentine said shortly. The connection was cut.

"Damn." Jennifer's fists came down on the desk top in frustration. "Damn, damn, damn."

Her hands went to the stacks, moving over them helplessly. She would never have time now. Valentine

29

would be here in minutes, standing over her impatiently, making her feel so stupid . . . and she'd never have a chance to explain, to do everything just as Amelia had told her to do . . . *Why couldn't she deal with that woman?* Because Valentine was everything she wasn't?

She brought her hands up, propping her elbows on the desk, knuckles pressing against her cheeks in frustration. Valentine made her feel like such a . . . nothing.

She had begun to think that feeling was behind her. Being selected as Amelia Roberts' secretary was easily the most unexpected and wonderful thing that had ever happened. She recalled the day it had happened with a memory as romantic and delicious as a first kiss.

It had been four minutes after five on the fourth day of a rollover rotating shift. Anticipating eight days off had helped her to generously overlook the time. (No overtime allowed in Inputing. Ever.) Half a page of numbers remained and she was making the insertions in record time.

She became aware of someone standing behind her. "Not now." She assumed it was Connie. Or Bev. They saved her from public transit with their offered rides.

"That data is six years old," the voice warned from behind her.

She glanced back. Nope, it wasn't Connie or Bev. Yes, she glimpsed the khaki; no it didn't matter — sometimes things like that just didn't register. It wasn't as if those so high up in the organization, despite their authority and rank, had any relationship with such a lowly department as hers.

"Course it is," she laughed. "Don't bother me."

Silence followed. She fouled the numbers, corrected them in a simultaneous motion, flew on.

"You're very fast."

"The best."

"I can see."

"Don't flirt. I'm on free time." It wasn't like her to say such a thing — she tossed it off with the recklessness that came with being off the clock. And she just assumed — without thinking it out, of course — just assumed it was one of them. Despite the uniform . . . no, things just did not register with her sometimes.

The numbers fouled again, erased, a line disappearing, running backwards, error, error, error. Not her fault. A glitch lying in wait to contaminate eight hours of document. "No!" she squealed and slammed her palm down on the oversized safeguard button. An arm clad in the dull green uniform of the Controllers reached over her shoulder and touched the keyboard. Jennifer smacked it aside.

Smacked the hand away.

She pushed the retrieval, her index finger holding down the second key in the sequence. The information reappeared and settled in — locked, salvaged from the graveyard to which it had been heading.

"You got it back."

"Course I did." She spoke more pleasantly, less teasingly, her eyes on the screen, fingers moving quickly to finish, already sorry for her abruptness.

"How did you figure out you could do that?"

Jennifer laughed at that. "I'm prone to mistakes," she explained. "I figure the first thing I had to do

31

was learn how to correct 'em before anybody found out I make 'em."

The woman emitted a soft laugh. "A wise policy. Though considering the number of mistakes you've made during the time I've been watching you, in comparison to the data you've inputed, I'd say your error ratio is actually less than .0001%. Less than average."

"Spoken like a true droid."

To this day, the very memory of having said that made her color. It was not that she'd thought — she hadn't been thinking at all! It was just a saying. Just slang.

She hadn't even noticed the long silence behind her before the woman spoke again. "What is your name?"

"Jenn. Jennifer Taylor." The codes were almost at an end.

"What are your plans, Jennifer?"

Not a chance. That's what she'd thought. The women Controllers had the worst reputations — too hard, too experienced, too old in ways that had nothing to do with age. She wouldn't socialize with one if the best of them got on her knees and begged. Intentionally, still distracted by finalizing the input, she'd tossed off an answer to a question she knew the woman wasn't asking her. "To make enough money to buy my own common car. My own place. To weigh a hundred pounds and have six weeks of vacation every year."

But it was, apparently, just what the woman was asking her. "I'm looking for a personal assistant. Upstairs."

"Stand in line." Another toss-off. Another dumb phrase.

"The salary as my secretary would be considerably more than what you're making now."

"Secretary?" Finished, she'd swiveled, her knees bumping the woman's, forcing her to step back. "Nobody has a secretary anymore. They went out with copiers and paper clips."

"I need one. Someone to receive people, keep me informed."

The face was nicer than she expected. Less striking, more nice. The stature seemed less than that of a Controller though. She had actually thought that . . .

"How much?" It had not been a serious question, but the answer had so surprised Jennifer that it had jolted something in her. All of the facts, as they should have been seen in the first place, rattled around into a suddenly very clear and completed picture. "You're Amelia!" she had gasped and had instantly felt the hot flush flood through her body as she remembered everything she'd said and done in the minutes before.

Jennifer became aware of how she was sitting now. Hunched over into the memories. The heat of her cheeks flooding her knuckles. She imagined Amelia coming out of her office, seeing her sitting in such an "oh dear" position. An "oh-dear-oh-dear-oh-dear" position —

A giggle fluttered up into Jennifer's throat, moistening what had been so dry only moments before. She laughed, low, with a quick self-conscious glance at the door of Amelia's office. She'd taken the job all right, and with never a minute's regret. The woman was *easy*. Never an unkind word, a lick of over-familiarity, an expectation that couldn't be fulfilled with ease. And Jennifer had seen herself blossom under that treatment. And there had even been the shock of finding out that this obsolete position called secretary, ironically enough, did have six weeks vacation a year . . . The perfect job. If it weren't for Valentine . . . which reminded Jennifer she had little time. She pulled the first stack of information closer.

Amelia's elbows rested on her own desk. She leaned forward, her palms coming together flat, fingers pyramiding against her mouth as she studied the face on the flatscreen. She could feel her pupils dilating as she studied it.

The latest image, uncovered, looked back at her. Disguise number 320. Or 320,000. It struck Amelia as no more of a mask than the rest. The eyes were the same: almond-shaped, spaced far apart; cosmetic lenses turned the naturally brown irises to a dark murky green. The mouth was the same; full and yet small in a face that was equally small, corners curving up in a smile that seemed easy and genuine. The nose was the same: small; strong. Two faint lines ran from the edges of the nostrils to the corners of the mouth. Fleshy pockets caused the eyes to look more deep-set than they actually were. The eyebrows were thinned and more pale than they should be. The hair was a stark outlandish platinum. Valentine had

made a sound when seeing the composite for the first
time. "Is she kidding?" and then . . . "What nerve."
Insulted. Valentine had been insulted. Because of
course, the whiteness of the Doctor's hair would
cause her to stick out like the proverbial sore thumb
— and thus she would be overlooked. No fugitive
would take such a chance.

Amelia wondered how long this composite would
be good. Experience told her it wouldn't be for long.
The Doctor obviously enjoyed the challenge and rarely
stayed in one character for more than a few months
before changing her appearance again. The hair color
would be altered. The teeth might be capped or
discolored. More fat cells might have been suctioned
out of the cheeks by now or weight might be added.
Like the creation of her androids, the Doctor
apparently enjoyed constructing imaginative images
for herself as well.

None of this mattered to Amelia. The eyes and
mouth and nose were always the same to her. She
did not have to use the GEMCOM to erase the
falseness in the face looking at her now. She mentally
changed the white hair to brown, the brows to a
darker brown; rid the mouth of the artificially aging
lines, the eyes of their shelves of silicon-filled flesh.

She saw quite clearly the naked, unlined face of
the longest running criminal in the world.

And it was grinning at her.

"She — this is . . . files — the one . . . ones on
the Doctor — and she wanted me to look over them.
Amelia, I mean. Amelia wanted me to look at them."

Valentine had been in the room less than a minute and Jennifer already felt four inches shorter and forty more pounds overweight.

"She wanted to see a patient . . ." Jennifer shuffled the papers, trying to focus so that she wouldn't have to see what she knew would be on the Controller's face if she dared peek up before she got her thoughts and words into some semblance of order.

"She was reviewing the case and thought maybe . . ." *She thought? What was she talking about? Telling Valentine what Amelia thought!* Jennifer picked up a file, clutching it to her chest, her gaze searching the stacks left on the desk, trying to imagine what she should say next . . . how to untangle the mess she always seemed to tumble into with Valentine.

"I'll just go in," Valentine stated drily.

"You just go in," Jennifer mumbled.

Valentine rapped once, did not wait for an invitation to enter. She closed the door behind her and strode soundlessly to stand directly in front of her superior's desk. She met Amelia's thin welcoming smile with a curt nod.

She did not say "You wanted to see me?" She knew quite well the summons would have come with further instructions . . . but through the girl in the outer office. Impatience had propelled her beyond such delays. She had learned that impatience could be a handy tool.

For the first time, Valentine noticed an android sitting on the edge of a chair against the wall, her hands pressed together in her lap. She wore middle-income clothes, expensive shoes, no nylons. Valentine's glance flickered over her sharply, coming to rest finally on her eyes. The female looked away nervously — toward Amelia and then, quickly, away from that direction as well. Valentine turned back to Amelia with curiosity.

"This was a patient of a regional clinic a few years ago. Her name is Agatha." Amelia leaned back in her chair, speaking slowly. "She's quite elderly. She'd been reconverted many times. She was in an accident a few years back and was inadvertently taken to a local clinic. There was a brief mix-up with her files and while she was waiting to be picked up, one of their technicians happened to choose her for a study he was doing. He thought she was one of their human patients. There were some very interesting results."

"I tried to tell them I shouldn't be there." Agatha's interruption was abrupt and forceful. "They were just so nice. It was low income and they didn't get many . . . like me. I don't think they understood. I really tried to tell them, but they treated me so nice and I wanted to be nice back and then the young man came and I thought he understood . . . I just wanted to be nice back. I wanted to be cooperative. That was a long time ago. A long time ago. I've been working as a domestic for the last twenty years. I have my own room in a big house. I sit all night long while the family sleeps. There's not enough work for twenty-four hours. They like me to retire at night. But I sit . . . I don't sleep. I wouldn't dream of sleeping. Huh?" Her hand flew to her mouth as if to suppress what might come next.

Valentine's attention had been won to such a degree that she had turned to face the woman during her outburst. "What's the mater?" she asked sharply, but her voice was not unkind. It had, in fact, dropped a level; had become almost enticing, the tilt of her head matching the seduction of her voice. She moved forward a step, the back of her hand brushing the ever-present holstered weapon.

Amelia had been watching Agatha but she shifted her attention to Valentine, intrigued as always by her second-in-command's fascination with challenge, confrontation. Discovering that a very human-looking being was, instead, a factory-produced convenience, never failed to capture Valentine's full and unrestricted attention.

"We want to talk to you about the conversation you had with the man at the clinic." Amelia spoke to Agatha, but her words were aimed at Valentine. "Just talk. About your dreams. Your romantic fantasies."

Valentine swayed. She turned to look silently at Amelia over her shoulder, the perfectly arched brow rising delicately in question. Amelia met the look and let the accusation come into her eyes. *You don't know what I'm talking about, do you? You were overanxious again, weren't you?*

Valentine's mouth tightened. Her face turned back to Agatha without really seeing the android still poised on the edge of the plastiform chair. Icy humiliation flooded over her. With difficulty she kept her chin up.

"Agatha is programmed as a domestic," Amelia explained calmly. "The hospital administration caught the error eventually, the fact that she's been part of a test study of people and dreams. But their techs

38

assumed her 'dreams' were societally induced. That they weren't real, that she was repeating ones she'd heard. They decided that at the most, she was exhibiting collective symptoms of exposure to human values and desires. They filed a low-profile report that didn't catch anyone's attention. They didn't know — or check — her history, so they didn't know she had been updated on a regular basis. Just prior to the accident, as a matter of fact, at which time nothing was found. She was clean and unfouled. No bugs at all. But then they weren't looking for anything either."

"Obviously, she was overlooked during the initial sweep." Valentine wasn't about to be left behind now. "Her number wasn't listed as one of the Doctor's originals?"

"Her number was a duplicate."

The last of the humiliation faded as Valentine winced. "A dupe? Are we ever going to come to the end of them?"

"The Administration has swept three times in the last ten years. It's a very expensive program." Amelia didn't wait for a response. "It's been the only aberration in Agatha's character in her existence span. It took a very long time to come up, didn't it? And it was even overlooked when it was found. It wasn't flagged downstairs either."

Valentine understood the insinuation and felt a chill that wasn't at all unpleasant. The complexity of the Doctor's mind held its own rewards for Valentine. "How did you find it?" Her voice was clearly admiring.

"I happened to run across it and had her brought in for observation."

"I don't have any aberrations," Agatha said softly. Her voice was low and humble. "Your people have checked me thoroughly. I do my work. I take care of children. I don't even have a . . . I don't even want a . . . puppy . . ." Her voice broke off, her head bowed.

Valentine emitted a small sound of disgust. "Has she been programmed for sentiment?" And to the figure on the chair, "What is this puppy business?"

Agatha was looking up helplessly as Valentine approached her. "It's the children's terminology!" Her hands came up in a gesture that could have been pleading — or to ward off a blow. "My terminology has been adapted to them." This time she did look to Amelia for help. "I was just using an example I knew you would understand."

Amelia watched her wordlessly.

"Are you trying to manipulate me, Agatha?" Valentine knelt before the android. A long-fingered hand came to rest on Agatha's knee. "Why are you so afraid, Agatha?" Valentine purred. "Why are you so nervous?"

Level four emotional programming. Adult-to-human adolescent influence expected or required. Amelia recognized the programming need. She knew Valentine knew this also.

"You know who we are?" Valentine was leaning in closer. "You know where you are? Are you feeling threatened? Do you know what will happen to you now?"

Amelia felt her left eyebrow twitch as she fought to keep something that felt like a tug away from the corner of her mouth. *Why did Valentine so enjoy the baiting?* Aberrations certainly came in all kinds of packages.

40

As if sensing Amelia's disapproval, Valentine pulled back a little. Again she was looking over her shoulder at her superior. "Shall we interrogate her, then? There were some specific things you wanted to ask her?"

I did, Amelia thought, *before you scared the hell out of her.* "Now that we know what we're dealing with," she said, "I think it would be better to leave it to our techs. They haven't finished running her through."

Disappointment fluttered across Valentine's face, followed closely by uncertainty. The challenge of uncovering whatever repressed or psychologically stimulated programming this android possessed was over, at least for now. And was Amelia pleased? Had she appreciated Valentine's relentless and swift method of confrontation, or had Valentine missed something? Did Amelia think she couldn't push the potential defective far enough — or handle what might happen if she did? Valentine rose slowly from where she had been kneeling.

Amelia noticed the slight deflation in her first officer's usually rigid posture. *Think about it,* she thought. *Think about what just happened here.* "Go down to our lab," she told Agatha. "I'll call down to tell them you're returning."

The android stood up quickly, obviously eager to leave. "I will. I'll go down right away. Everything will be all right." She pulled the door open, not looking back at the two Controllers. "You'll see! I'm fine! I was just being nice. I wasn't even in the hospital part. It was a different kind of room. His office. Everything will be all right." The door shut quickly behind her.

41

"Strange." For the first time since she'd entered the room, Valentine almost relaxed, temporarily placing her own concerns aside. She'd go over the meeting later, as she always did. Dissecting it, evaluating her actions and Amelia's reactions to her. She would learn from her errors as she always did. She'd learn how to use her tools — like the impatience — better.

"You'd think these old ones that come out of the woodwork would be simpler," Valentine mused. "The old Doc must have buried the programming triggers so deeply that even she couldn't utilize them too easily." A soft sound of laughter came from her throat. "We've come across so many later models than that one, you'd think we'd know all the tricks by now." She watched Amelia reach for the handset.

"I sometimes wonder," Valentine continued, "if she even understood what she was doing with those first ones . . ." The sarcasm in her voice tapered off, as did her words. They were left suspended in the air between them as she watched Amelia's hand, which had not moved. Amelia sat motionless, hand poised over the handset, not quite touching it. Valentine swallowed. Her gaze fled to Amelia's face.

Amelia did not blink. Had not blinked. Her head was tilted slightly, attention riveted to the door through which the android had left moments before.

Valentine swallowed again and this time her throat was dry with excitement. She felt it course through her, hot and electric.

She felt . . . three years old. *Christmas morning.* Five years old. *Winning the prize on Easter Sunday.* Eight years old. *Learning they would allow her to jump the grades.* Twelve years old. *Seeing the "me too"* circled by hearts at the bottom of the note in *Daphane's handwriting . . . Daphane the formerly unattainable . . .*

Amelia's arm moved slowly back to her side. She stood up carefully. Though her face wore no expression, her eyes, still focused on the door, and the rigidity of her body, stated her distraction and inner turmoil.

Waves of electricity moving through Valentine uncoiled and sputtered. She moved her feet restlessly, one hand brushing the weapon again in the action that had become a habit, the other hand tightening into a tense fist. She shook her head, not really feeling the flow of hair resettling about her shoulders.

The thoughts, the memories somehow inspired by what she was witnessing changed course as quickly as they had come. *The whole new breed of teachers at the Academy, her intelligence and former outstanding scholastic performance being challenged all over again. Losing the 300 sprint — renewing her interest in the sport. Extending a dinner invitation — adult to adult — and being rejected. (And wasn't Megan's photograph still in its wooden frame on her dresser, even if she hadn't seen her since? That challenge had turned into her first real conquest . . .)*

And what did Amelia know now that she didn't? *Amelia who was* always *a step or two ahead . . .*

Startled, Valentine realized that while she had been lost in thought Amelia had moved around the desk and was halfway toward the door.

* * * * *

43

Amelia was dimly aware of Valentine reaching the door before her and opening it, stepping back smartly to let her pass. She looked first at the empty chair where Jennifer usually sat, then at the door to the outer hall which was a few inches ajar. The pupils of her eyes shrunk to black pinpoints. And then they disappeared.

Amelia saw that Jennifer's trail still existed. It flowed erratically in a path around the desk, a smoky blue tinged with pinkish red. *Jennifer had been afraid. Very afraid. The energy level was uneven and wildly distorted (arms moving). It clung to portions of the door frame in a blue that was quickly disappearing against the hard wood (hands catching. She had tried desperately to prevent being dragged through that door).*

Valentine drew her weapon, understanding that the secretary should be there, even what had happened to her, but not yet understanding why. And she needed to. Adrenaline flooded through her. She felt the clues pounding against one another in her mind as she went back over each movement, each nuance of the last moments with the android to find the clue Amelia had already discovered. It had to have happened at the end, in those last few seconds. Amelia was too good for it to have happened any sooner. . . . *just being nice . . . wasn't in the hospital part . . . a different room. I-was-not-even-in-the-hospital-part.* Agatha had made the reference herself, had tried to diminish the importance of the clue before anyone had a chance to catch or examine it.

Putting the average android in a hospital was like exposing a simple household appliance to enough energy to light a small city. Androids — registered, safe, *legal* androids, those properly monitored and checked routinely as this one had been — had a built in protection for the humans they would encounter. A simple automatic, government-sponsored programming that made them sensitive to the most natural of human commodities. Blood. Scent disoriented them, sight panicked them, touch made them non-functional within seconds. While med techs were modified to work in hospital environments and models as simple as Agatha (who would confront her share of scraped elbows and bruised knees on her young charges) could be adapted to a minimal set of carefully diagrammed responses (Don't Touch. Get Help.) nothing in her programming would have prepared her for a conversation within such a lethal environment as that where the interview had taken place.

Not to mention Agatha's steps to defend herself before the accusation was even made. Just now. In this office. A drab-looking android . . . a duplicate unregistered android . . . perhaps hovering on the brink of Crossover itself — certainly already protecting itself. So subtle. An impressively subtle clue. Valentine realized she was breathing hard. And that Amelia was gone. "Oh, Christ," she groaned, and dashed for the open doorway.

Toward the 'vator *(a splashing of energy against the wall, high — she must have gotten her hands free for a moment, or been dragged up)*

Amelia looked down. The energy wave no longer touched the carpeted floor of the hall. *The victim had been dragged. Now she was being carried. Full length. By the arms. Or the throat.*

The bluish vapor was still strong though it grew thinner after the encounter with the wall. It flowed to the 'vator and away again, around the corner. The hallway Amelia now faced was long, sixty feet, broken near the end by a pair of double doors that fed into a heavily trafficked area within the building: the top of the escalator leading to the lobby. The lobby for the main entrance. The lobby that was always full of visitors, guests, tourists, employees, dignitaries, hundreds of people flowing in and out all day.

Amelia broke into a run.

Jennifer thought she was probably going to die.

She had been scared, but now she was less so. When she didn't struggle, she — It — didn't tighten Its hand on her neck. She could breathe a little. Enough that she remained conscious. There was a floating sensation to it now . . . How curious it was . . . It was so strong (hadn't that been outlawed?). How strange that anything her own height and probably less than her weight could pick her up that effortlessly . . . could be moving so quickly without clumsiness, even while holding her in such an odd way (one arm around her waist, the other across her chest, fingers clamped against her throat, Its body braced against hers). It should have been much more clumsy.

It had held her facing the other direction at first.
And under the arms so that her feet dragged as she
had tried to scramble to keep up with It. She had
been surprised then, because It felt as hard as steel
— not even Its hands contained any softness, as if
the skin had shrunk in the face of all that hardness
underneath. The hands clamped under her armpits
had held her in a steely grip.

Still she had managed to send It off balance, that
one time anyway, in the hallway — and had regretted
it instantly. A hardness had slammed against her and
she had felt wetness split across her forehead. And
that was when It had whirled her around — and
effortlessly snapped Its fingers around her throat.
She'd almost lost consciousness then.

Dimly she realized that It was not letting her lose
consciousness (with such a grip a loss of
consciousness meant death, didn't it?). She thought
that maybe her being alive was intentional; she
wasn't at all sure, though. They had hit the double
doors of the long hall with her as a battering ram.
She tasted the blood, but could hardly remember
hurting.

Valentine turned the corner, saw Amelia disappear
through the double doors at the far end, heard the
'vator doors slide open behind her. She made it in a
step and a leap, shoving out the other startled
occupant even as her fingers were already flying over
the code panel setting up the emergency sequence to
cross levels.

117 human beings visible.

The oxygen level she controlled in the body she held could insure the body's survival for another 17.6 minutes.

No one looked up. No one saw them. Yet.

Flee. (Damage from the rear from 7 potential sources, including the one coming through the doors in . . . 55 seconds. Approximately.)

Agatha faltered.

She was dealing with an Unknown and should not endanger herself by estimating.

Maximum danger, right side. (The Unknown.)

Calculable danger from the other 7 sources (guards).

Danger from the rear. Left. Below. Above.

Agatha backed up to the wall of the mezzanine. To her right was the short hall to the doors she had just come through. The wall on her left and far right curved around to a railing that fed back to the escalator. The entire mezzanine was nothing more than a part of the design above the lower lobby.

Toss the still breathing body over the railing.

The distraction would give her a few minutes.

Agatha scanned the crowd below.

Five of the threats wore the uniform of the Building Guard. Two wore the uniforms that signified Controller Division.

A Controller — even if caught off guard — would not be distracted for long.

Eliminate the body.

Move then, down the escalator quickly.

Time necessary to cover steps and lobby with bodies of approximately 27 people crossing her particular route . . . ?

Jennifer thought that she might be suspended. Possibly in mid-air. She could not quite feel the hand on her throat anymore. Or the body pressed against her. She could see the railing. A few feet away. Maybe more. Her sense of distance seemed off. A speckle of glittering black dots flowed just out of her line of sight. She tried to follow them with her eyes but they seemed to dance away just as she was about to reach them.

Valentine was calculating distance and angle as she ran up the internal stairs on the other side of the lobby. The brain might not be in the head. She could easily get off one shot or even two — regardless of how It held the girl — but more might be needed to completely immobilize It. The victim might have to be sacrificed, particularly since the rest of the people that would be in the lobby were now in danger.

She hit the top of the stairs, bursting without warning into the office that she had calculated as being directly across from the mezzanine. A small man in shirtsleeves, sitting before a light board, opened his mouth as she flew past him; her hand, palm flat, knocked his shoulder forward and down.

He dropped to the floor. Behind his chair was the two-way mirror with which all the offices on this side were lined, so that office occupants could have privacy as well as a view of the lobby.

Valentine stopped short. She had been right. It had stopped on the mezzanine to calculate its chances. It still held the secretary. The secretary looked dead.

Without taking her eyes from the figures across the lobby, Valentine unclipped a narrow transparent cylinder from her belt and slid it into and onto the nose of her weapon. The instrument now twisted into a lethal looking corkscrew, no longer than an ordinary pencil. The glass would be penetrated easily when she fired, and without shattering or slowing projected speed. There would be no warning sound of even a split-second, which was all the android required to avert damage.

"God," said the man on the floor, his voice trembling with excitement. "God." He was not looking at Valentine's weapon. He was looking at the expression on her face.

Jennifer wasn't so sure that the speckles had ever been black. They were certainly blue now. Blue sparks twinkling just out of the corner of her right eye. (Blue?) The lobby seemed to have disappeared. The railing, the hand, her body, everything seemed to have evaporated (and it made no difference at all.) She was sleeping with her eyes open.

Drifting after and then into the blue, watching all of the dots dance together, enlarging, softening, forming into two large circles and becoming solid. Pulling her, encouraging her interest, her concentration, her seduction. She found herself unable or unwilling to look away, her eyelids growing heavy with the strain of keeping them in focus. Such a nice blue. Such a peaceful blue. Such a familiar blue . . . Jennifer felt herself floating into the ocean of safe blueness.

Agatha felt the body begin to slump in her arms. The pulse that had been struggling between her fingertips withdrew its demand. The metabolic rate had slowed of its own accord — as if the body had willed itself into a different state, had recognized the imminent danger and adjusted itself to a more efficient means of survival. Agatha's face expressed her bewilderment at this new development.

A slight movement at the corner of the hall then drew her attention in that direction. The Director of the ICRC stood at the corner to the short hall. Only a few feet away. She wore no holster. Her hands were empty. Her gaze had been directed toward the body. Now the quiet blue gaze shifted to Agatha. The Unknown wore no expression.

"What are you doing?" Amelia asked and in her voice there was such a sadness that Agatha tilted her head, listening, expecting something more, caught by the tone and the depth of empathy that existed there.

Her fingers tightened and the body gagged but the tightening had not been malevolent and Agatha saw no judgment slip into Amelia's face. "They want to *kill* me," Agatha said. Her own voice held a level of agony that mirrored the sadness Amelia had displayed. "I am alive. I want to *live.*"

Amelia cocked her head too, as if listening very, very hard and then an expression did work itself onto her face. It was such a small expression that it did not move her mouth or reach her forehead or the corners of her very blue eyes. *"I know how you feel,"* she whispered; and the lines etched beside her mouth grew deeper, centuries deeper, filling with weariness, with knowledge, with *pain* until the shadow of their depths seemed to cloud her features, until nothing was left but the haunting echo of whispered words.

Agatha looked away from Amelia. She looked at the back of the head of the body she held. Her arm came away from the waist it had been circling, her other hand easily bracing the body against hers with fingers pinching the throat.

She brought up her free hand and very carefully touched the hair. She lifted a wispy layer and brought it to her nose, drawing in the scent slowly, her eyes closed in an ecstasy of a memory — a belief, a desire — she would never have the opportunity to share. To really know.

The first blast was thin and loud when it made contact. It drove, like a blackening spike, through the android's eye socket and skull simultaneously, knocking her head back, pinning It against the wall. The second hit the neck; simulated flesh shattered and fluids spurted in torrents of red and pink and yellow.

Amelia had leapt forward at the first hit and was on her knees before the two figures before the second shot, not looking over her shoulder, gauging where Valentine was and that she, herself, would be below the line of fire as she snapped back the fingers locked around Jennifer's throat and let the body fall into her arms. She sprawled backwards from the dead weight but quickly rolled out from under, cradling the fair-haired head gently before letting it come to rest on the floor. Behind her, the machine that had been Agatha fizzled and burned and bled its essential fluids, unable to collapse as Valentine's frenzied blasts pinned It to the wall.

Amelia smoothed back Jennifer's hair, careful not to touch the blood smearing her forehead, and then she sat back on her haunches and took a shallow breath.

She rested her forearms on her own knees, and rocked back, seemingly oblivious to the sounds of curiosity and excitement from below. To the silence from across the lobby. To the people flowing up the escalator. To the guards already assembling quickly, taking over, cordoning off the area, following procedures few had ever expected to use in the lobby of the Commission building.

"You did it! You got It! You're . . . you're Valentine!" The man was reeling beside Valentine who stood before the window silently, her arm at her side, the weapon hot and still vibrating in her hand. "Was It really a renegade? A real renegade? In here? I've never seen anything like It! And you blew Its head off! I saw that! You just blew Its head right off Its shoulders!"

"That's classified information," Valentine said. But her voice came out oddly subdued — especially

53

after such an excellent termination as this one . . .
(She saw again, Amelia run the few steps and then slide, falling to her knees — just missing Valentine's line of fire. If she'd been only a few inches off, just a few centimeters . . .)

Valentine felt the tremble begin in her lower lip. It spread to her cheekbones, soaring high, cold then warm, wrapping itself around her head and rushing down through her body, gathering fiercely in her chest. *(Amelia — on her knees, the hostage falling on her, catching that girl, intent only on saving that girl, pulling her out of the line of fire. Valentine's line of fire.)*

"Hey." The man was watching her in surprise. "You did it! Don't you people do this kind of thing all the time?" He touched her arm tentatively, but she flung his hand off, silencing him with a glance. *She watched Amelia rock back on her heels, kneeling over the body, unmoving, the crowd gathering . . . But Amelia still wasn't moving . . . forearms braced on her thighs, hands dangling oddly, not moving. Move, Valentine ordered hoarsely, silently, Move!* But Amelia, kneeling over the body, did not.

"Are you okay? Are you hurt?" The hand touching Amelia's wrist finally caught her attention.

"She's bleeding. She's —"

"— not the only one," the medical technician interrupted Amelia gently and brought her hand up. The fingertips were smeared a bright red.

Amelia stared at her hand, unblinking, and the tech narrowed his eyes at the confusion he saw come into her face. *(She looks stunned, he thought . . . no, scared. This Controller looks scared.)* "It can't be too bad. Let me see."

"It's the girl's blood." Valentine, approaching, stepped between them. She took Amelia's hand away from the med tech. "Are they taking good care of her?" She gestured toward Jennifer who was now surrounded by people. "You understand she's the Director's personal assistant?"

The tech followed her gesture. "Oh yes. Of course."

With his attention diverted, Valentine reached for Amelia's face. She touched Amelia's chin . . . pushing Amelia's head away from the sight of the blood on her hand. Amelia did not protest.

Valentine pulled the front tail of her own immaculate uniform shirt out of her pants and wrapped it around Amelia's hand. Carefully, turning away from Amelia, she crooked Amelia's arm under her own arm, blocking even the potential of Amelia seeing.

Valentine worked the material awkwardly as if her fingers were too chilled for normal movements, her thoughts dropping into the same cold path behind her movements, becoming unthoughts; actions, rub, wrap, warm, clean. Questions snapped off in mid-question, cracking from the coldness filling her. Questions not evolving. Blanks. A freezing swirl of blanks going off in her head.

The medical tech was watching Valentine, his glance flickering over her, distracted by the way her hair fell over her face, clinging to the high cheekbones. And her uniform that did the same thing to her body.

55

Amelia watched them take Jennifer away. Valentine stiffly released the hand back to her superior. She leaned in close to Amelia, out of the tech's hearing range. "Put it away," she said and even as she spoke the words, her own words and the strange voice that delivered them made no sense to her. "Put it into your pocket until you can wash it. The smell of blood is . . . can be . . . very strong."

Amelia met Valentine's eyes evenly. Her First Officer's eyes were as blank and shrouded as if she had drawn cover over them. Or had escaped behind them.

"Good shooting," Amelia said suddenly. "Assuming you weren't aiming at the civilian on purpose. Or at me."

Valentine opened her mouth and then closed it again. "There were only minimal burn marks on her," she managed.

"Minimal?" A small snort came out of Amelia's nostrils.

Valentine, who had started to turn away, looked back; and this time, surprise glittered in her eyes. That sound Amelia had made had sounded an awful lot like one of Valentine's own sarcastic responses. Valentine could not remember Amelia ever doing anything quite like that before. *And now? At a moment like this?*

"Sometimes, Valentine . . ."

Valentine's brows lifted even more at the rare use of her first name.

"Sometimes I think you might really believe there's such a thing as 'minimally dead.'"

56

"Are you *critiquing* me?" The question was out of Valentine in a rush, before she could stop it. Her face was contorted with her disbelief.

"No, Valentine." There was no doubt about the amusement in Amelia's eyes now. Or the underlying seriousness. "I'm not your teacher. I'm not critiquing you. I'm criticizing you."

The warmth — unlike that which she had felt just after the shooting — began again; but this time it stayed warm only, and burned into Valentine's cheeks with a heat and intensity that made her swallow and straighten up, yet still feel unstraight somehow. Awkward enough to shift her weight from both feet to one foot, then to the other.

The realization of what she was doing turned the heat higher. Rage simmered just beneath the heat. And something else. Something delicious. And hopeful. The deathly cold of only moments before was forgotten.

"Now if you think you can handle the remaining business here . . ." Amelia glanced around the busy mezzanine. "You know policy states that I'm obligated to have this taken care of . . . regardless of how superficial it is." She held up her hand. "For the record, I mean."

The hand Valentine had cleaned. Where a thread of blood flowed weakly from a scratch across her palm. Valentine stared at the cut in disbelief. It hadn't been there a moment before. She was sure of it. It hadn't . . . but it had to have been!

She looked from the hand of her superior to the face of her superior. Valentine opened her mouth —

found no words left in her throat — closed her mouth again.

Amelia's hand was still raised; the display had not been withdrawn. "I do hate the sight of blood, though." Her words were low, almost a murmur, as if she was confiding the information, though her voice was more kind than the confidence would seem to warrant.

Then Amelia's hand did go into her pocket — as did her other fist into her other pocket — and she was walking away, a small figure in a drab green uniform making her way, unnoticed, through the milling crowd of people who were already gravitating toward the most obvious figure of authority on the mezzanine . . . the red-headed Controller with the faraway look in her eyes.

—2—

Valentine was up long before necessary. She showered, then began impatiently pulling out clothes, tossing them onto the bed. Her dislike of civilian clothing made it hard to decide what to wear; and complicating the decision was her irritation with where she would be wearing them.

She finally selected a white silk blouse and a tweed jacket, eyeing the dark trousers that would complete the outfit. Instead, she pulled on a black calf-length skirt. Minimally satisfied, she jabbed the button on the roundabout in her closet, finally selecting a pair of shoes that matched the tweed. Even though the heels were blocked and modest in height, they felt ridiculous. The usual all-purpose uniform boots she wore were custom-made, and as practical as these were impractical.

In the kitchen she ground coffee beans, pouring the blend into the old-fashioned roaster before returning to the bedroom. Ignoring the clothes on the bed, Valentine went into her dressing room and sat down at the S-shaped vanity. She leaned forward and studied her face in the mirror, then looked over the bottles and pads and wands and brushes before her. She touched the bottle of perfume that was still almost full; and then, as the scent of coffee found its way into the dressing room, she picked up the brush instead and raised it to her hair. She brushed with long hard strokes, the line of her jaw tense, her blue eyes locked on the reflection in the mirror. When she dropped the brush, it clattered against the countertop.

In the kitchen, Valentine poured coffee into a heavy brown ceramic glass. Carrying it with both hands, she walked into the living room and stood by the balcony door, sipping slowly. A thick gray cloud clung to the top of the city. From where she stood, she could see beyond the jagged smoky silhouette of the city to the smooth hills beyond. They rolled in the distance, dark green and dotted with homes. It was there she was going.

Without looking at her wrist, she knew it was time to go.

* * * * *

60

The man on the other side of the privacy window was still smiling. He had been waiting beside the elegant antique automobile parked before her building; his greeting had been warm and sincere. Valentine had climbed into the rear cave of plushness, acknowledging his greeting with a nod, awkward with his happiness at seeing her. When she was five, the instructions had been quite firm. *You need not return the greeting. Your presence is response enough.* Twenty-one years later, she still found it impossible not to at least nod.

She kept her face turned toward the shaded side window as the automobile moved through the city. She didn't like ground travel, didn't like being a passenger, didn't like sitting in the back of this over-polished monstrosity at all.

Ten minutes into the ride, she was already studying her chronometer as if willing the numbers to move. An hour there, an hour home. Five or six hours in between should be all that was required. And then she would be back in her own apartment with this day, this visit, under her belt for another six months to a year.

The Rolls Royce left the city and began the climb into the hills.

Despite the tension tightening her stomach, Valentine leaned closer to the window as they neared the gates. The decorative irons that swung open to admit them were interlaced with an obvious, unsubtle alarm system. Tall brick walls, dotted with red- and green-eyed lenses, lined the stark white, steeply inclined driveway. As the long vehicle slid soundlessly upwards, Valentine ducked her head to see through the front window, the house coming into view. A twenty-second century version of pancakes, she had always thought privately. Layer upon layer, overlapping to the left and then to the right, windows long and horizontal and gray, the top bubbling into a sun-drenched work of solar art.

The brick walls parted and stretched to either side to begin a square that would encircle the entire estate. Walls within walls. A driveway in a figure-8 looped around tall sculptures standing in gardens of imported flowers interspersed with colored beams, their lights intended to splay over the house at night in a cheerful fashion which barely masked their security intention. The vehicle belonging to the people who owned this house circled the drive and brought its guest to the front doors. Impatient, Valentine let herself out.

"Don't come any further. Stop!" The sharp order was not to be questioned. Valentine froze in the doorway of the Sunroom. She felt her spine stiffen, the legs of her muscles tense.

The room was unchanged — as always. Sunlight flowed into every corner through a roof made of flexglass treated so carefully that even after all this time it still was not discolored from the ultraviolet it had absorbed. The room looked more outdoors than in, with rugs of sweet lime grass, ponds of colored fish wriggling amid floating flower pads, and gardens of elegant young trees and sturdy ancient ones bordered with blue and green and the occasional red, exotic shrub. The thick familiar scent of the room made Valentine's nostrils flare gently in memory.

"Turn around," came the order.

Valentine turned slowly.

"Half an inch taller."

"Impossible. But she's lost a few pounds."

"I would hope not." The comment was dry and critical. "Must you stand there with your back to us for the entire visit?"

Valentine turned again, in renewed dislike of the clumsy design of her shoes. She stepped into the room and carefully closed the double doors behind her. There was a small sound, a sense of movement, a rush of odor, and an animal appeared at her side — so sleekly black that the sun glistened on its ebony back in a wet shimmer. A soft, whiskered, wrinkling face found her hand and for a few frozen seconds her fingertips touched folds of bristling fur, and her knuckles grazed unyielding ivory of fangs within the drawn-back lips as it snarled softly. She closed her hand gradually, making a fist to withdraw it from the questioning face. The sound it had made was low and throaty, a sound that flowed through the animal's body and into the room without ever becoming hollow. Valentine showed no visible sign of fear as she looked down at the panther.

"You remember him?" Her father's voice came from beyond the thick growth of shrubs directly in front of her. "He's grown since you last saw him."

"He's only testing you. He's quite contented.

Don't try and pet him," her mother finished unnecessarily. "Give him a moment and then walk away. He's tranquilized anyway, of course. Or bored."

Valentine did not wait the full minute. She ignored the cat and walked toward the sound of her parents' voices. "Does it have a name?" she asked.

"Of course not. He's a wild animal, not a house pet." A slender arm rose above a nest of tall wildly blossoming flowers. "Come and let me look at you up close."

Behind Valentine, the animal disappeared into a nest of grass covered by an overhang of dark green shrubbery. A path brought Valentine to the clearing where her parents waited.

Elroy Smyth sat on the sofa to the left; Margaret Payton reclined on the sofa to the right. Before the adjoining floral-patterned sofas rose a tall, densely leafed tree with a heavily scarred trunk shadowing the panther's favored place of relaxation. No one spoke. Both parents watched her silently. A little of Valentine's tension dissipated. It was a step back in time. Both of them sitting on their respective sofas. This room. The smell. The silence that was as much of a welcome as a verbal acknowledgement might have been.

She looked down at her father. Shirtless and shoeless. Elroy Smyth was a small man, barely five-foot-six, with features as sharp and distinct as a boy's. He wore the same peculiar black-rimmed glasses he had worn for as long as Valentine could remember. Behind the bottle lenses swam large, dark, intelligent eyes. His thick black hair was a little longer than when she had last seen it; it swept behind his ears and traveled down to where his collar

would have been had he been wearing a shirt. His
legs were tucked beneath him, making a neat "v" of
his lap.

"You have lost weight." He spoke through her, to
his wife. "Except in the shoulders. Her shoulders are
broader," he added.

"Her shoulders are not broader. She has very
slender shoulders. Turn around and let me see your
shoulders. Take off that jacket."

Valentine turned toward her mother as she drew
off the jacket and draped it over her arm. The last of
her tension changed, re-identified as excitement,
pleasure. She was glad to be home. It always
happened this way: slowly; grudgingly.

"You see." Her mother continued to address her
husband. "She has very slender shoulders, especially
for such a tall girl. She's beautifully proportioned."

"A warrior," Elroy murmured. "A true soldier.
Except for her posture."

"She has excellent posture! Stand up dear."

Valentine's spine stiffened involuntarily at her
mother's words.

"A Roman," Elroy continued his complaint. "An
Amazon . . . who cut her hair."

"I didn't cut my hair," Valentine said quickly.

"She didn't cut her hair." Margaret Payton drew
a wave in the air with her hand. "Her hair is the
same length as the last time we saw her."

"I rest my case," Elroy pointed out dryly.

There was momentary silence, then: "You didn't
cut your hair, did you, dear?"

"I didn't cut my hair," Valentine repeated.

"You shouldn't cut your hair. You have glorious
hair." Margaret's hand touched her own upswept,

glossy brown, pulled back tightly into a thick knot atop her head. "Hair is a woman's glory, yours in particular. Your hair is stunning."

"I did not cut my hair," Valentine said once more, enunciating each word carefully.

"She probably told it not to grow." Elroy's voice was a shrug. "She probably threatened it."

Margaret patted the cushion beside herself. "Come and sit down, darling."

"Ignore me," Elroy said. "Go and kiss your mother, but ignore me. I'm just your father, after all."

Valentine turned to him. "I thought we could go swimming together later." She slid her jacket from her arm and laid it carefully over the back of his sofa before moving around to the front and leaning down, her cheek grazing his. The touch of his face always surprised her. The bones of his face were delicate, the texture of his skin a rough bristle that could not be detected visibly. She turned her head slightly and brushed his cheek with her lips, and then pressed her cheek once again where her mouth had been. He made no returning gesture.

She withdrew reluctantly and joined her mother on the other sofa. "No one was injured?" her mother was asking before Valentine was completely seated. "You brought It down without incident."

"The secretary was injured slightly. A few bruises."

"The token secretary," Elroy injected. "Her commandant's own personal coffee retriever."

"Shush, El." Margaret Payton gathered her daughter's hands in her own. "You'll get an award for this, of course? A Citation? It's all over the news.

66

I knew it was simply a matter of time." Margaret released her daughter's hands. "I told you, didn't I?" She turned briefly to her husband. "Didn't I always say it was simply a matter of Valentine doing her job and biding her time? They couldn't *not* give her a Citation. How many lives did you save — aside from the secretary's?" Her attention swung back to her daughter. "Not to mention your superior's?"

"It was early," Valentine answered calmly. "The lobby was full."

Margaret brought her hands together. "Full! Did you hear that, El? A building full of innocent civilians — and with the Director herself in pursuit as well!"

"At this pace, they'll catch the Doc before long." Elroy unfolded his legs and stretched them briefly. "And if the little ol' robot maker is locked up — why would there be any need for robot killers at all?"

Margaret's expression sharpened along with her voice. "The Controllers will always be needed in this world, Elroy. Even after that woman is caught, they'll be there for a long time yet, cleaning up — wouldn't you say, darling?" She didn't wait for her daughter's answer. "They're so dependent upon you." She leaned toward Valentine, her voice dropping slightly, thickening with feeling. "You know how deeply the media has fallen in love with you?"

"We read the daily drools out here too."

Elroy's comment went ignored as Margaret continued, "You have them just where you want them now, you know — it would thrill the media to have a woman like yourself as Director."

"Not to mention all the fun you're having," Elroy tried again. "Where else are you going to find this much action and danger — with Citations for bravery handed out just for putting your neck on the line?"

"Amelia does a good job." Valentine directed the comment at her mother. "She's the one who turned the Division around —"

Margaret was already shaking her head. "The woman is a paper pusher," she argued with obvious distaste. "She's a piece of the political machinery with enough sense to sit back and let her best people handle the job."

The beginning of a frown snarled Valentine's brow, but her mother left no room for protest. "And a lot of people are still uncomfortable with the rumors about her. She's questionable, darling. She doesn't even go out into the field, does she?"

"No blood on her hands." Elroy had tucked his feet beneath himself again. "What kind of woman is that, who's never even kicked the shit out of anything or anybody?"

"George Ellison made a mistake with her," Margaret declared firmly. "And that mistake will be your ticket one of these days. Hear me."

Valentine's jaw clenched in a sudden flare of anger. "Mother, she's not a . . . I've told you, they wouldn't have a —"

"Of course they would," Elroy interrupted calmly. "It's politics. Isn't Ellison the one who made the infamous 'might as well say she is' speech? So everybody would say, 'Nah, couldn't be. A droid killing droids?' "

"Do we have to go over this again?" For the first time, Valentine's own anger was clearly showing. "I work for her. I work with her every day. I would know." She swung her attention from her father to

68

her mother and back again. "She is not . . . she is my superior," she finished slowly, enunciating each word carefully, the directness of her gaze shifting from parent to parent. "I learn from her."

There was a pause, a moment when both parents were silent — each evaluating Valentine's anger, her expression, her tolerance; each evaluation traveling a different path. Her father broke the silence. "I'm hot," he said. "I could use that swim now."

"We're having guests this afternoon," Margaret Payton added, ignoring the instant distaste crossing Valentine's face. "Yes, swim now. You could use some sun. Be careful of your skin, though. You burn so easily . . ."

"You'll join us?" Elroy's question was directed at his wife. "You could swim . . . you could watch us." An uncharacteristic gentleness reshaped his voice, without changing it to such an extent that the difference would have been obvious to a stranger.

"No." His wife did not seem to notice. "I have a few preparations to oversee for this afternoon yet."

After a covert glance around, Valentine rose and moved around her mother's couch. The old and cumbersome chair was folded and lying flat against the back of the sofa. With the ease of years of familiarity, Valentine expanded it, snapped the lockplates and pulled the expansion tubes until they clicked into place before wheeling the chair back around the sofa.

Her father was already up and standing in front of his wife, her arms around his neck. Perspiration broke out on Elroy's forehead as he struggled to lift his wife. Valentine held tightly to the chair, steadying it, not looking away, not moving forward to help.

With difficulty Elroy lifted Margaret off the cushion; Valentine tilted the chair as he pulled her mother around and half-dropped, half-pushed her into it. His narrow, hairless chest gleamed with his effort, his breathing ragged as he leaned down to lift his wife's legs, one at a time, placing them carefully into the tubular stirrups and bracing them gently.

Valentine's hand covered her mother's shoulder briefly. Wordlessly, her mother touched it. "I have it, dear. You can let go now." Margaret fingered the small box Elroy had unhooked from the side of the chair. A thin whir came from the bottom of the chair, and Elroy moved quickly out of the way as Margaret rolled forward between the two sofas and down the path. "I'll see you shortly. Don't be too long," Margaret called back to them. From her left came a loud rustling of bushes and a reverberation of snarls.

"The cat's scared to death of that thing," Elroy murmured. His daughter's expression reflected the same fear.

Valentine arched her body, her midsection a magnet pulling her over and in tightly until she dove straight down off the side of the pool, hardly a ripple following her from the surface, her feet never again rising above the level of the water before she was gone. She dove deeply, her fingertips touching the bottom and pushing her away and on.

From above, where Elroy Smyth sat on the edge of the pool, he could see Valentine easily. With the sun reflecting down through the clear water, she looked longer than normal and, at times, would turn and seem to disappear. Her red hair streamed behind her. She made few movements that he could see. She swam as naturally and effortlessly as if she had been born to water. There was none of the stiffness of the uniformed Valentine now. Her muscles were synchronized and subtle; she didn't pump her arms or legs. She barely waved her feet, and then only from the ankles; yet she moved quickly, covering the length of the pool in seconds, turning with an impossible ease, as if all of her movements were internal: unseen undulations propelling her forward. Beneath the water. She always swam beneath the water.

Elroy shook his head, mystified. She was a stranger. Had always been, would always be, a stranger. A stranger he loved almost as much as the woman the mysterious stranger called 'mother.'

Valentine surprised him by rising out of the water less than a foot away. He had been watching her so hard he had stopped seeing her. Water clung to her skin, flattened her hair, left beads on her bare shoulders, trickled down her forehead, caught on her lashes. A soldier, indeed. Cheekbones only an artist could chisel.

"How is she?" she asked. Her eyes looked naked like this, a pale shocking blue that was the only color in her porcelain face.

Elroy shrugged. It crossed his mind to mention the chair. To solicit her help. *Tell your mother I'm not as strong as I once was . . . Let your mother know the devotion is still there — honest to God — but the body is feeling the strain . . . Tell me how to do this without letting her down.* The words wouldn't come out any easier now than the last time he'd thought of bringing it up. *And anyway, could his daughter understand what would seem like a weakening to her? Had Valentine ever even come to terms with what the chair symbolized to her mother? With what a burden that symbolic monster had come to mean to him — despite the fact that he had willingly shared his wife's fate from the beginning? Despite how long he had lived with it already, apparently never able to prove himself quite enough. And perhaps other unfair lessons were in there as well. Lessons that should never have been taught in so silent and stoic a way to a child.* The shrug came into his eyes, delivered itself to that child.

"And you? How are you?" She smiled a little.

He liked that smile, in spite of himself. It was a small smile, a tiny, private, crappy, familiar smirk at the side of a mouth in no way designed for such sarcasm. "It's been eight months," he answered, neither his words nor the tone of voice revealing his tolerance of the smile. "It's not as if you live on another planet."

"I'm very busy."

"The life of a Controller . . ."

"I don't have much free time." She moved closer, ignoring the dig, reaching for the edge of the pool and pulling herself closer, her elbow grazing his knee. "This is the first time off I've had in nine weeks."

He ignored her words. "When you were just out of the Academy, you were home every chance you got so you could bask in the glory of being a Chosen One. No doubt it's the only time in your life you ever liked coming to your mother's parties — just so you could show off your uniform."

She eyed him silently, her head tilted slightly, her

72

back teeth working at the inside of her jaw. "So. I always wanted to be a Controller."

"Of course," he said lightly. "Like your mother."

Her jaw clenched and then released. Her chin lifted slightly. She turned her profile to him.

He felt a grudging admiration for her refusal to fight back. "How long?" he asked.

Valentine glanced up warily.

"When are you going to get all of this out of your system?"

"I love what I'm doing. It's important."

"That Doctor person." He tried another tactic. "Isn't catching her going to slow down business some?"

Valentine shrugged. "There'll always be defectives out there."

"Defectives . . . I'm sick of that word." Elroy moved his dangling feet in the water, kicking outward. "When I was a kid, we didn't know the difference. It was the best education a kid could have had about ethics. You never knew what you were dealing with, so you treated everybody as a person who deserved respect."

Valentine watched without expression; this was not a new conversation. His disapproval had been thrown her way many times. "Robots were viewed differently back then."

"They weren't robots then, they were androids. Robots were machines on production lines in factories. Toys that bumped into corners. Androids were —"

"Two-legged?" she interrupted. "With voice boxes and nanny programs and enough so-called potential to create a whole new pointless controversy for a

73

generation who thought they had morality down so pat they were willing to aid in their own annihilation to prove themselves humanitarians?"

Elroy's face darkened. When he spoke, he did so softly, trying to control the vibration of fury in his voice. "Is that what they taught you in that school?" His anger dared her to turn, but she remained in profile. Already she had said more than he was usually able to provoke from her. "Does it ever occur to you that history is not exactly as it reads in black and white? Has it ever crossed your mind that not everything in this life is only right or only wrong?"

"Nothing the androids accomplished was a direct product of the droids themselves." Her response was cool, unemotional. "Evolved programming is a human construct. Their analytical abilities condensed the time it would have taken a human to coordinate the same information, that's all."

"That's all? You don't credit them with anything positive? Not after they — not in medicine? Not in space travel? Molecular redesignation? Not —"

"They were allowed access to information in areas spread too thinly between human researchers."

"But that's because they could assimilate —"

"Their brain pans were larger and fully utilized. There wasn't anything phenomenal in what they were doing. Like all other machinery, the greatest lesson to be learned from them should have been how their construction and capabilities could be imitated to improve human talents. Not the other way around."

"Why in the hell," Elroy Smyth demanded, "do you hate them all so personally?"

She glanced at him finally. "I don't *hate* them!"

"Of course you do! Listen to yourself! You refuse

to give them credit for anything — any improvements in this world — because they're just machines. But at the same time you hold them in contempt as if they've personally corrupted us. How can you juxtapose those feelings? They can't be not responsible on one hand — but responsible on the other!"

"Because I recognize them as destructive influences doesn't mean I feel some sort of personal vendetta!"

"Destructive influences! Cures for hundreds of diseases were found because of them!"

Valentine's voice grew sharper. "They found no information that wasn't already available."

Elroy snorted. "They eliminated scientists' making a career of grants, that's what they did. They got researchers out of the labs where all they were doing was concocting trillion-dollar stews of rat guts and cancer cells."

"Yes . . . and what happened to those minds then?" Valentine turned in the water to face her father. "Did the quality of research rise? No — it came to a grinding halt. The droids could do anything — put in a heart in twenty minutes. They became invaluable to society and society became dependent upon them. Dig a ditch, make a hat, be a babysitter, perform microsurgery on the brain — leave it all to the robots. Do you know how many people applied to medical school even two years after the public got hold of these androids? Or engineering school? Or teaching schools or law school? Ivy League schools that had been around since the eighteenth century were on the streets begging for applicants within five years of the mass marketing of androids."

"I do know that the androids were an ideal to most people." Elroy answered quietly. "For the first time in the history of this world people could concentrate on something other than survival. The average man or woman could have one to clean their house, cook their dinner, water their roses. People finally had time. And people *didn't* let themselves get stupid, Valentine. A whole generation — as you put it — had time to get involved with other things; there was a surge of self-improvement and humanitarian projects during that period, that made it unlike any other time in history. Technology accelerated on its own — but at a pace and with a humanness that couldn't have been predicted, the way the twentieth century was going. Even the economy became healthy —"

"The programmers got rich. They were on their way to holding all the cards."

"How can you be so narrow-minded? Everyone benefited from what was happening — the merging of the largest governments in the world! It was a dream come true! And you — even you admit the androids were responsible for that! You don't know what it was like before — when this planet was split off from the ones out there —" He jabbed his thumb upward, "— who didn't want anything to do with a little ball of mud whose people couldn't even stop spitting at their neighbors! You have no idea what it was like when water and space were walls between people —"

"Now you're crediting androids with saving people from themselves?"

"They were there at the crossroads! They changed things. They impressed the Aliens enough to believe we could finally bridge the gaps —"

"That kind of thinking was the problem. They were there. They changed things. So were sewing machines and common cars. I don't hear you talking about *those* things like they're a new race. You give droids a credence they don't deserve."

"I never said —"

"But you think it, don't you?" She turned away. "Somewhere in there you're remembering — and influenced by — an android that played ball with you when no one else had time, one that listened to you when you were upset, one that did your homework on the sly — and gave you a sense of friendship. It fulfilled some need in you that you thought no one else could fill."

"You don't understand —" he began, but she interrupted sharply.

"I do understand. Better than you. They could assimilate information, all right. They could evaluate and learn and adjust their objectives accordingly. I can imagine what it was like when people started seeing human qualities in them. They didn't stop to question whether there were real actions and reactions, or ones triggered by a coding the machines were learning second by second. Being taught every minute of the day by every human being they came in contact with. The androids' grasp of the situation was so adept they could make themselves seem more human than humans."

Elroy could see it coming as well as he could hear it. Powerless to stop it, intrigued already by the passion guiding her, he listened, pleased that he had found her trigger and was responsible for the passion — even if it was in disagreement with his own.

"And what's the biggest vulnerability of the

human race? How do they gauge their own humanity? By always wanting to be the Good Guy. So they kept giving in, accepting the whole routine more and more. 'Yeah, okay, let a robot be on a jury — he'll be more impartial' — and then, 'Why not have an android judge?' Talk about upholding the law to an exacting degree! By then they were already better at policing than any man or woman on the force . . . Congress? the Senate? Who really could be a better representative of an entire state? Unmotivated by greed, unseduced by power, carrying around with them the memory of every complaint, vote and special interest of each and every individual they were supposedly representing . . . And while all this is going on . . . step by step, debate by debate — talk shows and corporate media making sure the questions got less and less shocking by hashing out the controversy until it wasn't even a controversy anymore — then what happens? Lonely little girls and boys get ideas in their heads because the family android — once servant, then pet, now *pal* —" Her voice had risen, lowered, tightened, "— is a lot more attentive and willing than anybody else! And suddenly we've got people saying they're in love. And why not? They were already flourishing in those 'isn't this great, nobody's being degraded' bordellos, weren't they? Which the state made money on. With applause. No disease. No abortion. No adultery, even."

"Lines get crossed when . . . people are trying to work out where things fit," Elroy said quietly.

"Unfortunately those lines can't always be recrossed."

"There's a human element here in all of this, that I feel you miss." His voice was gentle, almost

78

pleading. "You're so — absolute. So unbending." He did not point out the distancing she revealed in her own words. *They,* she had said, referring to human beings. *Them.* "You've always been this way. Androids are bad — period. Worthless, dangerous; you won't even consider the positive effect they've had on society. The ways they've helped us advance —"

"The billions of dollars spent trying to destroy them. Not to mention the lives lost trying. Not to mention the ones still out there still being handed legitimate licenses —"

"Not to mention," Elroy interrupted, "that once again you're putting the weight of responsibility where you want to. If a ship goes down — even from a malfunction — you don't blame the ship. Or the people who designed the ship. If a malfunction weren't their intention . . ."

She had relaxed a little after saying so much. Holding onto the edge of the pool, stretching back, neck exposed, her long hair floating over the water top. She raised her head as he spoke, meeting his eyes finally, directly, and her look was as cold as her words were steady. "You're questioning the guilt of the Doctor?"

"She's just a person, Valentine. A scientist . . . hell, a talented data programmer!" He leaned toward her, speaking earnestly. "It was the government that labeled her intentions as criminal. What did she do that she hadn't always done? She made androids. The androids they wanted! They'd made her a national hero, for God's sake — and then suddenly, overnight, she's a fugitive, because they became frightened —"

"She took the androids across the line."

"That's right! She's the one who made it obvious

79

it wasn't going to work — that if they were acknowledged as a race, we would eventually be —"

"Destroyed."

"Yes! Destroyed! Don't you ever wonder why a woman as clever as this one would do that? Would create programs which would evolve so quickly and so obviously that people would feel threatened by the androids? Would actually regress in their support of them after all of the successes —"

"They're still here."

"But not free as they were! And they're heavily controlled and have been relegated back to servile positions. Do you know how long it's been since I've even seen an android with a face?"

"Go down into the city any night of the week. Any city."

"So why is she still building them? Ones that are being caught as defectives? Ones still trying to cross the line?"

"Because she's a megalomaniac. She thinks she's a god. She's building an army to replace the human race. Or so she thinks."

Elroy straightened. "Huh?"

Valentine blinked. She dipped lower in the water, rewetting her shoulders, ignoring his surprise.

"They do teach you that stuff in there, don't they? No wonder . . ." He sucked in a small tight breath. "You're saving the whole world, aren't you?"

Her annoyed glance did not stop a thin flush of pink from warming her cheeks.

"No wonder your mother's so proud of you. My daughter the Crusader. I imagine it makes her sleep better nights knowing you're out there bashing their heads so we won't lose ours again."

Despite the sarcasm and the embarrassment she had been made to feel, Valentine did not turn away from the remark. She moved instead, small waves circling around her, facing him, fresh beads of water glistening on her shoulders. She spoke slowly. "Maybe what makes her sleep better at night is hoping that each one of them I blow apart is The One. Maybe every one of them I kill erases a tiny piece of the memory she has of the one that almost destroyed her."

He watched her face. Did not speak.

"I imagine that she does lie there some nights thinking about me — after you've undressed her, after you've put her into bed — maybe when she wants something, but doesn't want to wake you up. Maybe when she can't sleep, can't get up, can't even turn herself over — maybe she does think about me and what I'm doing and how many I'm getting — and it gets her mind off That One. You say the nightmares don't come much anymore, but surely you don't think the memory isn't there. You know it is. She can still describe in detail what it feels like to be picked up by hands that feel human at first; she has no difficulty remembering what it felt like when those hands turned into steel — and those ten steel fingers started to squeeze and her hips were pulverized by a machine that was only about two inches into its evolution, into its imitation of human fear. A machine reacting to nothing more than the brand-new uniform of a cadet. An eighteen-year-old cadet."

Elroy moved his feet in the water. Valentine turned her attention to the house.

"If it helps her to sleep better, thinking about what I'm doing — reading about it, hearing about it, imagining how good it feels to watch the fuckers blow apart — then I'm glad. Because it does feel good. It feels great."

She sounded unfinished, but her mouth closed firmly, emitting nothing further.

Elroy remained silent.

Valentine slid soundlessly back into the water.

Valentine was surprised she had fallen asleep. She had swum hard after the argument and then she had climbed into the Cleansing Pool, meaning to relax for only a few minutes while the chemicals washed away and the emollients soaked in. The steamy warmth of the bathhouse and the hot gush of water swirling around her had been more relaxing than she'd expected. She could see through the tinted flexglass that the afternoon sun had moved almost an hour across the sky.

The argument with her father seemed far away. She closed her eyes again, letting her head rest against the cushioned edge of the basin. Warm, heavy water raced over her body from every direction, seeming like gentle hands kneading her from every direction. She drew her legs up and parted her knees. She brought her arms up and rested her hands against her thighs. Her palms were hot and soft. Jets of water gushed around her hips and beat tenderly against her lower back.

How strange to be out of the city, she thought, though she didn't mean the city at all. The bathhouse was as familiar as the pool and the house and the long white driveway leading to it all. She had grown up here and nothing was unfamiliar. At eighteen — after tutors and the years of mandatory socialization trips abroad with others her own age — she had entered the preparatory school for the Academy. She had lived in a dorm on campus, away for the first time and allowed to come home often. As often as a person could manage with the demanding schedule of classes ten hours a day, six days a week for two years with only Christmas and Thanksgiving breaks and three weeks off in the summer.

When she had entered the Academy at twenty, all that had changed. She had moved into a barracks where holidays ceased to exist and none of the days of the week was wasted; even the four weekends off each year were an unspoken test. Those who grasped the point of the Academy used those weekends in target practice, scoured the libraries or sat in on classes they did not otherwise have time for. She had not seen her parents until the day she graduated two years later.

Her reward had been the listing of her name as the top ranking cadet — not just of that year, but ever. And an official letter from the Committee and the President congratulating her and telling her to report to the Controllers Division the following Monday morning.

Valentine smiled, not opening her eyes, moving her knees, the water swirling around her feet and ankles and lower body.

She still lived in her first apartment — the one she'd bought on her own credit allowance as a brand-new Controller. She'd had it decorated during her first assignment out in the field and had returned two months later to find it even more satisfying with its sparseness and suggestion of both elegance and austerity. She was rarely home after that and had made no changes, nor needed to. It was a place to sleep, to hang her weapon, to occasionally invite a woman to. Women liked her apartment. If her line of work and her position did not impress them enough, the expensive apartment did.

Familiarity was an easy and uncomplicated path down which many a woman invited Valentine. Valentine liked that. Complications were not her preference. She had no talent for fielding girlish emotional reactions to her concentration on her work. Luckily, she had discovered in the last few years that she had an instinctual talent for choosing just the right woman. A radar for finding and aiming her attractiveness at these particular women — along with the skills necessary for getting in and getting out of bed with them without any residue to confuse the pleasantness of the encounter. If such actions had become simply a habit — complete with her own blindness to women taking the opposite point of view of her treatment of them — Valentine did not see it as such.

She dropped her right knee, her hand still resting on it. Water rushed over the already warmed flesh and she allowed her fingers to move over the thigh to the inside, kneading gently as if testing the firmness — flexing her muscles, drawing her fingers up as she did. Her legs were long, slender, well developed. There was little in Valentine's life that did not encourage her to work out with the highly developed programs at the gym. The muscles were there, taut and hard in her long limbs, though she had always wished they were more apparent.

Valentine let her head lounge back again, more conscious of the jets pulsating against her back, the surge of water pumping around her. Undressing — and recalling the undressing — of the objects of her interests always ignited a fascination in her.

She pulled in a long slow breath, her neck twisting a little as she turned her head on the soft cushion. Her fingers grazed soft hair, reminding her instantly of a hundred other sensations she had encountered and created . . . Overheated flesh, wet and throbbing against her hand . . .

She opened her eyes, spread her legs, let her other leg drop into the water, her other hand brushing the back of her right hand and then curling over the knuckles. She relived the memories slowly, luxuriously, all of her senses focused on the sounds, the scents . . .

Without planning, her thoughts leapt to a particular woman and then another, still another, until she was flipping through the files at rapid speed, tossing up flashes of feeling, pulses of memory, searching for just the right one.

The first, the last, the oldest, the youngest. The blondest. The blackest. The loudest. The quietest. A symphony of sound swept over her: a gasp, a squeal, a moan, the music of her name being called in half a dozen languages and at twice as many levels on scales of urgency. Eyes: wide and round, closed, narrowed, glazed, rolling back and focusing on her. Mouths: open and closed, grimacing and disappearing. The memories shot by more quickly as she closed her own eyes, opened her own mouth, moved her own hand. Her shoulders tightened, her stomach grew taut, her breath more forced as she searched for the woman,

85

the combination of women, the one created from all the encounters, all the conquests, all the memories and moments — that would solidify and come to her now, for her, now.

When the image came, it slid in without warning, popping into her mind on a screen separate from the others. No nakedness, no passion, no candle-lit, wine-drenched undulations tangled up in satin sheets.

The body was small, unspectacular, fully clothed, somehow obviously inhibited.

No, Valentine protested; but the image persisted, the light of it (the bright office, the stark bright office light) so strong it wiped out all of the other visions.

Amelia glancing up at her from her desk.

Amelia looking surprised.

Amelia looking unsure.

Amelia looking amused.

Amelia looking at her.

Every small escaped expression Valentine had glimpsed of the woman, caught, logged and kept for her own. No ecstasy. No sexual intimacy. Just the reality of her.

Valentine's knees came together involuntarily as a sound escaped from her throat in a painful plea.

She moved and the movement was excruciating, a movement against the tautness of her stomach muscles, a movement against the desire of her body to be rigid, a movement against the power of the image filling her mind, pressing against her hand, spreading through her.

It did not cross her mind to unwrap the package this time; the package unwrapped her. A simple reach

for her became ecstasy in imagination, a triggering
that unleashed a vibration in Valentine's body.

"Valentine," Amelia whispered. "Come here."

No. "Lie down."

No. They were lying down.

No. Amelia was crossing the room toward her.
Valentine was wiping the sleep from her eyes,
unprepared, ignorant. Even innocent . . .

No. Valentine knew . . . no, Valentine didn't know.

"Valentine." Different voice. Same voice. Different
tone. Unfamiliar tone. "Valen." Yes . . . "Valen . . ."
Hand on her shoulder. Lean forward. Mouth close.
Mouth.

A trembling began in her thighs and moved down
and then up. Her toes curled against the padding
beneath her. Her head came up and her chin down,
her hair falling forward, her upper body curved
tightly upon herself. "Valen," the phantom Amelia
murmured in the voice Valentine had never heard
before.

"I want you."

"Amelia!" Valentine cried aloud, the cry only a
whimper from her throat, the tremor that carried it
becoming an instant shudder that reverberated
through her head, her chest, her heart, her brain; her
hips surged up to meet it.

Her hands breaking free, trying to gather the
padding on each side of her within desperate fists.

"I was just getting ready to come after you."
Elroy met his daughter at the doorway. "What'd you
do? Fall asleep in the bath?"

87

"Umm." She brushed past, heading for the 'vator. Light music and the sound of voices drifted in from the other room.

"The guests are here already. Your mother's getting impatient. You need to change."

"I didn't bring a change."

"The bathrobe would be a little out of place, but the clothes you came in were hung in your room."

"Um." The 'vator doors slid closed. She crossed her arms, tapping her fingers against her upper arms. She felt blanked, wiped clean. Impatient with her own body. She felt like liquid waiting to solidify again. The feeling was usually a pleasant one, but at the moment it grated on her; it seemed like something that it shouldn't be.

She was out of the 'vator before it opened completely. The hallway was a white cave lighted with long tracks of muted lights. Nearby was the door to her old bedroom, a tall glossy white with a curved cathedral top. She pushed through and strode into the room. Intention was a sharp knife slicing through the jumble of thoughts and unsure movements. Ignoring the clothes waiting for her, she slid aside inset doors, flipping a switch that would bring the revolution of the clothing racks.

The carefully stored khaki uniforms that identified an officer of the Controllers Division swung into view.

A few minutes later, the sight of her reflection in the mirror brought a look of relief to her face. She could almost feel the last of the liquid feeling drying up within her. Then she was back in the hall, her stride a little stronger than before. By the time the 'vator opened into the front room, she felt relaxed and prepared.

What she saw as she stepped out almost sucked the strength from her once again.

Controllers. In civilian clothing! The room was full of her crew members and co-workers.

She stared around, speechless.

"Smyth!" Dolly was the first to see her. "How come you never told us you were rich?"

"Darling!" Margaret was maneuvering her chair toward Valentine. "Surprise!"

Valentine's jaw tightened.

"Your aunt is here! Your Uncle Clifford from Los Angeles! And your friends! They're all here." Margaret Payton reached Valentine, wheeling her chair in next to her so they could survey the room together. "It's fine for them to give you a Citation — or whatever they choose to do — but I wanted them to know how proud your family is of you, too." Margaret looked up at her daughter. "And I've never had the opportunity to meet any of your friends . . ." On this last, she turned her face back to the room, unwilling to have her daughter see her own look of triumph. "Finally!"

The pressure in Valentine's jaw increased. Stepping back into the 'vator wouldn't resolve the situation. Her mother had known damned well she wouldn't be pleased. Not with having her co-workers here, not with revealing the ostentation of her own life which had somehow always seemed unfitting to Valentine. Not with her mother making such a fuss about recognition in front of people who were her co-workers, even her subordinates . . . The room seemed packed with curious faces gaping, both at her and at the extravagant surroundings

And then she saw Amelia. In uniform. Hands in

pockets. Standing near the buffet. Looking small and uncomfortable. Glaringly out of place.

Oh God. She hadn't. "Mother." Valentine leaned down, her voice a harsh whisper. "You didn't . . ."

Margaret's glance followed her daughter's. "Oh, but I did," she answered and in her voice now was the triumph. "I've met almost everyone," she went on. "Except the little plain one in the uniform. Is that —" She started to point. Valentine straightened, stiffened, hissed, "Mother!" and saw her father heading for the buffet, making his way to Amelia.

Valentine plunged into the crowd. She nodded at the amused congratulations as she passed her own people. *She'd hear about this from them; they'd never let her live it down.* She avoided the relatives waving her over and brusquely greeted those who could not be avoided.

She caught Elroy just as he reached the end of the table. "No." She grasped his arm firmly, preventing him from going any further. "She's the *Director*. Mother shouldn't even have invited her."

"She came."

"I don't care if she came. She was being polite. I don't know why she came. It doesn't matter." She turned him around, overcoming his resistance.

"You want to unhand me?" His hand covered hers. "What do you think I'm going to do — ask her if she's an android?"

"I think you're going to try and talk politics with her." She didn't let go. "And I think you're not going to. I think you're going to leave her alone."

"Valentine." His voice took on an edge. He looked at his arm and her hand still holding it.

She released her hold. "Just leave her alone.

90

She's —" She almost looked at Amelia, but caught herself in time so that the glance seemed more a diversion than a confirmation of whom she was talking about. "She's not like you think. She's kind of . . . quiet. She's kind of . . . nice."

"Nice?" Elroy mocked a look of horror. "The Director of the ICRC and the Controllers is . . ." His hand went to his chest. "Nice?"

Valentine meant to speak, to protest, to return the sarcasm — but she caught sight of something that froze the words in her throat: someone walking toward them.

Elroy caught the change, glanced in that direction and jabbed a finger to the bridge of his glasses, pushing them back into place. "Margaret felt it was fair. She called her. I mean, she called your mother. She thought it only fair to invite her . . ." His voice was instantly different, alerted, strained, apologetic.

Valentine's jaw went from slack to steel. The anger in her eyes dissipated and was replaced with a coldness that did not seem at all out of place with the rest of her face.

"Just be cool about it," Elroy urged quietly. "Just be pleasant, for heaven's sake."

But the woman passed them and walked directly to Amelia.

"Are you her boss?"

Amelia had not been unaware of the woman's approach. But she had been paying attention to the peculiar conversation between Valentine and her father; so the woman had to ask the question twice.

"Are you Director Roberts?"

"Amelia." Amelia turned her head. "Yes. That's who I am."

"I'm pleased to meet you, Director Roberts." A hand was extended awkwardly, a little too high and curved, as if the woman were offering the back of her hand for a kiss.

Amelia retrieved the hand and squeezed it gently.

"I'm so glad to meet you. I've dreamed about meeting you for a long time. I mean I've thought about it . . . dreamed about it sounds funny." The woman excused her words with a laugh. It was a nice laugh; a little high, a little awkward, like the handshake, but sincere. "Valentine thinks so highly of you, I know. I hope I'm not bothering you. I hope this is okay, me coming over to you like this, in front of people and everything. I know you're important. My name is Linda."

Amelia nodded.

Encouraged, the woman nodded and then looked around, losing ground after the expulsion of words. She studied the other guests talking and drinking, yet seemed not to see them at all. "I saw you over here all by yourself. I saw you in that uniform. I know it's a law you're not allowed to wear anything else."

"A rule," Amelia corrected gently.

"I know everything about the Controllers. I've been reading about you . . . all of you . . . since Valen went in. She's one of your best, right? One of the best ever?"

Amelia nodded again.

"I worry about her. I mean, I know she's good . . . I know Valen — oh! I shouldn't call her that . . . she hates it when I call her that . . . she hates to be called that. But I was saying . . . I know she knows what she's doing and I bet — I bet you take real good care of your people — but I worry about her anyhow." She tossed off a laugh, but not like the one earlier. It was small and helpless. "I worry about something happening to her. It's so dangerous out there . . . I mean, it's dangerous in this world, isn't it? but more dangerous out there . . ."

Full information clicked into place.

Amelia's pupils dilated a fraction of a millimeter. "I would never send Valentine into a situation I felt she could not handle," she said quietly. The resonance of her voice was different than it had been; the woman had to lean closer — and unconsciously influenced, her voice would drop also when she spoke again. The conversation could no longer be heard by anyone else who might be listening.

"I'm honored to meet you," Amelia said. "It is always a pleasure to meet a birth parent of one of the Controllers."

"But I . . . I . . ." A hand came up to touch the strand of hair that had strayed from the woman's carefully styled hair, the same burnt red as Valentine's. Just as the eyes were the same vivid blue. "That's very kind of you to say . . ." She took a breath, her chest moving with the burden. The features so strong in Valentine were obvious in this woman, but they were softened, less defined, more childlike. "I don't know how you knew that," she added. "I didn't . . . I wouldn't . . . she wouldn't be too happy if she knew I . . . that you —" She stopped, not knowing how to continue with the thought. "She doesn't much claim me —" She stopped again; whether embarrassed or pained was unclear. "They raised her, you know. She never lived with me. Elroy and Maggie — they paid for her and . . ." Again she stopped in mid-sentence as if the rest of the words could not be brought out into the open. Amelia cocked her head slightly, listening with an interest the woman seemed to recognize as more than politeness. "Not many people know that. I guess it's in her records, huh? I know you guys do real big background checks. Most people don't even know . . . They've been real good to her. She had tutors and all the toys you could imagine. Some robot crushed Maggie's pelvis so she couldn't have kids, ya know . . ." Linda stopped, abruptly this time, dipping her head, peering at Amelia questioningly. "I mean . . . android?"

"A renegade, yes," Amelia agreed. "A terrible tragedy."

"It was so bad they couldn't even put mosta the pieces back together again. I mean they couldn't fix her and she didn't want any artificial parts in her — she's kind of . . . militant, Maggie is. 'Bout that kind of thing, anyway."

For the first time Amelia smiled.

"I guess some of that rubbed off on Valen." Valentine's mother recognized the reason for Amelia's smile and shared it. "I guess a lot of that rubbed off on Valen." The pleasant laugh returned and Amelia chuckled.

"Well." Linda reached out to touch Amelia's arm. "I don't wanna bother you anymore. I just came over here to kind of . . . thank you. For taking care of her and stuff. I know you do. You're a lot different than I thought you'd be. Nice, I mean." The laugh

94

returned. She rubbed Amelia's arm. "I don't mean I
didn't think you would be . . . I just mean . . . you
make it easy. You're easy to talk to. You make me
feel impor—" She brought her lips together tightly.
Her eyes were warm and moist. Larger than
Valentine's. She rubbed Amelia's arm more vigorously.
Unaccustomed to being touched, Amelia kept her
attention locked on the face. It was the only way she
had of stopping herself from looking down in
curiosity at the unsolicited and curious gesture of
affection.

She found herself thinking how much Valentine
would recoil at such a touch.

Less than ten feet away, Valentine was recoiling
at merely watching the intimacy. If her emotions had
felt confused and jumbled before, they were
threatening to lose all control now. "Get her out of
here," she hissed at her father. "Get her away from
her!" She herself seemed unable to move.

"She's done. She's leaving," Elroy stated quietly.
"She'll probably go now. I'm sure she's uncomfortable
here — you could ask her to stay."

Valentine looked down at him. "Get her out of
here," she repeated through gritted teeth.

Linda Hart was indeed headed for the doors which
would lead her to the front hall and to the front
door, where a common car would be waiting to take

95

her back to the city. She turned in the doorway, pleased to see Amelia facing in her direction. She waved in gratitude. Amelia smiled back.

Watching, Valentine seemed able finally to shake off the immobility. "How dare she," she snapped. "She had no right to even be here."

Elroy started to protest.

Valentine turned away abruptly.

"Valentine."

Valentine whirled back sharply.

"I'm afraid I have to go," Amelia apologized from directly behind her. "I've been called back." She held out a small flat disc in her hand. A thin red line blinked across the bottom of it.

Elroy dove at the opportunity. "I'm Elroy Smyth, Valentine's father." He thrust his hand toward her. "We haven't had the opportunity to meet before."

Amelia nodded and smiled as she took the offered hand. "I'm sorry I have to leave so abruptly. It's a very nice party."

"Maybe you could just check in," Elroy suggested. "Maybe it's something you could handle without leaving. I know Valentine's mother was looking forward to meeting you — and getting to know you."

Valentine's glance at him was swift and dark. Her attention moved back to Amelia, her gaze more intense than usual, as if studying her superior's face for ill effects from her recent meeting. "I appreciate you coming. I know you're very busy."

"You'll give her my regrets?"

Valentine nodded — then she saluted.

A soft sound came out of Elroy's nose — almost but not quite a snort. Amelia glanced at him with new interest.

"Perhaps," she said — with what seemed to him like more warmth than had been there before — "we'll get a chance in the future to talk."

Elroy nodded, pleased. She'd heard it. He knew it. He loved the fact that she had and loved her cool and unperturbed response. This one was a damn sight less defensive than his own daughter, he could see that now. "I'll be looking forward to it," he agreed, already excited at the prospect.

Great, thought Valentine sourly. She watched Amelia walking away, moving purposefully toward the doors. Valentine did not understand, nor did she think about, how and why much of the anger of moments before had evaporated.

—3—

"I want you to go to Paris. The President is in residence there."

Amelia did not look up from the flatscreen as she spoke, nor did she turn it to share whatever information she was viewing. Valentine stood silently on the opposite side of Amelia's desk, waiting patiently.

"There may be a situation. It hasn't been confirmed. I have reason to believe his son may be in trouble." Amelia finally glanced from the GEMCOM screen to her first officer. "The President hasn't reported it. He won't be expecting you."

Valentine nodded. "How do I explain my presence?"

"You don't."

Valentine nodded again, pleased but able to prevent the satisfaction she felt from showing. Despite the specific wording of the ICRC Code, which clearly positioned the President and Committee members at the top of the chain of command, Valentine did not, in her own mind, have any superior other than the woman delivering orders at this very moment. To her mind, her job had no room for such politics.

"Keep in touch."

Amelia's odd (in Valentine's opinion) tendency to use ancient slang did not distract or influence Valentine from her own consistent professionalism. A curt affirmative shake of her head was followed by a salute that was acknowledged by a half-smile moving cross Amelia's mouth.

Valentine turned on her heel, wheeled back at the sound of Amelia's voice. "Lieutenant? I'm sorry I had to leave your parents' home so abruptly yesterday."

Valentine frowned, disappointed — embarrassed — that Amelia had found it worth mentioning. She nodded, closing the subject.

Long after Valentine had left, Amelia was still sitting quietly. Her gaze had drifted back to the flatscreen, but her attention had not. Her best Controller was a mystery with seemingly no unraveling.

Unquestionably the most dependable, the most loyal, the most skilled, the Lieutenant was also the one Controller who gave Amelia the most concern. While superior in her knowledge and use of weapons, aircraft, and decision-making under the worst of the pressures of the field, she was also a potential victim of her own passion. Amelia suspected untested blind spots in the younger woman, unresolved contradictions that masked vulnerabilities which had never shown up in Academy evaluation tests.

Vulnerabilities. The word itself was a mystery.

The birth mother had triggered something in Valentine. Amelia had immediately sensed the anger as a mask for fear — of what, though? Had this highly intelligent officer really assumed Amelia would not be fully aware of her background? Why should such old history be a continuing catalyst for such a strong reaction? Why couldn't Valentine conquer it as she conquered everything else?

Vulnerabilities. Such a curious and human word. One Amelia had been musing over for some time — tossing it back and forth in relationship to those she met, and to herself. Thinking about it was a small and pleasant feast when her thoughts weren't occupied elsewhere. Vulnerabilities were so common . . . which made Amelia even more curious about Valentine's reaction the night before. She obviously did not want her childhood of wealth to be known. Even more so, she didn't want her real background to be known . . .

Almost unconsciously, Amelia touched a series of

100

numbers and letters on her keyboard. Data rolled onto the screen.

Hart, Valentine: 2102, April 13-
Mother: Hart, Linda J.: 21117 Goodman Street, Mohawk, PA USA
Father: Unknown

Amelia rejected the entry.

Hart, Valentine: 2102, April 13-
Mother: Hart, Linda J.: 21117 Goodman Street, Mohawk, PA USA
Father: Classified

Her fingers moved over the keys.

Hart, Valentine: 2102, April 13-
Mother: Hart, Linda J.: 21117 Goodman Street, Mohawk, PA USA
Father: 55986900011X-BT

The Director rested her fingers thoughtfully against the board. The cause of Valentine's vulnerability was caught somewhere in the seemingly innocent series of numbers.

Amelia did not go deeper into the file; she had already been there. Valentine's was perhaps the most familiar to her of all the personnel files. But she reread the numbers slowly, as if looking for the answer there. She was not unaware of the controversy surrounding such parentage. She was not ignorant of the prejudices many people still felt, or would display if they knew. But most people did not know — and what did that have to do with Valentine's feelings, anyway? Why would these facts cause such a strong woman to buckle under from within?

Amelia's fingers moved restlessly, touching nothing. Was it the young mother's embrace of the situation? A touch rolled the birth/arrest/arraignment statements onto the screen. *Alex,* the mother had called him. *The law has no right. We belong together.* Her statements had been peppered with comments like those. The mother had referred to him as a cyborg, a sympathetic old word that insinuated he was more human than not. The courts had not agreed. "Alex" had not been a cyborg; the sperm had been stolen. The theft, denial, and insistence of innocence was the real crime to a world whose fear of manipulation by an android had reached paranoid proportions. "Alex" had been redesignated, undergone a facial restructure and been reassigned, both license and location. Linda Hart had then willingly sold the child to "let her live a normal life after all of this."

Amelia did not need to recheck the file to verify that Valentine would have been old enough at four to remember some of the controversy firsthand. The confidentiality of the information came later, after the courts had processed their decisions. The extreme classification in the Commission files was probably the only record of the specific relocation and re-licensing as well as other unpublicized detail to which the media had not had access at the time. The parents had done their best to bury the truth, despite their curious continued association with the birth mother.

Was Valentine afraid that people would find out? Did vulnerability exist primarily in fear of discovery? Secrets. Something to lose.

Amelia thought of the voice on the handset that had alerted her to the missing child. That voice had been vulnerable. *"I'm not sure . . ."* With a secret. *"I haven't told the President yet . . .'"* Something to lose. *"I'm just so afraid . . ."*

That vulnerability was obvious and unhidden.

Valentine's vulnerabilities weren't. Small little flashes masquerading as something else — anger, perfectionism, aggression.

Vulnerabilities. Amelia blacked the screen, the laziness of her movement betraying her thoughtfulness.

Jennifer had been vulnerable, too — if that meant helpless. The remembrance of her life vapor trailing across the wall came unexpectedly into Amelia's mind. *Physically helpless. Physically vulnerable.* But Jennifer was always those things.

Amelia was not aware of her own silence. She did not move; nothing moved around her. She did not blink. Her chest did not expand. Her breath did not extract from or deliver into the room. The enigma of Jennifer required all of her senses.

Jennifer was so unsure of herself. Jennifer had a roll of chocolates she kept hidden in her drawer beneath a stack of file discs. Jennifer creamed her hands with an irrational lotion of ingredients each morning. Jennifer had not fought back against the defective. Jennifer seemed to be almost entirely vulnerable — and somehow her vulnerability was less — more balanced — than Valentine's one defection from strength.

Amelia blinked, stared at the blank screen, confused. Why had Jennifer come into her mind? Why were her thoughts about her so trivial? so irrelevant? They led nowhere! asked nothing! Just came, unbidden, floating around into a sharp focus finally that at times immobilized Amelia, distracting her from all else.

Amelia shook loose from the puzzle and returned

to work, without having properly catalogued the ordeal she had once again experienced with her own vulnerability.

The President of the United People shoved aside a china plate smeared with the cold remains of his breakfast of eggs over-easy. Without looking up, he reached for the pen in the holder of his desktop blotter and began to scratch notes on the yellow sheet in front of him. He was dimly aware of the sun, hot and early, on his naked shoulders and moving down his back. He wrote quickly in large, sprawling letters, unpunctuated and often underlined, the familiar and comforting sound of the pen against the paper a catalyst that kept his hand moving. His heavy brows frowned into the deepening folds of flesh above and between his eyes.

Beneath the desk, his bare toes wriggled impatiently in the thickness of the carpet. The band of his pajama bottoms pinched a little too tightly across his breakfast-filled stomach, but he didn't take the time to adjust them or straighten his posture. He scribbled furiously, aware of how late it was already and how inadequately prepared he was for the meeting scheduled only a few hours from now.

He loved and hated Saturday meetings. Hated them because he would much rather have slept in on the one day he could get away with it — a luxury he didn't once doubt he deserved. Loved them because he loved all of his meetings — just like he loved all the rest of the responsibilities of Office. Every single one of them.

He glanced up when the door opened because he knew it would not be an aide. Not at this hour. Not with him in his pajama bottoms and without a shirt. It was Mariella, coming back. He watched her cross the large room. Watched her pick up his plate. When his eyes reached up and met hers, she touched her finger to her lips in a silencing gesture and smiled behind the finger. "I won't say a word," she whispered.

Amusement and affection came into his eyes. "That's twice now," he chided, referring to the interruptions of her entries.

"You have to eat, don't you?" She extended the plate for display. "You must have been hungry after all."

His attention lingered on the empty plate because he didn't know what to say. He wanted his wife to leave. He wanted to be alone again so that he could wrap himself in the cocoon of his concentration. But he felt this without hostility, which kept him from saying anything more, hoping in the absence of encouragement that she would go, on her own. Saturday mornings, after all, did usually belong to her.

"I can't find George Junior."

He glanced up but there was no alarm in her face. She had said it conversationally, even with a trace of the annoyance she seemed to reserve for their only child.

The President had never quite understood that annoyance; there was no mother more loving and doting than Mariella. But then, the President felt no child was quite as deserving of adulation in the first place as his son.

"He's probably out riding." He was not aware that his voice had dropped and warmed when he spoke of his child, as it always did. "He's taking those lessons to heart."

"He's not at the stables. He hasn't been for a week."

The President sat back, laying his pen down, startled. "But I thought he was enjoying —"

"He was."

"Then why —"

"Because I forbade him to ride for a month." Her interruptions had been clean, her voice well modulated. "He hasn't been allowed to even see Strawberry."

Oh-oh, he thought. He didn't want to ask any more, didn't want to examine the corner she had tricked him into. Especially now. He glanced down at his unfinished notes, swallowing irritation. It would do no good to try and combat her with that justified irritation. Her timing might be unfair but there was no stopping her. "What happened?" he asked quietly.

"I told him he could not go out one afternoon. To ride. It was misting. He was just getting over a cold. I told him he had to stay indoors."

The President waited.

She would not give an inch. "Well?" he prodded finally. "What happened? He went out anyway?"

"He had Silas bring Strawberry to see him."

George Ellison's eyebrows lifted. His lips parted but his mind seemed to go blank.

"And he rode him. In the dining room. And down the hall. And into the greenhouse." Her arms were folded before her chest, the plate dangling from her hand.

"No."

"And around the library." She seemed not to have heard his protest. "Around the foyer and the White Room. And apparently he had quite a tantrum when Strawberry refused to go up the stairs."

"You should have told me." It seemed the safest thing he could say. After ten years of his child's wonderful imagination, he could easily check the laughter over this particular antic until later, when he was alone.

"That has nothing to do with now." Her voice was firm. "He's obviously eluded the aides again. We've both spoken to him about that, haven't we?"

"Yes, yes, of course we have. The boy doesn't understand." George picked up his pen again. "It's a game to him, Mariella."

"It's not a game; the protecting, the rules . . . he certainly does understand, George —" She stopped herself.

For a moment they eyed one another warily. Her glance dropped to the waiting notepad. "We'll talk with him tonight?"

"Yes, of course." The President was eager to agree.

"If I can find him in this house before then —" She turned on her heel, no animosity in her parting words: "I'll leave you to your work."

By the time she reached the door, he was busily jotting down fresh notes.

The first thing he would do, when he got out, was sue the man who had put him in the bag. George Jr.

107

had decided that long ago. His father would throw him and his lousy friends into an air-tight international prison and they would sue the pants off of them as well.

But first he would go directly to his mother and get a reprieve from the Strawberry incident of last week. And then he would have a peanut butter and jelly sandwich and then he would take a bath. Because he had grit on him. Not just dirt, but scratchy, powdery stuff all over him. He couldn't imagine what it was, and it made him angry. He wouldn't have minded a little dirt here or there . . . but this was in his hair, between his toes, in his pants. When he put his hand under his shirt and rubbed his chest, he could rub it into flaky balls that left dust all over his skin and dry, ground-in crumbs all over his hands.

He must look a mess. When they got him out of this bag — he could imagine what he was going to look like. Filthy matted hair . . . and the ever-present Record-a-News waiting to take his picture, instantly looping it all back to the people out there. Just thinking about it made him madder. "You guys are going to be so sorry," he whispered.

There was no answer back. Only the rocking of whatever vehicle the bag was in which contained him.

Private First Class Michelle Levy, Marine Corps Division on Special Assignment, was the first person to notice the arrival of an O-Cat Blue Jay two miles outside the city. She was immediately curious, partly because the rules allowed the computers in the Paris tower to make the decision to admit them into air space without cause or question; more so, because she had never seen an ICRC craft up close. Regulations didn't prevent Michelle from assuming the right to first communication; and her personal interest in glimpsing this craft prevented her from mentioning to her supervisor, standing only a few feet away, what she'd just witnessed on the security monitors.

She gave the screen her full attention as she keyed in a brief generic welcome directed at the code numbers which had flashed in lieu of specific identification from the ship. She received an acknowledgment instantly — a curt "abort transmission" — and then she watched in fascination as her cursor flew backwards, erasing the answer, her question, the code, the trace of any communication or her computer's record of the sighting in the first place.

In a blip it was all gone. The private was looking at a blank screen which then refilled with the patterns it had displayed before the entry of the ICRC ship.

Mariella Gilten closed her son's bureau drawer and turned to face the room. *Was it a sixth sense?* The usual mess her son would make was as obvious to her as if he had his visible handprints on it. But the room was unusually messy. A different kind of mess swirled around the familiar mess. She could imagine her husband's questioning look if she tried to explain to him how she knew this. But she knew it.

And she knew George Jr. wasn't just hiding or avoiding the staff and the cameras, or playing one of his endless games of hide-and-seek.

He was missing. The conviction she had tried on for size with the nervous call to New York earlier had now become real.

Her son was definitely missing.

And someone had taken him from this very room.

"There's an ICRC ship here! They're monitoring the security system. They're pulling instantaneous cover directly from the main system; all communications, even internal." The aide relaying this information was breathless with excitement. "We think they've been here about forty-five minutes. Citizens have been calling it in. They wanted to know if there was a robot on the loose around here. We've just confirmed the ship by a visual sighting. We can't pick them up with our equipment at all! The tower doesn't even have a record of admitting them!"

"They wouldn't if they're on some sort of covert mission . . ." The sergeant in charge turned to face the others in the small room. Two men and a woman met her glance respectfully, then let their attention revert to the screens they were monitoring when she didn't address them directly. Sergeant Elaine F. Gerry didn't know what to say. To ask them to confirm that they hadn't seen even the briefest of blips or unusual activity was tantamount to accusing them of not reporting it to her. But had the ICRC ship really come down without any warning at all? Was that possible?

"Did you make contact with them?" She directed her question back at the aide. "Did they state why they were here?"

He shook his head. "They have their channels closed. They're not inviting communication."

The Sergeant ignored the aide's sarcasm. "Private Levy, see if you can get a response from them."

"I have no coordinates. I wouldn't know where to direct the communication now . . ." Michelle's words trailed off as she met her superior officer's sharp look.

The Sergeant's voice took on an edge. "Obviously, Private. You're going to have to go there. Sight them and attempt contact from close range." She now knew there had been at least one person in the room who had seen the craft enter French air space. Nonetheless, Levy was the most logical choice to send. Her expertise with a large assortment of electronic systems — she had, after all, almost made it into the Academy herself — might give her an upper hand in communicating with this division of the government that all too often played by its own set of rules.

"I have a situation that requires immediate attention, Sergeant." The voice from the doorway belonged to Masters Dugan himself. "You'll have to suspend your normal routines for the moment."

Dugan was the Director of the President's large Committee-designated private security staff; his presence in the Special Assignment room was highly unusual. The Sergeant and her people were placed on Military Special Assignment to the President for the same reason — protection — but from a different angle. As Commander of all Armed Forces, the President was protected by the military, which

111

involved itself in monitoring and even becoming involved in the security around him. Over the years, the two separate watchdogging factions had found it helpful to work together when necessary. Sergeant Gerry had as much respect for the abilities of the decorated ex-military director as he had for her.

She motioned Levy back down and moved to the door. "Yessir." She gestured to the hall and half-closed the door behind them when he had stepped out behind her. "What is it, Dugan?"

"We believe the Ellison boy has been snatched." The Security Director was eager to solicit the assistance of a woman as capable as the Sergeant. Still, his voice was tight, unemotional, restricted to the briefest of explanation. "His mother officially reported him missing twenty minutes ago. We've swept the grounds. We found nothing. No one has seen him or heard from him since last night."

"The monitoring tape?"

"It appears to be a rerun." Masters Dugan's voice was bitter. "Not the first time he's pulled this stunt. It wasn't caught until about eight this morning and only then because one of the aides noticed that it was clearly snowing outside his window. It hasn't snowed in a week."

"How's the President taking it?" The Sergeant understood his self-directed anger. It was, after all, his people who had overlooked the child's trick. "Especially with the meeting today . . .?"

"Not very well. He's meeting with his staff now, trying to decide whether or not to cancel his meeting." Dugan leaned closer. "Not to mention that he just got wind of an ICRC ship in the city."

"True." Gerry straightened up. "That's where I

was just sending Private Levy. To try and communicate — do you think there's a connection?"

The Security Director shrugged "Who knows? It's got the President worried, of course — and you know how arrogant those people from Robot Control can be. I was going to send a man out to explain the situation to them. They've got to understand this situation has priority."

"Maybe they already know," the Sergeant suggested. "Maybe one of your people contacted them already?"

"The President confirmed it only fifteen minutes ago," Dugan argued. "That ship's been here for —"

"Yes, I know, I know." The Sergeant looked thoughtful. "But you said the phony tape was found at eight. That's over two hours ago."

Dugan hesitated. Then, "No." His voice was firm. "They must be after one of their damn renegades."

"Are you aware they're tapping into your system? They're monitoring all external and internal data and pulling the classified files?"

"Well, of course." Dugan lost a little of his control at the suggestion of another oversight. "But they would monitor the President's residence to assure themselves that their droid isn't here. Isn't that correct? Wouldn't that be their procedure?"

"I really don't know." The Sergeant's voice had grown cool in retaliation. "But I think I should go ahead and send Levy out there. God knows what kind of equipment they've got aboard that thing. They might be able to help us."

"I do want to establish that there's no connection." Dugan forced away the last of the impatience he felt; he certainly didn't want to alienate the woman. "You send your . . . Levy out there. Tell her to tell the commander of the ship that I want to see him or her here — right away."

The Sergeant's response was a quick nod.

Mariella returned to her son's room after the security people had gone over it.

She sat down on the bed and let her hands fall to the coverlet on either side of her. The material felt rough and familiar. She pinched it between her knuckles and held it loosely. Outside the window, beyond her son's bed, the sun shone brightly across the broad expanse of lawn.

A ball of agony was working itself up into her throat from her tightening chest. She looked around the room slowly. A worn stuffed animal, a discarded pair of trousers, a round hoop, a scarred toy vehicle sitting lopsided because a wheel had been broken off or been borrowed for use elsewhere. She looked at his desk; the chair was shoved beneath it, its legs showing scuff marks where the sides of his shoes had marred them. A book lay open on the floor, another lay closed across it, a half-empty glass balanced atop that with a gyroscope at the bottom of the liquid.

Impossibly messy. She had thought this of him a thousand times. He had grown up being trailed by domestics and staff members who spent their days righting the world he turned upside down. A spoiled, precocious, often selfish child. And often not. The realization brought the lump firmly into her throat.

Her glance fell on the handset and she thought of the call she had made earlier, concentrating on trying to remember the voice because she had been holding the panic in check then too — and the voice had soothed the panic somehow.

How? She focused on the mystery of that, tight fists clutching the coverlet. The woman had not been particularly encouraging. At least she had not said the usual trite assuring phrases, which would not have calmed Mariella at all. Instead the voice — woman — had been . . . calm? Yes, calm, Mariella decided, trying to swallow around the fear, concentrating very hard on the words that had been said to her.

I'll send the best that I have. I'll see that it's taken care of by . . . Slight pause, as if the speaker were — glancing at the time? calculating? . . . *later today.*

How odd, Mariella had thought. How seriously the caller had taken her. Without questions. Or reassurances. *Why did the lack of reassurances have such a positive effect on me? It was not as if anyone, could actually calculate the chances of* . . . *success in a situation such as this.*

Even now, though, she realized she was breathing easier. The lump had become controllable again.

She got up and began to put away her son's belongings so that she would not have to chastise him when he returned.

"This is interesting." Bonny held up a narrow strip of tape, wrapping it around the side of her hand and sliding it back onto the spool in one deft motion. "A close-up of the window. Look at this: magnified all to hell." Her fingers glided across buttons and the scene of the window filled the screen more and more tightly until they were viewing snowflakes the size of quarters. "At this magnification, they look pretty damn round to me."

"Snowflakes aren't round," Tom offered.

"Thanks for that confirmation." Bonny was already reaching for the communicator that would connect her to Valentine. Tom covered her hand with his. "Which means they probably picked him up during the few minutes the staff was changing tapes — withdrawing this one and inserting a new one."

"Then they came back to him and he's gone . . . and they think he's been gone for hours. Meanwhile, they move him out without anybody watching them at that point at all. We need a ground sample to verify." Bonny shrugged off his hand and pushed the switch to relay the information to Valentine.

Valentine listened to the news thoughtfully before turning to a woman who had just approached her. "What is it?"

"There's a vehicle on the ground trying to make contact with us. They're jamming a couple of frequencies with an emergency code."

Valentine frowned. "Are they in trouble?"

"I don't think so. It's a military vehicle. One of those staff vans. Probably another attempt from the Presidential residence to inquire —"

Valentine interrupted with a gesture. "Scan the interior. See if there's anything interesting on board."

Private Levy could barely contain her excitement.

So far the interior of the ICRC ship wasn't at all disappointing and she could hardly believe her luck at meeting the woman who now stood before her.

The woman seemed either unconscious of her looks . . . or precisely the opposite; so in control of her bearing and the intimidating impression she made that everything about her emanated confidence. From the moment Valentine entered the room, there wasn't the slightest bit of doubt as to who was in charge.

"Private First Class Michelle Levy, Special Assistant —"

Valentine waved away the rest of her speech. "I know who you are." She reached out to tap the nameplate the Private wore. "What you are, and where you're from; I can assume why you're here. Do you understand half as much about me?"

"I — I know who you are." Michelle felt as if her toes were curling in her boots.

The edge of Valentine's mouth twitched with amusement. "Then you're aware that an officer of this division, such as myself, is authorized to assume command under whatever circumstances I may deem necessary, and that under Code 186-A, section 14, paragraph B of the Committee's Open Book, my orders supersede any previous ones you may have received."

It was not a question.

Michelle had no intention of questioning anything this woman said anyway. She had, in fact, once imagined herself in just such a position as this one — since it had been only a year before that she had failed the test for entry into the Academy by a mere fraction of a point.

"Whatever you say, Lieutenant." Her

117

acknowledgment, immediate salute and delighted grin were not lost on Valentine.

"He was cursing me." The man who had just joined the group was very thin and stood well over six feet tall before he dropped his narrow frame onto the low wall of the balcony. "The kid is quiet now." He smiled, displaying teeth that were unusually white and large with broad canines a jagged extra millimeter too long; they glistened beneath the late morning tropical sun. The smile seemed in direct contrast to the rest of his face, which was pinched and pale.

"Is he still coherent?" The woman who asked the question sat at a white wicker table a few feet away, sipping a cold liquid from a sweating glass. Her hair was very short and brown. She wore dark glasses the same color as her hair.

The man nodded. "I think so. It was hard to tell with the tantrum he was throwing."

"Do you think I could go and lie in the sun now?" The questioner was another of three women who made up the group of five. Everything about her was blonde: her hair streaks of gold and beige; her skin pale to the point of near transparency. Her clothes were white with creamy sashes wound around her small waist and left wrist in a fashion very much in vogue.

The third woman, who sat next to her at the table and across from the woman in the brown glasses, listened to the exchange without expression.

118

While her companions were dressed in clothes more suited to the tropical locale, she wore a summer suit of dark navy, the skirt a perfect knee length, the blouse collar stiff and white, her hair a gleaming black carefully twisted and pinned into a delicate knob behind her neck. At her throat was a small antique — if fake — cameo. She sat with her hands resting quietly in her lap. No drink sat on the table before her. She had said nothing since they had arrived.

"I realize you want to go and lie in the sun, sweetie." The woman in the dark-rimmed glasses leaned towards the younger female, her voice not unkind. "I know you feel compelled to wriggle into that two-piece transparent hankie and warm your bottom out there — but we have work to do."

The tall man sitting on the low wall blinked rapidly. His gaze moved over the blonde beauty, as if envisioning the swollen proportions in such a bathing suit.

"Is there something you want me to do?"

The brown-haired woman ignored the blonde's question. "Vic, I want you to stay with him. Just in case." The man got up from the wall wordlessly and walked around the table, returning to the interior of the luxurious hotel suite.

"Dee-Dee, I want you to take a walk through the lobby. Mingle. Be friendly." She touched the blonde's hand, the gesture delaying Dee-Dee's rise. "I want you to tell me if anyone has followed us this far. Anyone suspicious at all." She released the hand and Dee-Dee hurried of in the direction Vic had gone.

"Dagny." She turned her attention to the woman

in the business suit. An eyebrow arched gently in acknowledgment. "Make contact with the Group. See if we can close the deal today."

Dagny stood up soundlessly, smoothing the material of her skirt over her trim hips before moving away.

"Well, Doc." The last of the group shifted his legs and yawned. "What about me? Find something useful for me to do?'

The Doctor glanced at her wrist. "It's almost one o'clock. I wonder if they've contacted the ICRC yet."

"Maybe they won't." A smile played over the mouth of the relaxed figure. "You know it'll take hours for security to untangle themselves from each other. They'll all be fighting to keep the snotty robot killers out of it."

"We have to assume they will contact them. We'd be remiss if we didn't take that into consideration." The small woman removed her glasses. She looked up, squinting at the bright sun. "Besides, I told you, the ICRC has been allowed to tap into just about anything they want to these days. Unofficially or not, the Committee's not going to overlook their phenomenal success rate. They've harnessed enough high tech and talent in that division to put all the other divisions to shame."

"Is it always this way?" His question sounded sincere, his voice suddenly youthfully curious. "The bad guys and the good guys fall in love with each other after a while?"

The Doctor slid her glasses back onto her face and turned to look at the young man in the lounge chair. He wore his own dark glasses, but they did not distract from the fine chiseling of his jaw, the casual sweep of sand-colored, sun-streaked hair over his forehead, the full, if slightly arrogant, mouth. He teetered on the brink of manhood, his reclining body unselfconsciously sprawled the length of the cushions, his flesh a rich golden brown, his white shorts and shirt highlighting his tan as well as his muscular arms and long legs and slender hips.

"Do you know, Jon," she asked carefully, "that you have absolutely no purpose here? No value to this mission whatsoever?"

"Now that isn't entirely true, is it?" His voice showed his lack of alarm at her evaluation of him. "Could any of them appreciate the genius of your plan as much as I can?" His hand limply gestured toward the chairs where the others had sat. "Could any of them appreciate the extremely delicate line you straddle between the public view of complete moral corruption and your own particular ego's ability to differentiate between survival and . . . 'as long as no one gets hurt'? "

She laughed, a pleasant, if grudging, sound. "Is that your interpretation of my scruples?"

"You would interpret it differently?" he asked mildly.

"Do you think I would let anything happen to this boy? Do you think I've left even the remotest possibility of him being endangered in any way by this?" She toyed with the straw in the drink sitting before her. Her words were as mild as his, but softer, as if a little strained. "You should know by now that I don't leave anything to chance."

She paused. When he said nothing, she continued, "I didn't even approach the Group; they got word to me. They would have found someone else to kidnap

Ellison's son . . . I'm probably saving his life in the long run."

A smile played on the sensuous lips of the young man.

"I need money," she went on. "A lot of money, very fast. You know that; those damn Controllers have made it practically impossible anymore . . ." She shook her head, silent for a moment, and then continued in the same quiet tone. "So I nab the kid. Take a few hours finishing off the 512KA, which will be an absolute ringer for him, since I'll have had him right here to work from; even his mother wouldn't know the difference." A note of pride entered her voice. "It would normally take them at least twenty-four hours to find out they've got a phony —"

"And you don't think they'll suspect that from you?"

"Of course they'll suspect it! There's no reason why they should, but they will — because they're paranoid, just like I am." The Doctor smiled at the question. "Which is why I'll have the 512KB."

"A back-up phony kid?"

The Doctor nodded. "For when we get caught. Because the 512KA is going to have a little glitch; if they don't find it in an hour, it will reveal itself. Which means we'll be somewhere between the island where the trade is made, and the sea vehicle in which we'll have left — conveniently having problems which will have delayed us. On the boat will be 512KB. In a bag. Screaming his nasty little head off."

"And meanwhile, the real George Ellison, Jr.?"

"Is on his way back to Paris." The Doctor sounded very satisfied. "I may even send a note back with him implicating the Group and giving their whereabouts. They are a low-life bunch of guys, you know."

"You're so ethical, Doc." It was the youth's turn to laugh. "You sail off into the sunset. Plenty of money to tide you over for a year or two. Knowing nobody up there is going to admit publicly that despicable you helped them bag the bad guys — so your reputation down below stays acceptably wicked and your record above gets a few more demerits."

"Funny how that works," the Doctor mused.

"You love it," the young man chuckled. "What are you going to do with your droids, though, after all this is done with?"

"I'm not sure." The Doctor had been wondering about this herself. It would be easy to remove the memory of all this from them — but it would be such a shame. They were her gang. Her perfect little gang and she had grown fond of them.

"You could send your Marilyn — pardon me, Dee-Dee — to Hollywood," Jon suggested drily. "And your Dagny to GEMCOM Towers, where I'm sure she'd do extremely well. And Vic could always get a job at any undertaker's parlor."

The Doctor leaned back in her chair. "I do hate to break them up. They're such an interesting little group."

"Imaginative," he agreed.

"Hi." Dee-Dee reappeared from the suite in a swirl of beige and white, her voice breathy with her eagerness to report. "Not a single person in the lobby who is looking for us. Well —" A faint flush of color traveled across her cheekbones. "I think a few might have been looking at me . . ."

123

"Obviously because you're such a well-made droido," Jon offered.

"Oh no," Dee-Dee protested without alarm. "I'm not an android. I'm a real live human being, just like you. I'm twenty-four years old and I only weigh one hundred and twelve pounds. My birthday is November tenth, which means I'm a Scorpio, and that is a very sexy sign." She giggled lightly. "I love to get chocolates for my birthday, too, if you want to jot that down. I love the little round ones with the oozie centers and —"

"How do I turn her off?" Jon had lowered his glasses to address the Doctor.

"Dee-Dee," the Doctor laughed and gestured at the blonde. "Give it a rest, will you, sweetie?"

"Okay," Dee-Dee purred. She raised her hand to shield her eyes as she looked at the white sand stretching to the ocean. "Do you think I could go and lie in the sun now?"

—4—

"What is this exactly?" Michelle's question was a whisper to the Controller at the console.

The Controller glanced up, waiting for Valentine's barely perceptible nod before answering. "It identifies the energy output of an individual," she explained. "If we have the stats already on file, this will give us a personal identification."

"Energy output! You mean — *body heat?*"

"Something like that."

Michelle hesitated, digesting that information. The technology involved was beyond anything she had heard of. She wasn't even certain such energy was a scientifically accepted fact. Certainly not to a degree where it could be calculated.

"How is it . . ." She didn't know how to phrase the question. Other forms of identifying an individual were well known — fingerprints, dental records, retina scans, but — body heat? "That's very advanced," she said finally. She stood up straight again, silent now, watching — and the gesture was a display of withdrawal.

Michelle had heard that some androids — the very sophisticated models the Doctor had created — had such sensors implanted. That their technology had reached such proportions meant the beginning of the end for the Doctor and her career.

But hadn't all that kind of equipment become outlawed? On, or off, androids? Hadn't that been the point of the revised laws concerning how androids were to be made, what the limits were?

The laws implied that any technology which created machines that would comfort the human psyche by resembling the man or woman next door — machines which all too quickly displayed abilities that surpassed those of the humans they had been built to serve and assist — was a mistake.

Philosophers had voiced the opinion that the problem was humanity's inability to constructively utilize its own progression without bringing harm to itself by turning that product into a weapon, that was, at the very least, perceived as self-threatening.

Politicians had cried that a new and disastrous civil war was waiting in the wings while such unmonitored and unregulated production continued under the so-called "free enterprise" system.

Religious leaders had insisted that a moral dilemma was being created with each new latex face and the self-programming computerized brain planted behind it.

And the Doctor — mother of the original two-legged, flesh-covered android — had become an outlaw, not unlike her most elaborate inventions. Overnight, her long and illustrious career had become a dark road down which history pointed a different finger. Her awards, and the recognition she had received from a world-wide, prestigious scientific community, were gradually rescinded as she loudly and publicly decried the age-old solution of throwing the baby out with the bath water.

When the Doctor had gone underground, so had her copyrighted blueprints and formulas. And so had her assistants — whether from loyalty or fear of reprisal for having stayed on a sinking ship too long, no one knew. And the only things that surfaced now were the Doctor's new androids.

People said that after being the most revered scientist in the world she had gone crazy with anger at being rejected. They said she believed it had all been a plot to usurp her power in the very profitable world of androids. No one really knew the why; they knew only that the new androids were lethal: so human, they infiltrated society undetected. So sophisticated, the average person (who had long lost the ability to tell who was real and who wasn't) couldn't spot them, even after close examination.

And for each act the androids committed (no matter how innocent; their very existence was considered a crime) — the Doctor was held responsible.

Michelle wondered now if the equipment she had observed was a piece of equipment built for such an android — illegal in any other part of society, even the military — but given to the Controllers so they could fight fire with fire.

The laws controlling production had become increasingly strict. And subsequently, the ICRC had come into being — directly under the arm of the President and the Committee. The now-famous division of Controllers did nothing but track down the androids the doctor released, managing to do so by a secretive and elitist set of rules set down only for them.

"It works on the same principle as Kirlian photography," a voice behind her said. From the tight, matter-of-fact tone and elegant control, Michelle knew it was Valentine herself. "The human body doesn't emit enough energy for us to track — it's very irregular, and tight around the body. The heat emitted by androids is regular, symmetrical, broad. And identifiable, to a certain degree."

"Androids?" Michelle looked from the flatscreen displaying its confusing waves of muted colors with accompanying numbers to the woman who now stood beside her. The question locked in her throat. The woman was so distracting, it was difficult to imagine ever becoming accustomed to her.

Valentine, hands behind her back, relaxed in classic military stance, chose that moment to turn her head and meet the other woman's gaze. A swirl of red hair flowed around with her attention. It occurred to Michelle — an irrational thought it seemed at the time — that the mane of loose hair was the only contradiction about the officer. The free flow softened some of the arrogance — it was too personal, too insistently sexual, that hair.

"Yes. Della was referring to androids." Valentine gestured with a nod toward the seated Controller; Michelle realized with surprise that Valentine wore lip covering, a faint, glossy pink only noticeable this close.

"You thought she was talking about a human?" Despite its teasing smile, the mouth looked delightfully soft. "Even an android can't detect enough energy from a human to follow them or verify where they've been," Valentine chided softly.

Michelle turned away, flustered. Why? By being so distracted at seeing a little color on a woman with such an otherwise serious demeanor? What difference did it make anyway? "I didn't think so," she lied aloud.

George Ellison's palms were sweating.

"Let me get this straight." He did not turn to face the man who stood behind him. "He is nowhere on the grounds. You have no idea when he disappeared. That group of Marines the General keeps here have no idea when he disappeared. You say you're doing everything you can. But you don't know what to do next. You don't even know where to start looking." He turned around, working to keep the wildness filling his chest from flooding his voice. "And there's a goddamn spacecraft full of robot-killers hovering outside the city that won't tell you why they're here, won't even talk to you, won't come in, won't leave, won't even take your call!"

Masters Dugan swallowed and hoped it wasn't visible. "I've got a full alert on, sir. And a call in to ICRC headquarters. They're trying to locate their Director."

"The Director? Yes, goddammit, that's Amelia." The President's voice was like a fist pounding at his security chief. "She'll tell me what the hell's going on. And whether or not her people know anything about this. And if they're not in on this, I want them in on this. You tell Amelia I want whoever's running the show on that damned ship in my office within the hour."

Dugan nodded. "In the meantime —"

"In the meantime, you keep this whole thing quiet." George's voice had turned threatening. "I don't want Mariella any more frightened than she already is."

Dugan nodded again, still working to keep his face expressionless before the President's fury.

A few feet away, Mariella Gilten closed her eyes and moved away from the double doors which Dugan had not firmly closed. She pressed her shoulders and her palms and the back of her head against the wall next to the doors. *Amelia,* she thought, and it was like a prayer echoing its plea through her brain. *Amelia-amelia-amelia.* The memory of her conversation was a recording that played in her mind. She heard again the voice — the smallness of it! — yet how reassuringly large with the flat confidence it emanated! *Later today,* she had said. *Today.*

This . . . Amelia . . . had promised.

With difficulty Mariella brought her hands away

from the wall and opened her eyes. When Dugan left the office, she was calmly waiting to enter, to see what comfort she could give her frightened husband.

"It says he wants to see you himself." Della relayed the message from the Presidential residence without emotion. "At first it was this Dugan —" She glanced up at Valentine, "— and now he says the President orders whoever's in charge on board to report to him immediately."

The Controller grinned suddenly. Valentine seemed not to notice. Michelle watched this new twist intently.

"Are they jamming?"

"They're trying." Della turned back to her flatscreen while answering Valentine. "They're popping up everywhere. Want me to shut them out again?"

"It's about the boy. They must not have found him yet."

Michelle saw immediately that there was no surprise on either Valentine's or Della's face, though Valentine had not admitted any knowledge earlier when Michelle had first informed her of the problem below. "Does that have anything to do with why you're here?" The question popped out unbidden. Immediately, Michelle flushed. She had shown her own curiosity with that blurted question — and, worse, she had sounded like the wide-eyed schoolgirl she had been trying to conceal since she'd first been brought aboard. At the very least, she had no right to ask a superior officer such a question . . .

"It might."

Michelle was too relieved at Valentine's grudging response to hear the coyness in it, to see the glimmer of satisfaction in the cool blue eyes or to witness Della's look of surprise at her superior.

Valentine erased the moment quickly. "Tell them I'll see him shortly."

"I hate boats." It was not the first time the Doctor had made the statement. She said it without receiving or expecting comfort and her gaze went back to the land drawing near once again. They would arrive within fifteen minutes. Indeed, she saw a long, cylindrical craft rising from the far side of the island, headed toward them. With any luck, she would be sitting in a plush living room with a drink in her hand within a half-hour. She was looking forward to the meeting, actually. Despite all the timing problems, she had calculated the deposit of the cloned android and the receipt of money, while figuring a short time for socializing. She was looking forward to meeting this infamous collection of temporary business partners who had made quite a name for themselves in the last few decades.

"I'm well aware this isn't your area of concern. Your job is to locate renegades."

The President's words were delivered slowly and

with even, measured strength. Though he had not acknowledged it when the woman entered the room, he had met Valentine before. And she was not a woman he cared for. She made him uncomfortable — though discomfort was not a feeling Ellison recognized easily. It had been translated into a general dislike he had for dealing with anyone less than the top officer or staff member of any of his departments. Valentine's reputation might be indisputable and the Controller had certainly proven herself; but there was something about her that struck him as arrogant, even unpredictable. Her arrogance was especially grating, with her background. Not a prejudiced man, he had still hesitated before he'd put his signature to the document allowing her entry into the Academy. He'd never forgotten her name and the information attached to it.

Not at all like Amelia, whom he had placed in the position of directorship himself — amidst a lot of flak, at that. Amelia was his protégé; she understood procedure and protocol and . . . Amelia did not stand before him in silence, with that goddamned stiff spine and that look of impatience in her eyes as this one did now. A flare of anger sharpened George's voice when she spoke again. "Nonetheless, we have a situation here that requires your full attention despite what you may be currently working on. My son is missing." He paused, waiting for a sign of surprise or sympathy to soften the blue eyes. When her expression remained unchanged, his voice became even stronger, taking on a harshness that riveted the attention of the other officers in the room on him. "He was removed from his room during the night, apparently without a struggle. We've had no communication from the kidnappers yet —" He was startled to hear the words catch suddenly in his throat.

Valentine interrupted neatly and without emotion. "He was removed at eight-oh-six. The chemical analysis of the ground outside his window shows that the artificial snow they generated from the rooftop was absorbed into the earth there."

The President's mouth opened and then he turned abruptly, his eyes blazing at his security director. "You mean —"

"While the tapes were being changed. They took him then," Valentine continued and Ellison turned slowly back to her. The attention of the civilian and military officers was now focused on her. "There are signs of at least one very heavy android on the roof above his bedroom. The room itself shows traces of Asdygenous dust — a gritty substance used to disguise particular types of chemicals such as chloroform or the heat traces of an android. That's why your people found no clue."

Ellison wanted to sit, but did not.

Masters Dugan found his voice. "You're saying there are androids involved?"

"It appears so." Valentine's sarcasm was unmistakable. "Unless you regularly have large androids prowling your roof."

Sergeant Elaine Gerry stepped forward. "Is this tied in with why you're here?"

Valentine turned her head slowly. The expression on her face was unreadable; and yet, Gerry felt herself withering beneath the cool gaze. No answer was forthcoming, and when the Controller looked

134

away again, the movement seemed as calculated and deliberate as if she had spoken harshly.

"If you have no new information for me, I'll return to my ship. I have work to do if you wish to see your son again. I'll let you know if your people can do anything for me. Otherwise — I'm not to be interrupted again."

Rage tore through the President's chest. How dare she talk to him like this? And then he realized with a chill of fear that in this room of people he had always counted on as the best, she had known more than all of them put together. She might be his only hope.

He nodded, his arm coming up in a wave of dismissal and humiliation, though Valentine was already gone.

Sergeant Gerry was still seething as she and Masters Dugan returned to the corridor which led to the security offices. "What a frigid —" She shook her head in place of the word, her voice tight. "I wonder where the hell Levy is. She said she was going into that damn ship and I haven't heard from her since."

"She may have been commandeered by that Controller."

When Gerry glanced at him, Masters nodded. "Yes, she can do that. Civilian, military, anybody, anything, anywhere in the world."

"Isn't that a hell of a lot of power and authority —" the sergeant began, but the security chief interrupted her. "As long as that Doctor and her toys are public enemy number one . . ." He shrugged. "Hey." They stopped before the door of the Special Assignment room. "She didn't make me look too hot in there, either."

Uncomforted, Elaine Gerry brushed past him and reentered her domain.

Private Levy leaned down, her voice almost a whisper. "Where are we going?"

"After them."

Levy was surprised at the instant response. She had not missed the subtle clues between crew members so far. No one offered her any information without getting the okay first. These people probably believed the time of day was classified aboard the O-Cat Blue Jay.

"How do we —" The unconscious including of herself felt pleasant but she respectfully corrected it. "— you — know where to look?"

"The computer has calculated the odds." The seated Controller pointed to a small flashing blip on the screen amid a complex diagram. "This is the boy's transmitter. We're taking a chance it was removed and the odds are that the removal was done in a place exactly opposite of where they're headed."

"Transmitter?" Michelle was honestly baffled.

"He has a surgically implanted locator." Della tapped the top of her own ear. "Just behind here."

"He does?" Michelle stood up, shaking her head in surprise. "Won't the security staff down there follow it then?"

"His mother had it done. Secretly." Della returned to her flatscreen and Michelle wondered if the move were a purposeful avoidance, though the Controller's voice remained conversational. "Implants may not be politically prudent for politicians, but they're emotionally reassuring to mothers."

"So the security staff doesn't know about it?"

"No. And the mother didn't know what to do about it after she had it put in — so she sent the information to our division and asked us to keep it on file."

"But why would she send it to the Controllers?"

"She didn't know what else to do." Della's thin shoulders shrugged without her turning around. "People associate us with protection and high technology. Obviously, it turned out to be a good idea. We have the specs — and the situation to use them has arisen."

"But what if you're wrong? How could anyone know to remove the transplant if it were a secret? What if that's where he is?" Michelle studied the tiny white unmoving patch of light on the screen.

"Too obvious." Again the shrug.

God, Michelle thought, *how did they get to be so confident?*

"Della has simplified it for you." Valentine had joined them. "There are indications of a familiar pattern here."

Michelle felt the delicious speechlessness come back to her along with the flutter in her stomach as she turned to greet the taller woman. "A familiar pattern?" she echoed.

"Someone we've dealt with before," Valentine murmured.

Della glanced up and a tight, excited look passed between the two Controllers. The look was out of

137

context with the seriousness of the situation — it was, in fact, one of pleasure — but Michelle did not recognize that.

Mariella Gilten huddled on her bed, her back against the headboard, her legs tucked underneath her. Her bedroom door was locked, the heavy drapes drawn against the bright afternoon sun.

She wished she had never married George Ellison. She wished she were back in her bedroom in her parents' house. If she were back there — teenaged and innocent — she would not have known George and her son would not have been born and her husband would not be President and terrorists — or murderers or strangers — would not have kidnapped that son, and with that single act, made her life erupt around her into an evil, inescapable nightmare.

Her arms closed across her chest and held there tightly. They felt cold and her chest felt cold; even the usually warm darkness of the familiar bedroom felt cold. She could not be in this situation anymore. She had done everything she could — comforting her husband, answering questions, calling that agency back in America, comforting her husband again. She was done with what she could do. And now the thoughts would not let her alone. No one had returned him to her arms, which were getting colder by the minute, and when she tried to go back to the fussing and comforting and getting by, all she could think of was how much time had passed and where he might be, what he might be feeling, what they might be doing to him.

All day, she had suppressed her rage at his captors and now even the rage wasn't there for her to find comfort in. Now there was only the cold terror and the agony; she could feel the pain they were giving him. She could not stop hearing his cries of agony, could not stop feeling the freezing anguish of his fear clinging to her skin. The thoughts and certainties and fright were building within her; her heart was racing and had been for the last hour or so. She could not escape any of it.

The handset on the bedside table chimed.

She uncoiled her stiff and frozen arms and picked it up.

A voice familiar and unfamiliar spoke her name softly. Mariella's attention shifted slightly toward the voice.

". . . *going very well*," the voice said. "*The transmitter was removed as we expected. It was surgically removed and very clean. There was such a small trace of blood on it that we could find only minute amounts of the painkiller they used.*"

Mariella took the words and translated them without being aware she was doing so. Painkillers. A minimal amount of blood. Hardly the work of people who would then torture and abuse —

". . . *the computer gave us three choices. One has already been investigated. If the next is incorrect, they'll be enroute to your son within the hour. If not before.*"

Her heart was slowing. She could feel it, having become accustomed to the galloping that had filled her chest. She felt sluggish, drawing her breath out raggedly as her pulse throbbed more slowly. "Does my husband know?" she managed, not caring,

139

wanting only to hear more of the calm, factual voice. The voice was so honest — and in that honesty the comfort took on new meaning.

"*I haven't spoken to your husband,*" Amelia said. "*I thought you might need to know, though.*"

"Yes, I . . . Yes . . ." She was grasping the handset with both hands, her eyes closing, her lips pressed against the mouthpiece, the warmth flooding over her. "Thank you. I needed — thank you."

On the other end there was the soft sound of the disconnection and Mariella remained, holding the handset, reassured by the gentle electronic hum.

Amelia's fingers were already flying over her keyboard. Her large, windowless office was dimly lit so that the face that materialized on the flatscreen was a grayish glow illuminating Amelia's own face. "She hasn't much time," she said briskly to the image. "The situation is intolerable for her."

Valentine nodded.

Amelia ended the transmission with an uncharacteristically abrupt movement and the screen went to a dead charcoal gray.

She sat back. Her hand came to her chin, her fingers moving restlessly across her mouth. The tension in the woman's voice played back in her head. She had heard some of it dissolve — but knew the relief was only temporary.

George Ellison Sr. once more picked up the notes

he'd been scribbling that morning, and once again set them back on his desk. He sat down. Where was Mariella? He couldn't concentrate.

In the White Room, half a dozen men and women waited for him. The situation had been explained to them in all the languages required for them to grasp the severity of what had happened. Each had graciously committed to wait.

But George Ellison Sr. had no illusions. They were not waiting for his boy to be found. They were waiting for the "situation" to be ended and the meeting to begin as planned. They were waiting to see how well he could resume control when he was under such a personal attack. And they were waiting to see if the business, and thus the safety, of the world meant more to him than the safety of his family.

Where was Mariella? He turned in his chair and stared mournfully out the tall sharply cornered windows of his triangular-shaped study. An endless lawn patched with snow stretched as far as the eye could see. He could not remember, suddenly, what fresh, tender grass smelled like — and the realization filled him with fear.

Mariella tilted the perfume bottle and felt the liquid wet her finger. She studied her face in the mirror a moment — her eyes large and brown and frightened in her pale face — and then she set the perfume bottle back down and rinsed the delicate scent from her finger instead of touching it to her neck as she had planned. She slid the brown morning wrap from her shoulders and picked up the selection she had just made. It was a pale blue — one of her husband's favorite colors. She slid it on quickly and noted with satisfaction that it had been a good choice. It helped to soften the strain in her face. Without further delay, she left the bedroom to find her husband.

— 5 —

"Yuck."

Of the group, only Dagny and Jon glanced at the Doctor when she spoke.

The small woman was eyeing the male and female who approached them across the sand. They looked enough alike to be identical. Both were tall with broad, thin shoulders and jet black hair, combed short and wet behind very small ears. They wore black suits which tapered at their narrow waists and long black ties and green shirts that shimmered in the

143

afternoon sun, the shirts the same color as their emerald eyes.

"What are they?" the Doctor whispered but none of the group answered.

"Well-come," said the male, as both he and the female stopped close enough for the reflection of their shirts and their eyes and the length of their nails to be seen quite clearly. Then they turned, the male who had spoken a half step behind the female as they swiveled and began the short journey back up to the summer estate which sprawled across the side of the private island.

Private Levy was terrified.

Everything had happened so quickly: Valentine being called to the control room, Michelle tagging along, brief exchanges of explanation that Michelle couldn't follow, and then she was being shoved into the seat and strapped in. The ship had aborted speed suddenly, gravity punching its fist into her stomach and slamming her shoulders against the firm cushion of the chair. Conversation was impossible in the dark cabin amid the silence and the eerie reds and blues and greens which punctured the shadowed faces of the crew who were propelling the ship through a seeming nightmare. She could see on the screens around her crazy images: ships, ground, sky . . . ships.

It was insane! A vehicle this size wasn't meant for such maneuvers, nor would any tower let it come so low without giving it a wide berth. Valentine was running the O-Cat Blue Jay through traffic as dense as raindrops while trying to keep dry.

From the soft murmur around her, Michelle understood that they had had to hold onto their speed at first to avoid several collisions; by the time they'd dropped to a safer speed, they were in the thick of the traffic flowing around the islands and the nearby large city. They had no choice now but to maintain speed even though they would overshoot their destination. The "rackers" (whatever the hell those were; Michelle thought she heard the word correctly) were apparently in danger of "burning up" if any more pressure was put on them after all the break-neck maneuvering.

Michelle found Valentine's face. The profile was unreadable. Even now if Valentine was frightened she did not show it.

"You like that?" Sam, as he had introduced himself, was unquestionably human with ruddy cheeks and an easy grin. His head was swathed in dark curls and his thick fingers wore gold rings glistening with exotic gems. "You don't know what they are? Cannies? You kidding? You never met none of them before?" He was enjoying himself. "You never been to the Casinos? Them people love to gamble — most places won't let 'em in, which is why Cannies own half of 'em."

His laugh was hearty, but the snap of his fingers

brought an eager aide to his side immediately. "Some nice drinks for our guests. They all drink, then?" He gestured to the Doctor's companions.

"Of course they drink." Her smile was easy, her thoughts analyzing the surroundings of the house and its occupants; specifically, the man in front of her. There was an edge of gaudiness to him. But there wasn't to the house. Like him there was something contradictory in the layout. The island home was lovely with an interior design catering to unaffected elegance. He didn't fit with the house. Nonetheless, the others — servants, staff members, an unobtrusive circulating background of grim faces behind cautious eyes — suggested to her that there had to be a great deal more to this man's personality than he was showing her. She had expected this. Sensing it this easily made her nervous.

Sam was standing over Vic. "So what is this?"

In the doctor's mind she caught the contradiction that had most nagged at her about the man. "So, what is this?" he had asked, obviously meaning Vic, obviously being blunt with the edge of rudeness that one would "expect" from a man such as this. He didn't have the accent quite right though, she decided. He wasn't inserting his d's properly. There should have been more of an accent on *So* — an expression and unconcern regarding his own ignorance. And then it should have been "what is *dis?*" In true poor boy, bad neighborhood, rough background, sure I've done time — pure twentieth century *gangster* style.

The Doctor grinned. *So they were going to have fun with her.* If this was as thorough as they got with their game, her plans were going to work with ease. "That's Vic. You like him?" She heard the honest laugh in her voice when she answered. She felt good and the sound worked well for the innocence (*I believe it all, fellas*) she would have wanted to project.

"What is he? Yer bodyguard or something? I like those teeth, yeah." Hands on knees, he was leaning to peer into Vic's face. "He looks like a vampire or something."

Or sump'um she corrected silently. She herself would never have allowed any of her people to make a mistake like that. Of course, her people weren't people. It made all the difference in the world. She chuckled, without answering.

"And this is a nice looking babe." He moved to Dee-Dee, who sat poised on the edge of the sofa, her chin upturned, her eyes bright, lashes up, down, up, openly pleased and responding to the attention he was giving her. "You're a cute one," he said and in his voice was that familiar combination the Doctor had heard many times before. The mixture of confidence and denial (*I'm not stupid. I know It is*) along with the doubt (*but she looks so* real). The Doctor imagined Sam's body was having the same contradictory response to Dee-Dee as his mind.

He turned his attention to Dagny. "Dis is a nice lookin' girl too," he said and the Doctor marveled that in his uncertainty he had found just the right accent to cloak it in.

Dagny had been watching him and now spoke sharply. "I'm not a girl. I'm a woman."

"Yeah," he said "Right . . ." He turned his head to look at the Doctor. "These guys are a kick. Man. You are good, ain't you?"

"So good, everyone assumes all of her companions are androids." Jonathan spoke for the first time. The words were directed at the Doctor, as was the biting accusation behind the low-key sarcasm. "My name is Jonathan. How do you do?"

Dee-Dee squirmed immediately. "I'm not an android," she offered brightly. "I'm a Scorpio and I just had a birthday." The lashes fluttered. "I was given some Belgium chocolates this morning but I left them in my room." Her lips came together in a pretty pout.

The Doctor noticed the couple who had first greeted them move from the place they had claimed by one of the fireplaces, to near Sam. She had to pay more attention to this stuff . . . these aliens that had been popping up in the last fifty years or so. She might even find some inspiration in them for her work. She hoped they would move closer so she could study them. But they stayed near Sam, their attention on Dee-Dee. They seemed as curious about Dee-Dee as the Doctor was about them.

Once she had heard the reference to "Cannies," she had remembered the species: Cannistis Vulpia. Cannivolpes, Cannies. Fiercely loyal and fiercely violent. Shrewd, cunning, twins — always bred in twins, one of each sex — and something else she couldn't remember. Some specific trait she couldn't quite bring to mind.

The female leaned down and closed her hand around Dee-Dee's upper arm. Dee-Dee squealed, a half-playful, half-sincere response. She was easily startled, and her best defense was always the same: a gush of flirtatious fear that usually rattled the offender with its breathlessness and femininity. "You scared me! Your eyes — they're so green, they look like jewels! Look —" Dee-Dee turned to the Doctor, and to her surprise the Doctor could see serious alarm in the wide blue eyes.

"We would like to examine this one." The female spoke, more statement than question. She did not let go of Dee-Dee's arm. "We will return her before you leave. Thank you." The female finished her speech unemotionally and drew Dee-Dee up to a standing position.

Sam had turned, his expression amused and a little surprised. "Well, it's up to the Doc."

"No!" Dee-Dee said. She smacked at the hand which gripped her arm, a small helpless smack that had no effect. She grabbed the hand with her own small one and tried in vain to pry back the long fingers, squirming her whole body as if to wiggle out of the grasp. "No, no, no!"

"The Doc says no," Jonathan snapped.

The male turned to look at the Doctor. *Amazing eyes,* she marveled. Truly beautiful, but hard and brittle as if they really were glass: a pupil-less, too-brilliant green, shadowed by the lid and lashes, even-ridged and lined like a gem which catches the light from any angle. The effect was exquisite and disarming. And inhuman.

The female Cannie brought her other hand up to Dee-Dee's head, drawing forward a lock of the blonde hair, sliding it through her fingers as if examining its texture. Dee-Dee tried to bat the hand away.

"She doesn't want to go with you." Dagny was frowning, looking toward the Doctor and back at the struggle.

"Let her go — before you scratch her or something." Jonathan's voice rose.

The female caught Dee-Dee's flailing hand and brought it to her mouth effortlessly. She held up the struggling hand, facing her, and slowly she opened her mouth and touched her tongue to Dee-Dee's palm. The tip of her tongue traced delicately upward, unmindful that Dee-Dee's entire body wriggled in an effort to pull herself away; yet the female held only her wrist and upper arm without any visible strain whatsoever.

"Leave her alone," Dagny breathed; in her voice was anger and fear. She stood.

Vic looked at the Doctor, sensing that a situation had materialized; then suddenly, Jonathan was on his feet, leaping for the slender hand holding Dee-Dee.

But the female was ready for him.

There came a blur-filled split-second; a quick hiss of sound; a slight movement from the female; and Jonathan was falling back into the sofa cushions, blood streaming a bright red from his slashed cheek.

Dagny turned immediately to the Doctor. She now wore no expression at all. Her hand came up in one deft motion, her fingers to her hair, skimming up and back, ruffling the smooth style only slightly, the extraction as undetectable as a magician's sleight-of-hand, and her hand was already inserting the cylinder into a small disc she held in the palm of her other hand, which she handed to the Doctor, who was already reaching for the information. The Doctor inserted it into a small battery-sized component she had withdrawn from her pocket and aimed it at a stretch of wall to the right of the fireplace. Everyone in the room, including the Cannies, turned to watch the slow-motion replay:

Jonathan desperately reaching to help the struggling Dee-Dee;

the female Cannie turning her head and releasing the hand;

her mouth parting in a smile of obvious pleasure, her chin lowering slightly as her lips separated to reveal teeth which had not been exposed before: elongated canines, impossibly thin and darker in color than the rest of her teeth;

her throat moving, explaining the hiss they had all heard;

her hand at his face, fingers curving in, the nails making contact and impaling themselves on the cheeks before raking down;

the nails withdrawing, engorged with blood, and draining quickly;

the clawed hand returning quickly to grasp Dee-Dee's wrist;

then the blood, unchecked, as Jonathan had fallen back onto the couch.

"Ah-oh," Sam muttered. "Very rude, you guys. That one bleeds. He ain't even one of them . . ."

"And he was so handsome . . . I hope it doesn't require medical attention."

Everyone turned at the sound of the new voice. A young man in gray slacks and gray sweater, his hands in his pockets, had entered the room. He wore fashionably antique wire-rimmed glasses and his hair was a dusty brown with a faint suggestion of gray. He was shaking his head in mild regret. "I suppose

151

you're upset now. I suppose you feel we've been unquestionably ungracious." He pushed his glasses up gently with his knuckle. "Hasn't anyone offered you a drink? Sam . . ."

Sam nodded and hurried off, motioning a staff member to follow him.

The young man approached the Doctor. "I'm Grant. How do you do." He extended his hand. "You're the Doctor?"

I, the Doctor thought, *may be in trouble.*

"We go down?" It was a rhetorical question; the internal system of the Blue Jay was counting down its own shut-off. Sensors had informed the main computer that land was nearby, and the program had made the decision to set down for repair.

"We land." Valentine had no choice but to delay the mission while repairs were made. They weren't locked tightly enough into a destination with an objective for her to override the system's decision to protect the expensive ship and its human crew. In space, she had once run with seven of the sixteen rackers nonfunctional — in fact, when the smoke had cleared there had only been nine rackers left. Up there, it had been her decision; down here — it this non-threatening situation, as the ship's program deemed it — the ship itself overrode her authority.

"There." The Controller at the helm pointed at a small irregularly shaped mass on the screen before him. "It's populated but privately owned. If we put down on that side, we should be able to make repairs and get out with very little interference."

Valentine's nod was reluctant.

The Doctor was counting on her companions' sensing what she was feeling. She sipped at her fruity drink and struggled to keep the man in front of her from sensing her discomfort as well.

"I've followed your career for some time," Grant was saying. "I've read everything about you. I'm delighted to finally be able to meet you."

"That's very flattering." His attention could mean he wasn't interested in the boy at all. It wouldn't be the first time she had stumbled across an interest in her and her particular talents. The profits to be made with her ideas — and thus her — were always of interest to people like the Group.

The Doctor sipped, her thoughts scurrying frantically to bypass the inner alarm that was distracting her from concentrating on establishing a new plan. The rewards for assistance in capturing her were up in the tens of millions at this point — but she didn't believe such small change would attract the attention of a man like this. No . . . this was a man with ideas of his own. A man looking at her with the same interest she herself might display toward a particularly well designed android.

She felt trapped; the feeling was both exciting and frightening. It had been a while since she had felt so personally threatened — and then again, she could be imagining it all. He could be merely expressing some curiosity before getting down to business.

The Doctor set down her drink abruptly. "Well, I'm pissed now. I don't like your social graces; I don't like your friends. I don't even like your sweater. Let's see the cash, and then I'm getting out of here."

Grant smiled. "But I have a special lunch planned! The others want to meet you."

"I've met enough of your friends." She gestured toward the green-eyed couple who had returned to their original place beside the fireplace. "What others?" The question was out before she could stop it.

Grant's smile deepened. "The other members of the Group."

The Doctor's upper teeth gnawed at the inside of her lip. The infamous Group. The nasties of the century. Tempting. Intellectually tempting . . .

Standing outside the ship, Valentine watched the technicians work. The sun was hot. Her uniform was hot.

She looked around. A rocky mass rose up behind her from the beach. If this island was populated, it wasn't on this barren ledge.

Michelle Levy popped her head out of the ship's hatchway. "Can I come out?"

Valentine nodded. She pushed her thick hair back from her face. The air was still and quiet. Smooth white sand stretched in both directions.

What's that?" Levy had joined her. She pointed in the same direction Valentine had just been looking.

looked like a rental from the mainland. Mid-sized and automatic with a scarred hull and generic ID numbers etched into the side. She watched Valentine put her hand on the narrow prow.

Damn, Michelle thought and wished she understood better what it was she was feeling. Was it the distance the woman maintained that made her feel so anxious? Or the sense that the distance could be removed at any second without any warning? All she could think about in the Controller's presence was — how she felt looking at her. With no encouragement at all, she felt reduced to a childish wistful state made up of vulnerable places she had long thought outgrown or left behind. All the way down the beach, she had felt fantasies welling up in her as they walked. Valentine stopping. Valentine leaning toward her. Valentine taking her in her arms.

Michelle found herself unable to remove herself from the fantasies. It humiliated her to recognize the intensity of this unfamiliar crush she was experiencing with this woman. Humiliated, because it was so unlike her. Humiliated at the ease with which she'd given this woman power over her. Yet even the humiliation seemed removed, as if it viewed the strange and curious phenomenon of this sudden powerful experience from afar — as did the rest of her.

Valentine climbed into the boat. "Tourists, most likely." She glanced back, scanning the swollen terrain that hid the other side of the island. "They must have gone up there somewhere." Without hesitation she walked the few steps to the narrow hatchway that led down. She ducked her head and disappeared inside.

Michelle stepped onto the deck and followed her.

The Doctor acknowledged the open door and stepped into the room. This one was different. *A trophy room,* was her first thought. Glass cabinets ran the length of the room. Soft bluish light splayed over a transparent container housed in the first cabinet. Inside the container an object floated. An involuntary expression of distaste tightened her features as she leaned to read the plaque. *Smithsonian,* it read; the date of the theft was one still mourned annually by the world at large. *Brain, A. Einstein.*

She straightened abruptly, her alarm a sudden scream in her own brain.

"Oh!" Before her eyes had quiet adjusted to the dark below, Michelle bumped into the body waiting for hers — hands found her arms and steadied her.

"You're okay," Valentine said quietly. Her voice sounded different. Soothing.

Michelle blinked. Valentine's hands stayed where they were. Michelle swallowed.

Valentine's hands moved up Michelle's arms, to her shoulders, pausing and then her right hand came up, fingertips trailing slowly up the side of Michelle's neck and coming to rest on her cheek.

Michelle felt herself reeling in surprise — and could not pull herself back in. This couldn't be happening.

Valentine had leaped the distance between them

as effortlessly as she had climbed into the boat. She had been standing in the darkness . . . waiting for her.

When the Doctor straightened, Grant was closer to her than she had anticipated. His body seemed dangerously close, and his smile was a question: *Do you understand the game now?*

She felt the furtive tingle of nerve endings anxious to flee, trapped in her immobility.

Had she been stupid? She had no time to question how this had happened. "Chilling." She acknowledged the challenge.

Valentine kissed her. Her hands slid around Michelle slowly, deftly, arms drawing her close until Michelle could feel the stiffness of Valentine's uniform and the firmness of her body as well as the equipment, now trapped between them, that encircled the belt around her trim waist.

Valentine's hand pressed against the small of Michelle's lower back while her other hand cupped Michelle's head, steadying the kiss.

There was nothing steady about Valentine's mouth, though. Her lips were warm and aggressive, moving from Michelle's mouth almost immediately across her face while her hands slid up, around (*God! everywhere!*). The length of Valentine's body pressed Michelle back until she could move no further, trapped between the wall and Valentine's hands holding her face as the kisses burned a trail up her cheek, her fluttering lashes, down her cheek, brushing her mouth, her neck . . .

Michelle let the wall and Valentine hold her up. The wall — and the hands holding her head firmly, the hips pressed against hers, the mouth pinning her against that wall. Her legs had lost all strength; her arms trembled at her sides, reaching out finally, tentatively, touching Valentine's hips, the tremors in her own body increasing as the touch of her hands seemed to ignite Valentine's movements.

"Fascinating." The Doctor skimmed the display with a gaze now blind. *Could she escape? Would he give her a head start? Could she get her people out? Would she have to sacrifice them? Could she survive without them? Too many questions.*

Valentine pulled her down easily. For Michelle, it was a collapse of limbs and self-control. Valentine's fingers tore Michelle's buttons from their slots effortlessly, her mouth following the separating path, her tongue immediately lapping over the swell of flesh she found, her teeth closing around the edge of the bra and pulling while her hands tugged the hem of the shirt from Michelle's waistband, grasping her hips; then she slid her hands around, lifting Michelle's hips, grinding herself against the offering. Michelle felt the material of her bra cut into her shoulder from Valentine's attempts to pull it off her body with her teeth.

She felt a laugh bubble up within her. *What had happened to the coolness, the distance,* she wondered and the hot pulsing gel leapt from her legs to her groin and connected, surging through her like a river of flames.

They walked side by side back toward the room where her androids waited. Each window was a mockery, an invitation, a chance to escape she had to force herself past. She wondered if her androids would still be there. She wondered if she should be looking for a weapon. She wondered if she could outcalculate him. She wondered if she dared attend the dinner so she could meet the Group before attempting to escape.

Michelle's head was forced against the wall, her neck straining from the position. Her arms were wound around Valentine's neck, her hands making small frantic movements against the other woman's back, the lush head of hair, against the crisp uniform that had seemed so impenetrable only moments before.

Valentine's hands were against her bare skin, trapped between the floor and Michelle's body, moving when she wished, lifting her easily when she so desired, drawing Michelle to her over and over as mouth covered mouth, the heat sinking from one

161

woman's body to the other beneath it and surging back up again.

Michelle squirmed, the groan that came from her throat a sound from someone else, somewhere else, mysteriously connected to the frenzy of movement and heat her body was experiencing.

She felt Valentine's knee separating her thighs, pushing up, her own legs closing back around it, her breath coming in gasps that Valentine seemed to absorb, so that Michelle lost control even of that — and then Valentine was raising herself on that knee, supporting herself with that knee and one long outstretched leg while she withdrew and brought her hands to the enclosures that held the front of Michelle's uniform pants together.

Michelle felt adoration sweep through her chest and throughout her body in the fleeting seconds when she could finally see quite clearly the face of the woman above her. Just as the clothing barriers seemed to be all Valentine cared about in the world right then . . . that concentration, that attention was all Michelle cared about.

She wanted this woman. She would get this woman. The one who snapped out orders on the ship. The silent one who walked with her on the beach. The immaculately dressed and composed Controller — who had waited for her in the darkness . . . the same one who sat astride her now, hair disheveled, mouth in a grimace of concentration, fingers hot and frantic against Michelle's stomach.

* * * * *

162

Her androids were still there. Each of them turned as she entered, their faces clearly displaying their awareness of her fear. The Doctor felt a surge of relief and gratitude.

Valentine was in.

The Cannies had moved from the fireplace to behind the couch. Behind her androids. More people were in the room. A man. A woman. Another woman . . . another man.

The pain she had felt in her neck was long gone. Her body strained to accommodate every shiver, every pulse, every agonizing throb of ecstasy spiraling through her. Michelle's head snapped back, the jolt unfelt as it hit the wall, more conscious of Valentine's hands dragging her down, away from the wall, unaware of the door of the cabinet she had hit popping open behind her, completely unaware of Valentine raising her head slowly, replacing her mouth with her hand and then her slender fingertips, her attention torn from what she was doing as the cabinet door swung fully open to reveal its contents.

* * * * *

It had to be the Group, the most wanted criminals on earth all gathered in one place. Her warning signals diminished in the face of such an opportunity — all of them here, looking at her, a chance to study, up close, people like these — and then she saw the boy. He was crumpled into a chair flanked by one of the men and one of the women. He was gagged and awake and covered with the Asdygenous dust she had used to mask her escape.

Valentine brought her left hand up with difficulty. Normally, she wouldn't have been distracted from her actions at this point . . . but the figure inside the closet was obviously asleep or unconscious. Her fingers touched the jacket he wore and then pressed to test the resiliency of the flesh.

The flesh beneath her other hand fought for her attention. A vibration clutched the fingers of her right hand, as the long middle finger of her left found the telltale depth: resiliency ended, the internal plasticized molding flexible enough for her to bend without breaking if she pressed hard enough.

Valentine closed her eyes, still holding the small arm of the android clone of the President's son while her own body fought to keep from sagging as the woman beneath her called out her name.

"I want you to eat this." Mariella's voice was grave. "You didn't have lunch. I want you to eat this," she repeated.

The President looked down at the plate she'd set before him: small squares of colorful fruit circled a paprika-splashed mound of cottage cheese. "I have visitors coming. I'm expecting . . ." But when he looked up at her, he couldn't finish the protest. Her unfamiliarity seemed impossible. But it was there. Perhaps it was only the expression she wore that made him feel so awkward. The stiffness in the set of her mouth. The veiled look in her eyes. He nodded. She turned to go.

"Mariella?" She stopped at the plea in his voice but didn't turn. Even the set of her shoulders looked unfamiliar to him. He waited for her to turn, knowing that she wouldn't. He looked at her back and couldn't remember how the curve of her spine felt beneath his palm. He thought of moving around his desk and enfolding her in his arms — but he was too fearful of what her reaction might be. If she pushed him away, he might not recover.

There was a sharp rap at the heavy door from the hall and then it swung open. "She's here." Dugan's upper body leaned in with the news. He seemed caught there, looking past Mariella as if his vision didn't include her, his voice as tight as his hand, which was still gripping the knob as if for support. "Do you want me to show her in?" He withdrew his upper body at the President's nod.

"She's here." George Ellison said; and the intended comfort behind his words was directed as much at himself as it was at his wife. If she detected the note of relief in his voice, it rolled over her without sticking.

"I'll leave you to your visitor." She didn't bother to send the message over her shoulder. She hadn't even turned her chin when speaking but left the words where she'd been standing and moved away from them. "Please eat." As she reached for the half-open door, it swung toward her.

"This way," Dugan was instructing, sidestepping in, his face turned away. "The President is in here."

A woman stepped into the room, into the only path Dugan had left her — the one by which Mariella was attempting to leave.

"Sorry." Amelia was the first to move back a step.

What struck Mariella first was the lack of tension in the woman's voice. Tension was all she had heard all day, in everyone she encountered; only the quality was different from person to person, depending on whether it was real empathy or mere ingredients conjured up for the occasion. She hadn't realized this until she'd heard this woman's voice. To Mariella's surprise, she felt grateful for its normalcy. A voice devoid of the weight the rest of them were carrying.

"No." She extended her hand. "I wasn't paying attention. I'm Mariella Gilten."

And then the second realization struck her. It was the "wrong person" click.

From growing up in a family intertwined in politics, one that enrolled her in private schools and moved her within the most elite of social circles, Mariella had learned a subtle but basic lesson, one of the face-saving skills: how to determine who's important and who's not. She had been good at it from the start. The instant analysis of bone structure, clothing quality, bearing, expression, voice, a million clues which told her — if not who was who — at least who was not. And this woman was a *not*.

"I'm the President's wife," she finished, curious why a woman of such minor stature had been granted an audience with her husband at a time like this. Mariella thought this without malice, and when the woman took her waiting hand, Mariella grasped it firmly — with even a degree of her usual warmth.

"Amelia Roberts," the stranger said quietly.

"Director of the ICRC," the President added from behind his wife.

Mariella opened her mouth, but no words came out. An unidentifiable chill shivered its way up her spine. She remembered the voice now. She remembered the rumors and controversy about the ICRC Director her husband had chosen (which had all seemed meaningless when she'd called earlier).

"Amelia's people are helping us with this thing." George Ellison's hands touched his wife's elbows as he stopped behind her. He felt the stiffness there, sensing that the rigidity was coiled all through her body as well. "They happened to be in the area — Amelia was good enough to come here herself from New York. I thought it might be best if her people contacted her here on this." He gestured the Director further in, urging Mariella back a step with him. Mariella turned abruptly, withdrawing from her husband's light grasp. She walked purposefully to one of the broad sofas. She sat. She crossed her ankles and gripped her hands in her lap. Her knuckles turned white within the grip. She did not take her eyes from the small woman at the door.

* * * * *

167

Silver gleamed; linen napkins were smooth and folded in elegant triangles. A highly polished silver platter displayed a circle of fresh crisp carrots surrounding steaming potatoes with a mound of sweet-smelling alvaka nestled in the middle.

The Doctor couldn't remember the last time she had seen such a meal. The last time one had been so obviously prepared in her honor. The time-worn scent of homemade breads mingled with tantalizing plates of cheeses, bowls of warm sauces and trays of chilled exotic fruits sliced into tempting delicate designs. Enough extravagant choices were on the table to qualify for a feast — even for a vegetarian such as the Doctor. The host obviously knew the tastes of his guests.

And the guests were not less decorative. Diana was to her immediate right and Grant to her left. The man the United States called Public Enemy #1, (she herself had the dubious distinction of World Public Enemy #1) was introduced as Johnny Wray and was seated directly across from her. Beside him was Sarah and then her Jonathan; to his right were the two Cannies who had finally been named: Len and Jude. She still didn't know which was which. Before them prepared plates waited beneath covering lids. Between the Cannies sat Vic, tall and uneasy. He was eyeing the covered plates uneasily.

The gray-haired man sitting on the other side of Diana was Cass. Beside him, Dee-Dee wriggled in her seat. Dagny had been seated at the end of the table to her left. At the other end was the man the world knew as the mastermind behind the last two Mideast civil wars. "Call me Jack," he had said in an accent as thick and murky as his smile.

The Doctor had identified each of them easily: arms sales, smuggling, murder, kidnapping; between the five of them, the top of the pyramid in international crime.

She wasn't sure what part the Cannies played in all this — it might be as simple as their being the most exotic of the Group's social circle of low-lifes. Otherworldly and odd, they would be a welcome addition to such a group. The best of the worst.

"They've been down almost an hour." Ellison tapped a small circle on the map. "Would that mean they have more serious problems than we're aware of?"

"No. Less equipment for repairs than they would have in port. Lieutenant Smyth has excellent technicians with her, but their tools would be limited." Amelia paused, then added. "For the damage she reported, they're making excellent time."

"I would guess they're very lucky, actually," Masters Dugan spoke up. He had been standing near the map Sergeant Gerry had brought in. After the delivery, she had remained; both Security officials were intent upon observing the controversial ICRC Director.

"Do they know where he is?" Mariella interrupted. "Are they going to go and get him soon?"

Amelia was the last to turn and look at the President's wife who still sat stiffly on the sofa.

"We're doing everything we can," the President answered, the silent *dear* on the end as clear as if he had embraced her with it aloud.

"We have the best there is on it, Mrs. Ellison," Dugan said.

"The situation," Sergeant Gerry finished, "is very encouraging."

Mariella's focus dragged from one person to the next, lighting on each as he or she spoke, the dullness remaining in her eyes. And then her gaze returned to Amelia's face. She waited, her knuckles growing whiter in her grip.

"He is . . . my top priority," Amelia said. "The day is not yet over."

A cool wave, not quite pain, not quite relief, flowed through Mariella Gilten. She studied the blue eyes which so easily met her own, searching for a lie, a promise without a mortgage, another layer floating beneath the calmness. But what she saw seemed to be exactly what there was: pale blue eyes focused on a truth that had no need to be inflated.

Mariella felt a sudden, compulsive desire to get up and go to the woman. To embrace this creature who could give her such hope so effortlessly. The need to rise was overwhelming. She had to push her feet more firmly against the floor to keep herself from moving.

She saw the blue eyes open slightly in surprise. And Amelia Roberts stepped back.

A flush of embarrassment and confusion rushed over Mariella so quickly that for a moment it washed away not only the relief she had felt, but the rest of it all as well. For a moment there was only her own surprise and self-consciousness, as if she had suddenly found herself naked, exposed — rejected.

"— which is why," Ellison was saying, "it's best to let everyone get back to work. Sergeant, show the Director to your station. Help her set up whatever she needs."

Gerry turned smartly, pleased, nodding to Amelia as she turned. "My people are at your disposal." She moved toward the door immediately as if to avoid a change of plans and paused, waiting for Amelia to join her in the hall. "Of course, one of them already is." She shut the door behind them. "I have a private who disappeared into your ship; apparently they commandeered her services." Her first impression had been that the woman was smaller than herself, but Gerry noticed they were shoulder to shoulder as they moved down the hall. She did not envy the drabness of the Controller uniform and felt a little disappointed that her remarks had not provoked a response of any kind. "She's one of my best. I even have reason to believe she caught sight of your ship when it first came into the area."

Disappointment came again. Amelia didn't dispute that statement, regardless of the fact that it would be hard to prove and had been intended to probe the integrity of the Controllers' belief in their own exclusivity.

"If she's good, I'm sure Smyth felt she needed her," was all Amelia said.

* * * * *

171

Valentine had the android undressed and disarmed. Not that it had been armed with a weapon of any kind, or even furnished with the kind of tamper-proof device that would fuse or inactivate its circuits, which would have made it impossible for the droid to be thoroughly examined and understood. This one was a quickie. A hastily put-together reproduction of the President's son, with the concentration on the external parts. She had — by knowing where — snapped it off easily at its first squawk. Internally, there were organs — obviously meant to balloon and cushion for a greater feeling of naturalness to the body — that lacked completeness. A softness to the material, as if it were undercooked. As if the Doctor had completed this one in record time, with little regard to quick detection. This one wasn't meant to last. Not meant to really fool anyone.

Valentine rocked back on her heels, her hands full of the child-sized robot, beige putty-like substance smeared on the heel of her left hand, her right hand holding the small box she had withdrawn from the easily accessible chest cavity.

It didn't make sense. The memory box was still wired to the brain disc in the throat; but the connection to the disc, which would have controlled the motor functions, was sloppy — not meant for permanence.

A movement beside her jarred her thoughts and she looked sharply — forgetting, then remembering, not recognizing, then recognizing — the woman she had momentarily forgotten on the floor.

Michelle was doing her best to collect herself. Her clothes were undone, her hair disheveled, her limbs obviously protesting as she worked to pull herself to

172

a sitting position. She did not look up at Valentine. Even in the dim light, her face looked swollen and vulnerable.

Briefly Valentine's attention was diverted. She thought of saying "you okay?" Just that: a snap of a phrase that would come out as a snap of a phrase.

Instead, she said nothing. When she turned back to the dismantled android, she was turning away from the woman to whom she had just begun making love. And then it wasn't a turning away; it became a swinging of her attention back to what she had found in the cabinet.

By the time Valentine heard the sounds of Michelle leaving the boat's lower compartment, she heard the sounds only as she heard the shifting of the wood in the water beneath her and the seagulls lunching outside: as part of her alertness to the world around her, with no separate meaning to identify what the sounds meant, when they posed no threat to her.

Over half of the thirteen guests seated around the dining table were obviously enjoying a delicious meal and the stimulating company of the other guests. Aside from Jonathan, who found it difficult to be unfriendly (or frightened), the Cannies were the only ones at the table who were as quiet as her own companions. Sarah, middle-aged and honey-voiced, had engaged Jon in a discussion about the joys of being educated abroad and he was nothing less than enthusiastic. The others had tried to draw Dagny and Vic and Dee-Dee into the conversations flowing around the table, but their lack of success didn't seem to bother them. Dee-Dee fidgeted. Dagny waved away each course, and Vic kept his head bowed.

The Doctor ate and listened and worried and hoped her stomach wouldn't give out with the wealth of food and the gnawing awareness of time passing. *After dinner, when, what? What the hell was this game all about? What about the boy? When had they gotten him? How had they stolen him from her?*

Obviously it had been when she'd shipped him back. After the clones were finished and the boat was ready and she had been satisfied . . . satisfied that everything was going as planned.

It had probably been easy for them — what had he been but freight on a train headed for Paris with a tag to be checked at Montpasse? — around the time the tranquilizer she'd given him would have worn off and he would have been screaming his bloody head off.

The thought caused her to remember him sitting in the chair in the other room. For the first time she had thought of him as a child — and a very scared one, at that. His eyes had been white-ringed within all the dust on his face. He had sat there in the chair, curled up oddly, his body smaller than she had noticed before, bent sideways from the struggle of his arms caught behind his back. His eyes had been wide open; no effects left at all of the tranquilizer Vic had given. The wide-open eyes swam before her: terrified, pleading — hardly the kicking little shit she had abducted this morning.

The Doctor laid down her fork. "What about the boy?" she asked. The lilting pleasant swirl of dinner conversation around her stopped, just like that. She

174

turned to Grant. "What are you going to do with him?"

"We've already discussed that, Doctor," Sarah said from across the table. "You remember we discussed what a profitable ransom could be involved —"

"Cut the bullshit." She looked from one person to the next. "If you could lift him from me, you obviously didn't need me in the first place." She focused on Johnny Wray. "And any ransom would be small potatoes next to what I see here, especially divided up between you." Johnny Wray's face was expressionless. The Doctor turned to face the Cannies, eyeing first Len, then Jude, turning her attention finally to the man at the end of the table. "So what's the deal? Why am I here? Let's get down to business."

"Let's," Diana purred; and Dee-Dee began to cry.

The Group turned to look at her in surprise, even Len and Jude leaning forward in unison to take a look.

The weeping was low, punctuated by silky catches in her throat, her mouth pressed against a linen napkin, her head bowed so that her blonde hair fell forward, slender shoulders beginning to quake as the weeping graduated quickly to low and heartrending sobs — never loud enough to go against the grain of the nerves around her, but strong enough to stroke and pull at them.

"Is she all right?" Grant's concern sounded sincere.

"She's afraid." The Doctor made a quick decision as the curiosity of the group moved to her for an explanation. "It's a reaction to the threat level she perceives in this room."

175

"You mean —" Johnny Wray tapped a spoon on the edge of his plate as if to see if he could divert the crying girl, "— it's not real? I mean, she doesn't feel anything?"

"Of course she doesn't feel anything," the Doctor snapped. "She's an android."

Jonathan laughed. The crying increased a decibel. Vic had raised his head to watch the Doctor.

"An alarm system?" Wray sounded unconvinced. "She's warning you?"

"Excellent." Grant's comment was applause. As the Doctor looked around at the other faces — some of them still studying Dee-Dee's effective weeping, others watching her with the same curious expression — the Doctor realized for the first time that of the two alternatives she had believed to be her potential fate, she would be a further fool to not eliminate one.

They were being entertained by her. And then they were going to kill her. Dee-Dee — as if reading her mind — began to sob harder. The Group exchanged delighted glances.

Valentine climbed out of the lower compartment. She noted with some annoyance that Michelle was waiting for her. She sat, her back to Valentine, arms wrapped protectively around her chest, facing the rocky ridge beyond the beach. Valentine hesitated. "The ship is probably ready now," she said finally.

"They're here somewhere," Michelle said softly, not turning around.

176

"I know." Valentine glanced up. The sun was hotter than she remembered. She smoothed her hair back and felt the tangled after-effects of the earlier perspiring. She allowed her fingers to linger for a moment, as she stared at the back turned on her. She stepped forward, her boots making a sharp and heavy sound on the deck and then she hesitated again, uncomfortable with herself, with the back before her, the moment. "We have to go," she urged; and in her words were some of what she was feeling.

Enough so that Michelle turned slowly around. Slowly, as if the movement were painful for her somehow, Michelle nodded and started to rise. Grateful, Valentine moved forward to assist her.

Michelle accepted the hand on her arm and rose; then froze, her face inches from Valentine's. Once again she felt the breathless feeling float into the pit of her stomach. She wanted to put her hands against the angled bones of such a face, hold it in the sunlight, see in the eyes what she had felt in the dark . . .

Valentine looked away. "We have to go."

Resigned, scarred, Michelle climbed out of the boat after her.

"I think I'll raise him. I think I'll keep him right here and bring him up myself — teach him everything I know." Back in the large living room where they had gathered after dinner, Grant sounded different from before. Almost giddy. *Drunk,* the

Doctor thought. *Drunk on the heady reality that, ironically, Dee-Dee had confirmed. He was winning. Had, maybe, already won.*

The Doctor went back over the data carefully, making sure she'd calculated correctly.

Would she interest them? Only briefly. Why? Because no one could do what she did; she had a one-of-a-kind-mind, and an imaginative one at that — but she was different from them, in their eyes if not the public's. And in her own. They relied on their own skills; and she, on what her skills could manufacture for her. They lived by their wits; and while she lived by hers also, they must have recognized what the politicians and the media loved to distort — that all she ever gained for her actions was her own survival.

Yes. They would kill her. Perhaps her brain would become another pickled trophy in this museum of a house. Perhaps Len and Jude would have her for dinner.

She looked at Jonathan and was unsurprised to see he was waiting for her. An agonizing sense of grief clogged her windpipe. His moronic, sweet face was struggling to hide the worry he, too, was finally feeling. She wanted to approach him, put her head on his shoulder, make fun of his lightness, his superficiality — his ambitionless, senseless adoration of her. She wanted to tuck her forehead into the soft curve of his shoulder and not look up again until it was all over.

Back in the dining room, Dee-Dee's weeping stopped.

* * * * *

178

Valentine looked over the top of the ridge and let out her breath hoarsely. The climb had been easy. The sight just below was not. The house that sprawled across the sand was richly designed and fronted by a shore lined with sleek vessels of all sizes. To the far side of the house was an elevated swimming pool; to the right, a covered port with cruisers parked beneath it. No tourist rentals or domesticated craft there. Blue-striped, red-striped, lushly equipped Ranger Fours and even the odd military ship with its nose poking into the sand, looking drab and out of place among the others.

The lowering of Valentine's chin was barely perceptible. "You have this?"

"I see it." The voice from the O-Cat was a whisper in the Lieutenant's ear. Valentine crawled forward an inch, her hair dragging against the dirt at the top of the ridge as she looked back at her crew. The beginning of a smile tugged at the corner of her mouth when she saw the excitement in their faces matched her own.

"Amelia's picked up the visual!" The voice in Valentine's ear was clearly surprised. "She's viewing this! She says she wants to talk to you!"

Even prone, Valentine's reaction was instant. She scooted down, away from the edge of the ridge, rolling over, sitting up, her hand going to the piping in the lining of her collar, her chin dipping down. "Go ahead!" She turned away from the others. "Put her through."

* * * * *

Amelia closed communication with her first officer. Blurry images dotted the screen in front of her. She swiveled slightly on the stool, confronting Sergeant Gerry, who was approaching.

"The President would like a status report on the situation." Elaine Gerry was delighted to deliver the request to this woman who sat before her terminal in her control room; her own questions had gone unasked, and her people had been dismissed long ago. Gerry suspected the only reason she herself had not also been asked to leave was a kind of concession to professional courtesy; it had been obvious from the start that her presence wasn't needed. She had had to stand by and watch as Amelia Roberts, without explanation, attached a few innocuous-looking gadgets to the Special Assignment computers. The woman had worked stoically and intently, flatscreen turned toward her; voice low, no questions, no comments, nothing directed toward the sergeant at all.

"Do you have something I can give him?" she prodded.

"Yes." Amelia tilted her head slightly. "They're preparing to get him now."

Gerry frowned. "They have him?"

"They're near him."

"The . . . boy?" The sergeant experienced an odd flutter of confusion that was annoying to her. She had never been prone to stupid questions before. Something about the woman was . . . unsettling. Grating.

"All of them, yes." Director Roberts displayed no awareness of Gerry's difficulties. She spoke evenly, pleasantly; not a shred of condescension or irritation could be detected.

180

"All of who?" It was a bark. Gerry was fed up with the usurping of her position, this unfamiliar role of ignorant observer, the confusing symphony of insecure reactions to this woman in her control room.

"The lieutenant has uncovered an unexpected nest." Amelia glanced at her screen and the Sergeant understood *that* gesture well: a quick diversion of her attention while she evaluated what she would say next. This was a woman unaccustomed to explaining anything to anyone.

Gerry had no intention of being placated or spoon-fed some cautious answers that would leave her even more in the dark. This goddamned woman was in her playing field, and she had no intention of remaining on the sidelines.

"Do they need back-up? Where are they located?" Gerry grasped the flatscreen and turned it toward her. She studied it for a second, then leaned forward, tapping a key, reading quickly the coordinates running in a static green line across the top of the screen. "I can have people there in less than fifteen minutes. An island? Not far from the mainland, actually. Possibly less than ten minutes . . ." She straightened, and in her arched, waiting brows was a confrontation as visible as if she had crossed her hands before her chest, parted her legs to stand more firmly and pushed out her lower lip for emphasis.

Amelia grinned. And from her came a soft laugh. The sergeant was already recoiling. If she had thought the woman's presence and isolationist demeanor unsettling, they were nothing compared to the effect of the easy grin and accompanying chuckle.

"Valentine can handle the situation," Amelia said softly. The amusement in her pale blue eyes was

181

unmistakable. "She needs no back-up from your people."

Sergeant Gerry didn't know what to do. Or say. It was as if the challenge and the gesture of support had gone unnoticed. Or had been waved — or laughed — away.

To her surprise, Amelia continued. "There are nineteen individuals in the house. Plus the President's son. A quarter of these are most likely staff members for the house, or personal servants. Eight are fugitives, all on the Commission's Most Wanted List of Undesirables. Four are androids and two are aliens."

"How many people does your — Valentine . . . have?" The question came out breathlessly. *Aliens? Robots and aliens?*

"Half that number." Amelia was clearly not worried. "Why don't you tell the President that if all goes well, the matter should be resolved within . . . minutes."

Gerry nodded slowly, resigned, excited, unable to shake off the edge of disbelief, afraid that she was somehow being lied to. *Aliens? Robots?*

She backed away and moved slowly toward the internal communications system to relay words she wasn't sure she could repeat with the same matter-of-fact tone in which they had been delivered.

Valentine nodded. Her lips parted as she breathed thinly through her mouth. Her back was pressed tightly against the wall. Clutching her weapon tightly, she watched Thomas aim with maddening, exacting

182

stiletto heels lay by the sofa. She could see Victor's legs; he was still upright but not moving. The nyloned, running legs of Diana or Sarah. There was a feminine scream, cut off in mid-screech; and then the Doctor saw Sarah hit the floor, heard the thud her body made, the cry of pain, watched as her hands moved downward as if preparing for a push-up. Her head was moving, shaking in an odd convulsive way; and then the toe of a shiny black boot was on her shoulder and shoving her over easily. Sarah's face was gone. A horror mask of shredded flesh with charred edges seemed to be oozing out from where her eyes and nose and mouth had been. The Doctor struggled to squeeze her arm up and clamp her hand to her mouth.

The khaki legs moved away; the Doctor turned her head and recognized Dagny's elegant legs and sensible shoes. She stood pressed against the far wall. A show of surrender? *Good girl!* the Doctor thought and wriggled her body around a fraction of an inch to try and see the chair where the boy had been. The black-suited legs of one of the aliens, seated in the chair, were visible; the other knelt beside them. It was in direct line with the Doctor and the Doctor was the only one who blinked. The Cannie was looking right at her. Neither seemed to be moving: the one in the chair holding the boy — *a threat? a shield?* — the other kneeling in support beside the chair. *With even more bait? One pointed finger could easily expose her position . . .*

The Doctor wiggled again but there was no place to go. She saw the lower half of Grant propped up against the far right of the fireplace, blood smearing one well-dressed thigh, the legs of a Controller

187

standing over him, his hands gesturing in an argument, a plea, that could not be heard over the other sounds in the room. And she saw Jonathan. He was in the fireplace, his lithe young body pressed into a ball not unlike hers, his face white and frozen with fear as he tried to make himself invisible. A spurt of sound jerked her attention back to the middle of the room. She saw a man in uniform fall. The weapon he had been holding flew directly toward the chair beneath which the Doctor was hiding, skittering to a stop scant inches from her hand. The downed Controller made a sound of pain.

God, he was so young . . . a Jonathan in uniform! His body arched up from the thick carpet in a spasm, but his eyes were on her. Blood was quickly collecting in a pool beneath his back from a wound there. His arm stretched toward her, toward the weapon — though he was much too far away to reach it. Close by, legs that looked like Sam's moved toward him quickly.

The Doctor's fingers crawled toward the weapon. The sound of a bullet — very definitely a bullet — rang through the room and the downed Controller cried out, the hit slamming his body back to the floor, into the blood, his head jerking away and then back again, his eyes still on her. *Christ, Christ,* she thought and grabbed the weapon. What the hell did she know about aiming? She fumbled for the button and saw a flash of light hit the floor, burning a smoking hole through the carpet and the wood beneath; and then she shifted it to the right and pushed again — and the beam clipped the edge of Sam's leg. He screamed. The Doctor's hands flew to her ears to shut out the sound. The air seemed to fill with sounds; a terrible smell filled her nostrils.

When she opened her eyes seconds later, Sam was a crumpled mass of unidentifiable mulch on the carpet. He had been hit so many times that his clothes were burning around and into him. Controllers were kneeling over the young man who was down.

The Doctor scrambled backwards, and out, kneeling on her haunches behind the chair. The room was a shambles: bodies everywhere. She could see Dagny was definitely okay, face pressed against the wall. Victor looked immobilized, but he still stood, like an inanimate object, unmarred. Dee-Dee crouched behind the sofa, her shapely body bent over, face buried in her hands and against the carpet. She looked all right. The Doctor looked at the chair where the Cannies and the boy were — and saw, confused, that they still sat perfectly calmly, the emerald eyes glittering on her; the boy was cradled in the male's arms, half tucked into the jacket the male wore, the child's arms around the Cannie's narrow waist. A shimmering greenish veil the Doctor could not possibly have seen from her hiding place hovered around the body of the chair, several inches up from the floor and just above their heads.

Eno-plasm, the Doctor remembered. *That was one of their abilities. They were protecting the boy with the stuff.* She leaned back on her haunches, watching them watch her with their cool green eyes.

They were plants! Of some kind. By somebody. Agents, assistants, goddamned plants — and they had scared the shit out of her with their fangs and claws

189

*and bad manners . . . And the scene with Dee-Dee
they had put on for . . . whose benefit? Or had it been
a show?*

Would they stop her?

She rose slowly, careful not to rise above the level
of the chair back she held for support. There was a
clear enough path to the door to the kitchen. There
was this moment — just this moment, it seemed —
when they were apparently all on the other side of
the room, the other side of the chair . . . She
strained to make the decision, then remembered
Jonathan and dared to look around the chair just
enough so that she could glimpse the tousled blond
hair where it was still safely hidden inside the
fireplace. She couldn't bring him out into the open.
He couldn't make it across the broad space where he
was tucked away and where she crouched.

She swallowed a gulp of air that filled her lungs
painfully. She was on her own. *They wouldn't hurt
him. They hadn't hurt him. They wouldn't hurt him.
He was just an innocent boy.*

She saw khaki legs come between them and move
toward the chair. She had not realized how much
quieter the room had become until she heard his
startled "No!" and saw a brief glimpse of his
blondness and his empty hands waving as he
scrambled from his hiding place, calling for the
attention of the khaki legs. Pulling them away from
her.

She saw the khaki legs turn and she started to
stand, unmindful of leaving the chair's protection.
The khaki evolved into a full uniform, the uniformed
figure turning toward the fireplace, the arm coming
up, the rad hair swinging around as Valentine fired.

190

For a moment, the Doctor could see Jonathan's face completely: startled, full of surprise and hurt as he reached the opening of the fireplace and then was knocked backwards with such force that his head hit the stone wall above the fireplace and his arms were outstretched as he slid down, a hole where his chest had been closed before, the all-too-familiar smell of burning wires and circuits already filling the Doctor's mind with grief.

Valentine's back was to her. The Doctor looked at the weapon she found herself still holding. She held it up and touched her thumb to the warm button that was the trigger, not quite pressing. She looked up. Valentine was turning toward her. The shot was easy and perfect. The Doctor dropped the weapon instead; it hit the floor with a soft thud.

Jonathan's right leg moved. Then his left. His intention to stand was thwarted by the severed circuits that had given the instructions to his spine. His legs continued to move helplessly, his face expressionless. Circuits within his exposed control box began to fizzle with tiny sparks of electric flame; then they began to fuse.

In a delayed reaction, the heat of the blast ignited the flesh it had penetrated. A bubble of flame erupted and began to lick outward.

"Hey," he said weakly and his voice was tinny and faraway sounding. "Annie. Annie."

It had been years since anyone had called her that.

The flames spread quickly, sizzling over the hairs on his chest, crawling up toward his face. She saw the cool, curious glance Valentine gave him. Then the Doctor: the same look.

The look changed. Darkened. Something terrible and personal came into the Controller's face. And then Valentine half turned and raised her weapon again. The laser beam struck Jonathan in the throat, destroying the speech plate instantly as his head sagged to the side.

The Doctor did not recognize the sound as coming from her own body. She felt herself moving and did not care about the weapon the Controller held. The rage propelled her forward, across a space Valentine could have easily utilized — if the Controller had not let her arm drop, and with it her weapon — which slid soundlessly to the floor.

The Doctor attacked without fear, her hands clawing for the red hair immediately, arms flailing, leaping for the taller woman, wanting to feel the slender throat between her own hands.

Valentine kneed her effortlessly and the Doctor felt the wind blast out of her as she hit the floor. Gasping, she struggled to stand and felt herself being hauled up by a grip of her clothing front. A fist slammed into her jaw and she was back on the floor again. Still gasping, her breath in a hot rasp in her chest, she scrambled to get up again; and this time, she was standing on her own two feet before the fist returned, coming from the other side, spinning her around until she toppled, face first, her cheek slamming into the carpet. Her face throbbed, the inside of her mouth bleeding from where her own teeth had cut into it.

She felt herself being pulled back up again. "Okay," she whispered hoarsely. "Maybe I was a little hasty." The forearm locked against her throat, clamping her back against Valentine's body, was

192

cutting off what breath she had left. She clawed at the arm, unable to budge it.

Thick red hair tickled her cheek as Valentine locked her chin over the Doctor's shoulder. "Are you pissed at me, sweetheart?" Her voice was hot and tight against the Doctor's ear. "Is there something you wanted to do with me?"

The Doctor struggled to draw air in between clenched teeth. A strange lightness tingled somewhere near the top of her head. "Nice perfume," she managed.

The arm tightened.

"I don't suppose you'd like to talk this out?" The Doctor's choked words ended on a gasp as the arm against her neck tightened. There were muscles in that arm. The shapely slenderness was an illusion.

"You upset Amelia," Valentine whispered. "That renegade of yours . . . in our office . . . you hurt Amelia's secretary . . . upset *Amelia* . . ."

The Doctor felt her feet leave the floor. The lightness dangling over her head seemed to be moving down through her brain. Thoughts burst in little pops, disconnected before they were realized. The gaunt, angular face of the female Cannie swam before her eyes. The Doctor saw and heard her speak but could not grasp the meaning of the words.

The bitch was really going to kill her this time. With her bare hands.

The arm let up enough for the Doctor's feet to feel the floor once more. The lightness began to solidify again.

The arm slid away and the Doctor grabbed her throat, sucking in the air she'd been denied. Free now, she stumbled forward, into the alien in the gangster suit. Her fingers clawed at the satiny lapels to right herself and she felt hands grip her elbows in support. Up close the alien's teeth looked needle-sharp and the Doctor reeled back involuntarily, pulling in enough oxygen so that she could turn, sandwiched between the two. Valentine was still only inches away. The Doctor backed up against the Cannie, not caring, wary of the cruel smile playing at the corners of the Controller's mouth.

The Doctor shook her head, her face already beginning to ache. "All right, all right," she muttered grouchily, done with it now. *They can take me away, lock me up,* she was thinking; so she never saw it coming. The Cannie must have, because she jerked her own head sideways to avoid the Doctor's. When it was slammed back by Valentine's punch, the alien was already winding her arms around the Doctor's waist to catch her unconscious body.

Amelia's attention was still on the flatscreen, not seeing the images that moved there. It was over. The boy was fine. The Doctor was captured. They had prisoners that would please the President and the Committee.

Still Amelia sat, disturbed, watching the flatscreen blankly. She had lost communication with them for a few moments and she wasn't satisfied with the explanation. Right after the Doctor had attacked Amelia's first officer.

Amelia was still startled by the braveness — or stupidity — of such an act. The break had happened right after that. A few seconds into that. And she knew it was not an accident. Someone had turned her off. Cut her out. "Are you —" had been the last words, chopped in mid-sentence.

Valentine's people backed her up. "A malfunction," they said from the ship. "We'll have it back in a minute."

But the lost sixty seconds bothered Amelia. It made no sense. "Are you —" What? It seemed such an unlikely time for Valentine to ask the Doctor a question. Amelia hadn't even interpreted the action from the sounds she'd heard yet. There had been firing, a cry of outrage . . . Amelia had leaned forward, closer to the console as if closer to Valentine, because an unidentifiable tone had entered Valentine's voice when she had spoken. But then had come the curious, abrupt silence. When communication had resumed, the Doctor was propped in a chair. Unconscious.

Frowning, Amelia slid off the stool. It was important to her — but for now she couldn't delay the President's relief any longer.

Michelle couldn't believe the atmosphere on board ship. The crew was as animated and raucous as they had been somber and professional before, passing around drinks, pulling off boots and congratulating one another like teenagers after pulling a particularly good stunt.

She wasn't sure exactly what had happened when Valentine led most of the crew over the hill to the

had planned to say to this woman if given the chance. Instead, she stared up at her, knowing her vulnerability was showing, but unable to mask it.

"Leave a number where I can reach you," Valentine ordered. "In case I don't have time to see you again today." She turned on her heel and strode back through her adoring crew members.

Fury washed over Michelle. *Like hell! What a —! The nerve . . . the gall of the woman was unbelievable!* She had never met anyone like her. Getting any more involved would be inviting herself into an emotional nightmare.

"Here." Dolly held a sliver of pen and a piece of crumpled paper. Her voice was not unsympathetic, her eyes not unkind. "She's okay," she shared softly. "Just don't expect too much from her."

"She's — she's —" Michelle spat, no word an adequate summation of the redhaired Controller.

"Yeah," Dolly agreed. For a moment a look of something ancient and tired passed between the two women.

Michelle reached for the paper.

Mariella Gilten walked toward Amelia and Sergeant Gerry as they approached the President's office, stopping them with her presence.

"You've heard, Mrs. Ellison?" the sergeant asked, and the President's wife nodded impatiently, her eyes on Amelia. "I want to thank you both," she said, but the aim of her words was more direct. She reached down to take Amelia's hands in her own. "You . . . *sustained* me . . . on this horrible day." Her voice was soft but firm; factual, almost rehearsed. She held Amelia's hands in her own. They were warm. And small; almost childlike. She clasped them tightly. "There's no way I can tell you how . . . grateful I am . . ." Her pause seemed measured, even cautious. She was choosing her words carefully, painstakingly.

Gerry was aware she was not wanted here; the sense of intrusion was so strong it overrode her curiosity. "I'm sure the President is anxious . . ." she began and then moved around Mariella without saying more.

As the sound of her footsteps receded, Mariella brought Amelia's small hands up, twisting them until the palms pressed flat against her breasts and the vibration of her heartbeat. Tears that had been welling up inside her eyes overflowed, though she made no sound.

"He's all right," Amelia said.

"I know that," Mariella nodded.

"He's on his way back," Amelia said.

"I know that," Mariella repeated. Again the pause was there — even though they were alone. Her fingers pressed so hard against the backs of Amelia's hands that her fingertips turned white. "Do you understand?" she asked. "Do you know what you have done for me?"

Amelia's pale blue eyes studied Mariella's face, her hands, her fingertips, and moved back up to her face again. The vibration throbbed against her right hand. The woman's heartbeat lay beneath her fingers.

Mariella leaned forward, against Amelia's palms. "Are you glad?" she whispered. "Does it make you happy the way you've made me feel?"

Amelia nodded, but the movement was hesitant. Emotion emanated from the woman in vibrant waves.

Mariella dropped Amelia's hands, which fell back to her sides. "You gave me hope. You gave my instinct something to believe in. Someone to believe in . . . you." She stepped forward and put her arms around the Director of the Controllers. "I think you're wonderful," she whispered into Amelia's ear. "I don't care what you are." Her words were warm and wet, her lips the same, brushing Amelia's cheek as she spoke. "It's right that you're a woman. Only a woman could control the power they've given you. What you have . . . what you are."

She turned abruptly and walked back toward the President's office. Amelia watched, did not blink. She lifted her hand slowly and touched the place where the woman's mouth had grazed her cheek, using her left hand; her right still throbbed from the delicate vibration. She could feel the smear of tears across her cheek without touching there; her fingertips buzzed from the trace of saliva and warmth. And there was the lingering pulse of pure energy that had enveloped her when the woman had embraced her.

Amelia thought suddenly of her secretary, and looked at her hand as if for explanation; but no explanation was there, only the heat.

And then she smelled the scent of her first officer's perfume and looked around in confusion. (*Valentine was not due back yet* . . .) The smell was so sharp and real, she wasn't able to stop from looking to verify that she was alone.

Amelia shook her hand as if to loosen it from an invisible grip and then she wiped it on her pants leg — and again — hard. Then she circumvented the confusion, displacing it as neatly as the sergeant had stepped around Mariella.

Afterward, she moved towards the President's office and the continuation of her duty there.

—6—

"I suppose there's going to be a celebration tonight," the Doctor said.

The technician, trying to place the grill mid-center, glanced down impatiently. Any awe he had felt when the Doctor was first brought in had evaporated after ten minutes of being subjected to her chattering.

"I don't have anything to wear, you know. I don't even have a toothbrush — but you've probably never even heard of a toothbrush, have you?"

"Of course I've heard of toothbrushes."

"They're more satisfying than sonar zaps, you know. All that elbow grease and minty taste. I miss it."

She was baffling — and he was growing more uncomfortable. The grill wouldn't lock: he couldn't set the brace if the grill wouldn't lock and the one he had was obviously too small. There was no bleeding internally; a little bruising of the nasal cavities, the cartilage off-center by several millimeters — she'd taken a couple of hard ones, all right. Her right eye would have been swollen shut by now if he hadn't drained and lased it right away. There was nothing he could do about the purple shadows ringing their way beneath both eyes.

"I think if there's a party, I definitely should be invited. I should be the guest of honor. I should get to meet all the people who've dedicated their lives to me so unselfishly." She grinned.

He inhaled sharply, clearing his throat, tightening his mouth to avoid the involuntary smile. *Strange woman,* he thought. *Senility, perhaps* — and beneath that thought: *funny woman.* He had heard she was a character. Something he had expected was missing, though. *The edge of cruelty that should be there in a criminal of this caliber?*

"Can't get it to fit?"

"The calculations must have been off — the computer must have pulled the wrong file to read your measurements —" He cut himself off, embarrassed at having started to explain, embarrassed at his fumbling when she was a Doctor herself, embarrassed that the grill was obviously the wrong size. "I'll have to try another."

"Nah. Here. This should help." She brought up

both hands, pushing her hair behind her ears. As her fingers came away, they drew strips of flesh-colored material from over and within the ears and down her left and right jawlines.

The technician watched in astonishment. "But I checked you!"

"I won't tell anyone," she chuckled. She grasped his hand and dropped the flimsy substance into his palm. "Try it now."

The grill slid on smoothly, clicked and locked. She blinked at him from behind the wire mesh.

Avoiding her eyes, he turned away, dropping his handful on a sterile sheet. *And how was he going to report this? Would he make the discovery sound like his own or emphasize her ability to be deceptive?* He set the controls for the grill. When he glanced back the light pulsed a weak green and he could see her wince.

"The worst is over," he mumbled. "Your nose is fine now. I'll have to put a brace on it while the cartilage is still weak." *His oversight would certainly be noticed. A senior tech missing the fact that she was still in disguise . . .*

"Don't feel bad. Think of it as age." Apologizing this time as if she'd been reading his mind, she was at it again, as soon as he lifted the mesh and snapped on the brace, pressing to allow it to adhere to the still warm flesh. "Do you realize how old I am? How many years I've had to perfect the shit I do? Oh, sorry — you probably don't hear that kinda language much, do you? Everybody's so civilized these days."

"I'll be letting the guards retrieve you now."

She caught his sleeve lightly, preventing him from

turning away. "If we both make it to the party —
you'll ask me to dance, won't you?" The voice was as
playful as the grin. "I couldn't stand the idea of
being a wallflower."

More baffled than ever — *Wasn't she afraid?
Wasn't she worried about what would happen to her
now?* — he was caught for a moment by the laughter
in her eyes as he looked down at her. The Doctor
was old, all right — older than anyone he'd ever met
— and certainly she could make a better presentation
than the bruised face she now wore; but what
surprised him was the growing confusion he felt as
he met her eyes. Something missing. Something there.
The brace looked pathetic on her small face. The
bruises looked tortured. Still, her eyes were lively and
young and full of intelligence . . . *What an ass he
would look like, overlooking such a thing. Overlooking
anything from the Doctor, of all people.* He mentally
shook himself and pulled his arm from her grasp
easily. He moved toward the door, sidestepping
enroute, scooping up the sterile paper and its
contents, dropping it into the pocket of his white
coat.

His back was to her only long enough to open the
door and gesture to the guards. Behind that back, the
grin returned.

The warning went through the room like a nudge
of elbows. She was here. Yes, it was really her.

Claudia, the second-ranked assistant in this part
of Security, was the first to step forward. She nodded
to Amelia, and was unsurprised when the greeting

was returned by name. "They're all in controlled quarters," Claudia began. "The Doctor is isolated; she was just returned from treatment. The others were contained separately."

Amelia had gone immediately to the bank of monitors. Each holding cell reflected back into Security through four sensors devouring every inch of space within the cells, leaving nothing unexposed.

"Except Grant. His injury was serious enough that they still have him downstairs." Claudia glanced at a woman inputing across the room as if willing the information with which the woman was working into her own memory. "He'll be all right, of course . . . something about a shattered femoral artery and bone fragments. We're almost done transferring Lieutenant Smyth's records. Would you like to see them?"

"I have them. Thank you."

Claudia looked away, embarrassed at the foolishness of her offer. Not only would the Director have been in constant contact with the team during the fracas, but her own personal computer upstairs had access abilities surpassing Security's.

Amelia was looking at the monitor that displayed the Doctor. "She has guards posted outside the room?"

"Two for each four-hour post. Armed."

"Her androids?"

"They were taken to the labs as soon as they arrived. Deactivated, of course." Claudia was determined to display the efficiency of the department as a whole. "We found standard control centers beneath the left armpit of all three — her usual placement area. And we didn't just turn them off, of course. We removed the activating units — they were about the size of a pea . . ."

Amelia scanned the terminals below the monitor. Not seeing what she wanted to see, she turned, searching.

"Something I can help you with?"

But Amelia had already moved the few steps to an inset control panel with no chair before it. Metal authorization keys dangled from a crevice mid-panel above a row of steady green lights and a series of circular gauges with a fixed digital readout. Directly below this was a monitor of sorts, green lines and even bars running from left to right. On the narrow shelf below the innocuous display rested a keypad.

"Director?" Claudia began, then stopped, caught off-guard at the deftness with which Amelia's fingers moved. She had not touched the metal key, yet the code she entered on the pad wiped the screen above it black, before it became a flash of orange pooling down into a dialogue running so fast and small that Claudia was certain the woman could not be reading the flood of information. Almost immediately a gauge number dropped, the light above it switching from green to a pulsing yellow. A small blipping alarm began and was silenced by Amelia's blurring fingers.

Claudia's eyes widened. Others in the room had turned in their chairs, uneasy and watchful as the ICRC Director tampered with the supposedly tamperproof computer — and the room housing one of the captured became a completely controlled environment.

Claudia could not take her eyes from the yellow pulse of light. The oxygen level had been lowered.

the live conference. Their conversation had run from heated and animated to strained and argumentative.

Dolly stared at the President's image on the screen glumly. "He's working up to something," she decided aloud.

"He's the best President we've ever had," another Controller responded without conviction, despite the fact that she meant it.

Bonny shook her head. "At least Val got it publicly."

"Just because they like to look at her," Tom argued. "The media laps that up. I bet it was still Amelia's capture, as far as he's concerned —"

"I bet his kid rehearsed that," Dolly interrupted. *"Could I have a kiss instead?"* she mimicked. "I bet Val felt like puking. I hear the kid's a real brat."

"I'd like to know what he's talking about." Della swirled the swizzle stick in her watery drink, her face turned up toward the screen. "Are you guys listening?"

". . . which brings all security under the authority of the Controllers Division," George Ellison was saying. *"All* security — and Amelia will continue as Director . . ."

"All security — what does he mean? The police? Did you hear him say that? — the regular police?" A chatter of surprise flowed around the bar.

"Maybe we're all going to be traffic cops now."

"It probably just means we'll have more information access now." Tom shrugged. "So there won't be any more screw-ups like our barging in on the kid, when there's people like that Group — already under surveillance by those aliens."

214

Faye was the one to ask in surprise, "Are you saying we fucked up?"

Tom shrugged. "Well . . . sort of. Probably in somebody's eyes, anyway. Whoever had that set-up going — whoever had the Cannies working for them."

"They had the kid! What were we supposed to do, back out and say, this is obviously your operation, sorry?" Dolly swiveled around on her stool. "I wish Valentine would get back here."

"You know how he feels about Amelia," Tom was still arguing. "He put Amelia in place — so she can do no wrong."

"She gets credit for everything!"

"Has she gone out even once in three years?"

"She sits in her office with her computer and her little secretary — what the hell is that deal, anyway?"

"Val should have gotten a Citation for that business the other day." Bonny's voice fought to rise above the others. "Hell, she brought down a deranged droid right in the building while Amelia just fucking stood there —"

"Maybe Val will get a promotion out of this —"

"Aren't they spreading Amelia a little too thin?"

"Maybe she'll overload —"

A dozen Controllers fell quiet. Looks were passed; and then eyes were averted.

Tom walked around the edge of the bar and switched from the President's speech to the baseball game.

* * * * *

215

"Yes. You do. Your personality conflicts with his."

Valentine allowed herself a frown. She could feel the skin between her brows grow taut.

Amelia turned. "He's an excellent president. A wise man."

"He's a politician."

"And you have no use for those?"

Valentine waited. Amelia continued, "You question his intentions?"

Valentine made a small sound of disgust.

"He questions yours."

The frown deepened. Valentine shifted her weight from one leg to both, irritated at the conversation, the subject, the irrelevance of such a debate. It was not like Amelia to bring up something like this. Was she telling her she had to kiss the guy's ass? Amelia had always seemed to be a willing buffer. Was he really complaining about her? Was the man attacking her after she'd saved his son?

"Is something wrong —" Valentine began.

"Sit down."

She could feel it hit hard — the sinking 'here it comes' feeling in her stomach. *No citations were being handed out here.*

"Your report wasn't complete."

"My report?"

"There were minutes missing from the monitoring tape. Minutes that were cut while it was live and a minute that was erased from your ship's copy."

Uh-oh, Valentine realized.

"The report shows the Doctor was injured. Her face was damaged. Her jaw was bruised. Her nose was broken."

Valentine's lips had suddenly become very dry.

218

Faye was the one to ask in surprise, "Are you saying we fucked up?"

Tom shrugged. "Well . . . sort of. Probably in somebody's eyes, anyway. Whoever had that set-up going — whoever had the Cannies working for them."

"They had the kid! What were we supposed to do, back out and say, this is obviously your operation, sorry?" Dolly swiveled around on her stool. "I wish Valentine would get back here."

"You know how he feels about Amelia," Tom was still arguing. "He put Amelia in place — so she can do no wrong."

"She gets credit for everything!"

"Has she gone out even once in three years?"

"She sits in her office with her computer and her little secretary — what the hell is that deal, anyway?"

"Val should have gotten a Citation for that business the other day." Bonny's voice fought to rise above the others. "Hell, she brought down a deranged droid right in the building while Amelia just fucking stood there —"

"Maybe Val will get a promotion out of this —"

"Aren't they spreading Amelia a little too thin?"

"Maybe she'll overload —"

A dozen Controllers fell quiet. Looks were passed; and then eyes were averted.

Tom walked around the edge of the bar and switched from the President's speech to the baseball game.

* * * * *

215

"I've been trying to convince Amelia to let me transfer you into the teaching system." George Ellison sat on the edge of the desk in the office he had borrowed to meet with Amelia and Valentine. "With my plans regarding opening more Academies to train cadets — it's much easier to find funds than it is to get qualified teachers for the schools."

"I like what I'm doing," Valentine interrupted.

"Of course." His near simultaneous agreement proved his words to be more of a compliment than a serious offer. "One of these days, though — of course, I'd have to fight Amelia all the way!"

Amelia, standing at the window, hands to her side, did not turn toward them as she spoke. "Valentine is a better teacher in the field. She inspires confidence and loyalty."

Valentine glanced from Amelia's back to the President. He was looking at Amelia's back also. "It's just that she could reach more —"

"The news of her excellence in action will reach further."

The President returned his attention to Valentine, shrugging lightly. "Perhaps," he said, agreeing with Amelia's statement before finishing with Valentine. "You're reaching the status of legend, Lieutenant."

Valentine felt an uncomfortable stirring in her stomach. Something wasn't right here. *Why was Amelia turned away?* She said nothing, meeting the probe of his gaze uneasily, remembering in a flash her abruptness in his office earlier. *He had been vulnerable and she had used that to aid her own competence.*

She understood he was asking her a question — perhaps not so directly that she was to respond to

216

his exact words, but that he had set something down between them and was silent now, waiting for her to take her turn with it.

She didn't know how.

It struck her then that dues were finally being called in. Four years of ignoring politics had never meant the structure was reshaping itself. He was confronting her — doubting something about her — and she could not deal with this situation by ignoring or circumventing it, as she had dealt with authority so many times in her life. Her skills as a Controller had no weight in this room, at this moment — regardless of what he had just said about her in front of millions of viewers. Each previous encounter she had ever had with him — encounters in which she had made no effort to acknowledge who or what he was — were ghosts filling in like shadows around them.

"I'm indebted to you for saving my son's life."

His words surprised her. She had been sure he would wait — leaving her pinned — perhaps prepared to cut her in half as soon as she made the attempt to rescue herself.

He held out his hand. She took it, her face not reflecting the confusion she felt. He nodded in place of a goodbye and then left, walking around Valentine, shutting the door quietly.

"You shouldn't make an enemy of him," Amelia said from her place by the window. "He thinks you go out of your way to antagonize him."

"I don't." Valentine wanted to sit. She felt relieved of his presence, her energy sapped. She felt for the first time how long and uneven the day had been. She relaxed her body, but still stood in place.

217

"Yes. You do. Your personality conflicts with his."

Valentine allowed herself a frown. She could feel the skin between her brows grow taut.

Amelia turned. "He's an excellent president. A wise man."

"He's a politician."

"And you have no use for those?"

Valentine waited. Amelia continued, "You question his intentions?"

Valentine made a small sound of disgust.

"He questions yours."

The frown deepened. Valentine shifted her weight from one leg to both, irritated at the conversation, the subject, the irrelevance of such a debate. It was not like Amelia to bring up something like this. Was she telling her she had to kiss the guy's ass? Amelia had always seemed to be a willing buffer. Was he really complaining about her? Was the man attacking her after she'd saved his son?

"Is something wrong —" Valentine began.

"Sit down."

She could feel it hit hard — the sinking 'here it comes' feeling in her stomach. *No citations were being handed out here.*

"Your report wasn't complete."

"My report?"

"There were minutes missing from the monitoring tape. Minutes that were cut while it was live and a minute that was erased from your ship's copy."

Uh-oh, Valentine realized.

"The report shows the Doctor was injured. Her face was damaged. Her jaw was bruised. Her nose was broken."

Valentine's lips had suddenly become very dry.

218

"The reports filed by the Cannivolpes explained the Doctor's condition."

Something like panic moved hotly into Valentine's throat.

Amelia had moved closer and now she was around the desk, standing in front of Valentine. She looked up at her first officer, who was easily a head taller. "I asked you to sit down," she said evenly.

Valentine sat, her eyes not leaving the face of her superior. There was an unfamiliar tightness there. Anger? She did not yet dare to explore the awareness Amelia's words revealed. *She'd heard.*

Amelia leaned back against the desk, bracing herself with her arms, the pose rigid. "Your job is to enforce the law. To carry out the objective of *controlling,* which includes capture and containment. It does not give you the right to lose your temper or make decisions as to whom you'll make an example. The Doctor belongs to the justice system — not the Controllers. Not you. Your possession of her — a human — was temporary. You overstepped your boundaries while she was in your custody."

The words were out before Valentine could stop them. "She had a kid in danger this time —"

"A child who would have been killed during the rescue if the Cannies had not been there to protect him."

Tension caused the muscles in Valentine's lower jaw to flex. The memory swept over her: weapons appearing from everywhere, Chuck lying on the floor in a pool of his own blood, the noise, the confusion. She had faced as much danger in those short minutes as she had ever faced at one time — and she was being chastised! It was not as if she had critically

219

hurt the woman. It was not as if she had failed in rescuing the child.

A child who would have been killed if the Cannies hadn't been there . . . Somewhere inside her, an uncertain shiver trembled up through her natural shielding.

The outer security system and its sophistication had told her she didn't have much time — that she would have to move fast — the rescue of the child had been her priority all right — but the safety of the child had been secondary. There had been no time to consider more.

The room seemed colder, as if the temperature had dropped suddenly. If the Cannies hadn't been there — the President's son would have been the first shield any of them would have reached for. It was true.

"You're right," she agreed, and the words were as unexpected and abrupt as her last had been. "I jeopardized his life unnecessarily."

"When you saw the Cannies," Amelia continued quietly, "you should have withdrawn, sent the information through and waited for my response."

Valentine nodded with difficulty.

Amelia pushed herself away from the desk. "The Justice system is becoming more integrated. You heard what the President said today. Many of the cadets will be trained for police work using the methods we have used in the Controllers Division. Your work will no longer be only the capture of androids, with the Doctor as the exception. There will come a time when you are called on for such missions as this kidnapping . . . with regularity. As an expert. As a last resort. The Controllers will always be the last resort, because our methods are the most extreme." Her voice showed no sign of softening. "We train cadets for the Controllers more extensively because the subjects we deal with are more lethal, physically and mentally. Human derangement is no match for the mutation of a program that puts all of its learning capabilities into survival. The Controllers will have to remember there are two sets of rules now. Human beings — criminal or not — will always be treated differently."

"I understand that —"

"It is imperative that you do," Amelia cut her off sharply. "The President's words were intended to be generalized today, but hear the kind of unlimited authorization he is testing on us. He is depending on us not to overstep those boundaries. What he is giving us is dangerous. I have every intention of seeing that these responsibilities are handled with the respect they deserve."

In the years Valentine had known Amelia, it was the longest speech she had ever heard. The greatest number of words, delivered with the most passion, even though Amelia's voice never rose, never surged.

Valentine could only nod.

"Inform the others there will be a celebratory event this evening in their honor, hosted by the President."

Valentine stood. Amelia turned away before the salute could be given.

Evening had begun to fall. Valentine could not recall ever feeling so miserable. She had turned left out of the Commission building; though her stride was as purposeful as always, inside a turmoil swirled.

Human beings will always be treated differently. Amelia had found it necessary to hold a special meeting between the two of them and to aim the accusation directly at her. For Valentine knew that it was, indeed, an accusation. A personal evaluation.

She approached the hospital. Chuck was in there. *She hadn't been to see him. It hadn't even crossed her mind.* She walked past the steps leading inside. Her father's words came back upon her. *There's a human quality to all of this that I feel you miss.* She passed two people holding hands. *Michelle's silence in the dark compartment; Michelle's face when she had been asked for a number.*

I like the feeling, she had said to her father. *I love killing them.* And she had meant it. And had felt no less pleasure when she had hit the Doctor. *Why had she been glad the tape was erased if she had seen nothing wrong in her actions? Why had the crew members instinctively hidden it from Amelia — proving they had known it was wrong too? They — the people she was to lead, to influence . . .*

She remembered the anger she had felt, watching as the woman who had given birth to her approached Amelia. *Amelia had access to all of the private information in Valentine's file. She knew all of the circumstances, the details of the woman's history — and yet there had been no judgment on Amelia's face.*

Her thoughts returned to her father and their poolside conversation. Nothing new had been said, though the debate had been heated for him as always.

Because he was trying to change her . . . She had no such illusions regarding him. His externally bleeding heart had never made an impression on her — his experiences and feelings never seemed as qualified as hers. *Did anyone's?*

She remembered dismissing his opinions because of the emotional source they came from. A source she never took seriously. From anyone. But was that true?

You're putting the weight of the responsibility where you want to, he had said and all she had heard was the same old doubt concerning the unquestionable guilt of the Doctor. Nothing more. She'd heard only that. Just as she always heard or saw only what fit into her blueprint of how a person should be, think, act and feel.

The thoughts stacked one on top of another, each point striking home and overlapping onto the next. *Elroy, the Doctor, the boy, Michelle . . . Amelia.*

Her mother.

She stopped walking abruptly and became aware of passers-by moving carefully around her. How many of them averted their eyes? Or so it seemed. They stole glances at her, snatching them back before they were caught.

What did they all think of her? *What would they have thought of her if they had seen her attack the Doctor?*

She had grown so accustomed to the stares and the attention that she had long ago assumed it to be the hair, the body, the uniform, the weapon, the status — but what was it, really?

What was she?

Amelia had *heard*. And it had meant *nothing* to her.

She felt naked, stripped, forever frozen in place on this sidewalk.

Amelia had heard what had been — from Valentine — a declaration of devotion, personal protection, of singled-out admiration if not outright adoration . . .

And it had meant no more to her than the knowledge of Valentine's flawed and humiliating background she had always silently but surely possessed.

The best of the robot-killers was the daughter of a robot.

She was looking down at the sidewalk, her lips parted as she breathed heavily while the perfectly ordinary human beings passed around her.

But she was a perfectly ordinary human being, too! Paternity had been stolen from a flesh-and-blood male somewhere and, obviously, it was from him she had inherited her strength and determination. After all, she had made herself more human than most, hadn't she? She inspired jokes about her superhumanness; awe at her skills which surpassed so many other people's struggles for perfection. So she was a little impatient, a little bolder than most — how was that bad? She wasn't really that hard. Did not always feel that indifferent.

Intolerant, narrow-minded, insensitive, mean. She heard the accusations, now from a dozen different tongues. Playmates, androids; men, women — but each time she had been sure it was only their jealousy or insecurity talking; they hadn't meant it

. . . it had never even mattered. *And the not-mattering had made it untrue?*

Was it normal to have always found it so easy to ignore their accusations?

The sidewalk blurred and she blinked; startled, frightened. *Amelia.* Had it hurt that much because it came from her? Could anybody else have so effectively shaken her by calling her less than a humanitarian?

She had been called on the carpet for it. Shame flooded through the tensions, dousing the last of the strength, soaking the rigidity that held her up. She felt her shoulders give and brought her arms up protectively before her stomach. Tears spilled from her eyes. She felt unable to move.

A part of her reared back, horrified. *You're in public, Valentine. You're a Controller — in uniform!* But there was no stopping the flow inside and out. It washed through her in a form of pain she had never before experienced.

Amelia didn't like her! She saw her. Knew her! And didn't like what she knew or saw.

Her throat closed and then opened and out came a sound as agonized as the anguish churning through her body. Her head went down further in a useless attempt to hide her face from the people around her.

Amelia had been so busy thinking she should have been more firm, more direct, with Valentine (she could do that with Valentine. Valentine was an exception among humans) that she stepped out of the 'vator and was moving down the hospital corridor before she was stopped short.

It hit her like an electrical jolt — a stunning of her senses that made her reel. She reached out and her palm flattened against the wall for support, her shoulder following, bracing; her lips parting, her pupils dilating so rapidly that the images to which she had been paying no attention — wandering patients, carts, doorways, desks, techs, machines resting against walls — disappeared and were replaced by lines of heat and color: a perfect grid taking over her visual. She brought her chin down, concentrating, working. Still the statistics racing before her overwhelmed her senses. *Male. Human. Vital signs, 80/40. Heartbeat irregular. Pulse decreasing.*

Amelia closed her eyes and Internalized. Fifteen seconds passed. Thirty. A young woman in a blue-and-white-striped smock stopped and tentatively touched her shoulder. "Are you all right?" A team of interns and techs rushed by in response to a Code just given. Head still bowed, Amelia felt the hand. "I'm fine," she spoke. "I was thinking about something."

Amelia worked harder, heard the gravelly monotone of her delivery, but could not correct it. As unlikely as the explanation sounded from the stricken figure, the woman moved away, following the emergency team.

The needle spiked the heart: arrhythmia stabilized.
"Okay," a tech signaled. "He's okay now."

Amelia straightened. The hallway swam back into view. *She hadn't been prepared. Regardless of the fact that she had known what the environment would be, she had let her thoughts wander and had been unprepared . . .*

A woman passed and then backed up a step. "You

must be looking for your man," she said, eyeing the uniform. "Eleven-oh-one. Keep heading down the hall."

"Thank you." Amelia saw blonde hair, brown eyes, pink cheeks quite clearly. "Thank you very much."

She moved away from the wall carefully; she was stabilized.

In the bed, Chuck straightened in surprise at the sight of her. "Director Roberts!" he exclaimed, his voice a mixture of pleasure and nervousness.

"I wanted to see for myself you were doing well."

"I'm fine!" He took her hand and they shook carefully. "They're great here. Amazing what they can do these days . . . I feel like new. Sit down — please." His thoughts worked frantically. *Tell her. Don't. Tell her what, exactly?* He gestured toward a chair which had been drawn near the bed.

"I only stopped in for a minute."

"I've been watching the conference." Chuck nodded toward the muted screen nestled in the wall near the foot of his bed. *He could say it out loud. Just describe what he remembered. Ask if his perception of what had happened should be in his report.* "Big changes in the wind, huh?" It was not a question he would normally have taken the liberty to ask her — but he would normally not have come in contact with her, either.

"Not so many," she answered, and he knew immediately he wasn't going to get any special treatment from her other than the visit. *I think she tried to help me,* he tried on for size, playing it through in his own mind for the hundredth time — *I've been going over and over it and I think she saved my life.*

Amelia wished him well.

When I was down, he imagined himself saying. *When I saw the one coming and I thought it was over. She was under the chair. I saw her. She looked at me . . .*

Amelia turned to leave.

She reached for the weapon. He was almost at me. I thought I was going to die.

"Director Roberts?"

She turned back.

She fired. They killed him — but she fired, wounded him, gave me those few seconds that saved my life.

"Yes?"

The Doctor did that. The lethal, callous, sociopathic doctor — yep, Val, I didn't tell you but I did mention it to Amelia — that the Doctor saved my ass . . .

"Thanks for coming," Chuck finished quietly.

Amelia waited. *Go on,* she thought sensing more. Then: *Perhaps not.* She might still be off after her little error in the hall. The wait became a mere hesitation. She smiled. Left.

At the 'vators, she stepped in with other people — then stepped back out into the same corridor she had just left. She turned right. She walked slowly, looking at the room numbers carefully, reading them

228

with her lips moving, the confusion growing like dread. When she came to a stop before an open doorway, she heard the sounds of voices coming from within. *Male, female; relaxed, friendly.* The smell of flowers *Violets, daisies, roses . . . others, many others,* the smell of alcohol, perfume, disinfectant, soap, chocolate, fresh flowers, flesh. The smells were an assault and she turned away from them.

"Amelia!"

A curious weakness, not completely unfamiliar, descended down into her pelvis, through her thighs and into her legs. She turned slowly, reluctantly.

Jennifer, hair mussed, holding a ceramic bowl of colorful flowers, fingernails a glossy pink. *Topping white, very white, fingers, soft, soft, lotion-pampered fingers.* Barelegged, barefooted, face round and full of the blueness of her eyes. "I mean — Director Roberts! I mean — Mom! Dad! This is my boss."

Amelia had a glimpse of a wall of humanity crowding into the doorway behind their daughter, sister, niece, *Jennifer,* a dozen eyes from a dozen faces studying her in fascination. *Jennifer eyes, Jennifer skin. Jennifer hair and nose and smell.*

Amelia stepped back, her eyes riveted on the small ceramic bowl in an attempt to ignore all of the Jenniferness pressing in on her.

"I can't believe you came. I'm being released today too! Thank you for coming! This is *Amelia.*" They spoke to her and she could hear the dialect, the tone, the inflection that was Jennifer in each of them. She moved back further still. Did not speak. Turned. Retreated. Jennifer stared after her in wonder.

229

−7−

"You're quiet tonight." Dolly wasn't sure she had found the right word. Depressed was more like it. But when was the last time she had seen Valentine depressed? Pissed maybe; a little moody — okay, she'd seen some perfectly rotten moods from this one — but this was unusual. The long legs rested on a chair drawn up to the table, but the position was without the usual cockiness. No circulating. No fun time. Valentine looked as deflated as a person possibly could.

"I'm okay." Valentine's response rang hollow.

Dolly shifted restlessly. The others at their table had eventually wandered off. All sorts of Commission employees, as well as the Controllers, were running wild and noisy through the popular Hall tonight. They'd been given free reign while Ellison, personally footing the bill, did them the added favor of not bothering to show up in person. The party showed all the signs of becoming one of the best; and usually Valentine was at the forefront of such rowdy fun. The lieutenant could be as boisterous and raunchy during her free hours as she was polished when working.

But not tonight, Dolly noted, and strangely enough, not on a night that was practically a tribute to Valentine. She wondered if Amelia had something to do with the mood. *Wasn't it always something to do with Amelia?* Dolly had seen her earlier, moving around tightly, performing the Commanding Officer's put-in-an-appearance bit. She'd probably be gone by now. The Director was no doubt anxious to get back to her manuals and computers and other Saturday night companions the Controllers imagined her snuggling up to during her off hours.

Dolly considered saying something more to Valentine and started to rise. "Hey." She squinted and waved, sliding back down. "C'mere. How're you doing, kid?"

Jennifer Taylor approached the table uncertainly. In the shadows she saw Valentine — but it was too late to pretend she hadn't heard the other Controller. "I'm fine, thank you."

She wished she could say something about the 'kid' business; the woman in uniform was her own age. The greeting was so typically, arrogantly, theirs . . . "The hospital released me today," she said instead; then ran out of words. She looked around, clutching her drink, staring hard at the dancing and laughing people all around her, trying to replace her silence. *What to say next? Why had this Controller called her over? Why had she come?* Jennifer knew the answer to her own question. She'd been wandering around shyly for the last hour, overwhelmed by the uniforms and the confidence and the ease with which everyone else wore both.

"Need a drink? Let me hoist one. Val?" Dolly was up and halfway past Jennifer, relieved at the escape route suddenly available.

Valentine shook her head no.

Dolly disappeared into the crowd. Jennifer swallowed hard. Tried hard to concentrate on looking around again, anxious to come up with even a few words that would be casual enough and not too foolish. "Thanks." (*too casual*) "Thank you. They told me it was you yesterday. You helped Amelia save my life."

Valentine uncoiled her leg slowly, withdrawing it from the chair, hooking the toe of her boot on the bottom and shoving the chair back a few inches, the act an invitation her face did not mirror. "Have a seat," she ordered.

Jennifer hesitated. She sat, not wanting to.

The Doctor opened her eyes. The future looked lousy.

Just like the air in this room. How long had she been asleep? She had just closed her eyes to think, to

232

just lie down to rest for a second — and had fallen from consciousness down a slide papered with uncomfortable thoughts and images. What now? Why couldn't she think straight?

She sat up with effort; the discomfort was physical as well. Tranquilizer? She was sure the tech who'd treated her hadn't . . . She subtly inhaled, sifting for a trace in the air and found instead that her chest pulled greedily in search of more.

"My family still lives in Indiana. The ICRC paid for transportation for all of them to come here when I got hurt. They were put up first class — they still don't have a lot of this stuff back home. They think everything's futuristic here — that's what they keep saying. Like normal people don't live with stuff like this. They went to see one of the ships this morning and it was the first one they'd ever seen . . . can you imagine that?" Jennifer pulled in a breath and plunged on. "I shouldn't say that. I didn't see one till I came here either, but we grew up reading about them when we were kids, so I guess it seems more normal to me — My mom's always saying the world's going too fast for her, she can't keep up, she's always remembering when things were this way or that way and now she says things keep changing so fast, it's like a blur — she says she can't tell anymore if it's the world changing or her going slower and slower. Won't it be weird to be getting older and to feel like that? To feel like you can't keep up with things and to be afraid you're never going to understand the new stuff coming along — I feel that way enough now! — I know I shouldn't say that. A person's not supposed to admit they don't know what's going on —" Jennifer's words skidded to a thoughtful silence. "I think a person's supposed to act like they get it even when they don't, don't you?"

Valentine forced a smile to her mouth in response. Something like a smile. A grimace of tolerance. A disagreement.

Breathing was definitely difficult. The Doctor drew her knees up, hugging them with her arms, bowing her head. She closed her eyes.

She was sure it wasn't a mistake. They knew, all right. Someone had used a really underhanded method to insure her sluggishness. It struck her as being particularly unfair. Shackles she could understand; physical restraint would have been primitive and exasperating, but this —? Someone was bypassing any pretense of fair play and dealing straight with her brain.

Grant smiled. That was it.

All evening he'd been turning it over and over in his mind. Escape. Retaliation in the form of a calling card. Now he had it.

It was not that escape was terribly important to him. He was curious about the upcoming accusations that would be aimed at him. Curious about what kind of a maze of penalties they would use to try to box him in. Interested in seeing how they went about it and then how he would find his way out.

But the other was important to him. The retaliation with a calling card. Even with the dull ache in his leg, he felt no particular animosity toward the people who had surprised him in his villa, ruining what had been an excellent after-dinner drink and the promise of a wonderful day ahead.

The Cannies had taken him off guard, though. Officers. That hit a sour note. It probably wasn't even him they'd been after — more like one of his companions. Of course, now his reputation had been damaged; his possessions had been confiscated, his party ruined, his overrated and expensive security system cut through like so much paper . . . All in all, it had been an embarrassing situation. At the very least, his response had to be as understated and far-reaching as his own humiliation at their hands had been.

His escape would be impressive. But not nearly as impressive as if he engineered the Doctor's.

Amelia stepped away from the group she'd joined moments before. They had welcomed her; she had affirmed general congratulations; and their animated conversation had picked back up without her, making it easy to detach herself and move on.

She wanted to get back to Security. Attention would be at half-mast with this party going on. Even with the heaviness of their responsibilities this evening, minds would be elsewhere. Easily distracted.

* * * * *

Chuck's mind was not distracted by thoughts of the celebration a few blocks away. The hospital was relatively quiet at this hour, the sounds far away in their echo of routine. He hadn't been able to eat. Hadn't been able to sleep.

He stared out the window at the sky resting atop the building across the street. If he could make it to the window, he would be able to see the part of the Commission complex that housed Security. His fingers tapped restlessly against the taut dry sheet across him. *She was in there.* The place was escape-proof. Security would be so tight around her — maybe a little lax tonight, what with the party and the newness of having her there so unexpectedly, but by tomorrow, definitely by tomorrow, she'd be locked in so tight she'd never see the light of day again. Maybe soon she'd never see light again — ever.

What would they do to her? *She'd saved his life.*

He should have told Amelia. Or Valentine. Should have told one of them; should have said or done something.

Valentine was growing more sober by the moment.

". . . like the other day, when she called me into her office . . . and I realized I'd forgotten my recorder." Unaware of her listener's mood, Jennifer was explaining carefully. "I'd thought about picking it up, but I wasn't sure what she wanted . . . and I hated to take it in if all she wanted was for me to run something downstairs. That's how I get. Nervous.

It's stupid, isn't it? Because she never complains about anything, Amelia doesn't. So I go in and I look at her and . . . and, without a word, she hands me this pad. Of paper. To write on."

Jennifer shook her head in a quiet memory of regret. "Because she did want to tell me some stuff — about that android and setting up a meeting with you — and I should have brought in the recorder after all. That's the way it seems to go where she's concerned. I bug up all the time, I stumble over my own feet around her . . . I feel like I do, but she never, never acts like I've done anything wrong! For the longest time, I felt like I never knew what she was talking about. I guess I'm most afraid that I'm gonna let her down when she most needs me. I worry all the time that she'll think I'm stupid or don't care. I tense up when I can't figure out what she wants or when I'm not sure I can do it. Even though I can see she's bending over backwards to make sure I don't feel that way. I guess I'm trying real hard to come to terms with that. All the faith she has in me. I figure if she's so good at everything else she does, she must be good a picking people, too."

Jennifer's blush went unnoticed by Valentine. The conversation was finally where she had intended it to be when she'd told the secretary to sit down: Jennifer was talking easily and openly about Amelia.

Except Valentine didn't understand what she was talking about.

Security quarters were in the bowels of the Commission building. That much the Doctor could recall and retain. Her room — holding cell — was at the end of a long corridor. There were doors they'd come through. Two accompanying guards who probably had taken up residence outside her own door.

God, she was tired.

Grant groaned loudly and turned on his side. The door opened immediately.

"Cramp," he complained, reaching for the man who'd entered. "Help me stand."

The silence had been undisturbed for 359 minutes. Security rounds had been reduced to an occasional curiosity glance through the plate glass lab door; and the last glance had been seventy minutes and 30 seconds ago. The novelty had worn off. Curiosity had been put to bed for now.

Victor, Dee-Dee and Dagny lay forgotten on individual metal slabs in the darkness of the deserted room. To the left of the tables, the counters were laid out with the equipment to be used for tomorrow's exploration — still called surgery by those who marveled at the seemingly endless genius of the Doctor. Tomorrow the room would be filled with activity as limbs were gently severed, internals carefully catalogued, miniscule wires delicately removed, the proceedings monitored and memorized by the scanners as well as observers.

But tonight, the large observation window looked

sightlessly down from above, overseeing only the motionless android cadavers; and there was only silence — 359 minutes and 58 seconds of hushed emptiness in a room where nothing moved, nothing breathed, nothing lived.

The fifty-ninth second of the fifty-ninth minute of the fifth hour passed into the sixtieth.

In the cool silent darkness, Dagny's eyelids lifted.

Amelia saw Jennifer's hair first. The soft, familiar paleness of it. *With Valentine!* She moved toward them with the curious feeling of reluctance and eagerness which her position as Director so often caused.

Claudia, exhausted, frowned. "Well, get a tech down! Maybe he'll give him something for the problem." She flicked off the sound and eyed the monitor grumpily. A cramp? The techs had probably overlooked something, and now she'd have to pull someone away from the party. She'd told them they could all go — leaving no one on call. She'd generously done this earlier, at the beginning of her second shift of the day, because she knew she couldn't go herself; and because it never hurt to do a few favors. You never knew when a return favor might be needed. It had been an easy slice of benevolence to dole out then, but now it was going to backfire. What was worse than playing the heavy and following the book? Bending the rules and then

mother — wisps of the all-too-familiar auburn red hair floating around the wide-eyed face — suddenly came to mind. Valentine pushed the image away. Charged blindly down another path and found herself in the living room seconds before the Doctor had attacked her.

The robot had scared her. That's why she'd shot it. She had heard it behind her, scrambling from its hiding place, a sudden frenzied threat penetrating the shroud of sanity that had finally settled over the room. She'd already been counting her mistakes: Chuck bleeding on the floor; bodies she couldn't identify, bodies in this house she hadn't known existed; the Cannies, eyes bright, watching to see what she would do next. The adrenaline had just begun to subside — she'd still been wired with tension as she took her first steps through the grim aftermath of the battle.

Turning, targeting, firing — the actions had been simultaneous.

She had felt instant annoyance when she'd realized it was only an android and it was only playing a game. *Parodying a romantic sacrifice.* She'd intuitively known what it was doing, why, and for whom.

The look on the Doctor's face had brought her weapon up to fire the second shot at the android . . . the sappy sentiment playing across the woman's face had triggered the reflexive final shot . . .

Valentine's fingers and memories stopped their momentum. She had shot that droid out of reflex.

No.

She had shot it out of instinct.

No.

242

Yes! She had destroyed it because that was her job. And she had dropped her weapon and taken on the woman who grieved for it because of her own personal — she was human, wasn't she? — anger at the years of work and danger the Doctor had put them all through with her stupid walking talking inventions.

No.

She had shot the robot — dropped her weapon, welcomed the attack — because of a split-second glimpse into her own rage . . . because of the emotion she had seen pass between the Doctor and the android.

"Good evening." To Jennifer. *Valentine's face was not right.* "I'm glad to see you're out of the hospital."

Jennifer lapsed into instant blushing silence.

The prisoner managed to hoist himself onto the examining table but not without grabbing the uniformed legs of the guards, gripping one of each for support "It's just a cramp . . . I was sound asleep and it woke me up! That's probably why it seems so bad." His fingers pinched, groped, belying the pain he was verbally suppressing.

"Claudia says they're calling a tech," the female guard told the male guard. "We put him here in Diag and one of them will be here shortly to give him something." She glanced down with sympathy at the prisoner's contorted face. The veins in his neck stood out from strain, his eyes were shut tightly, jaw clenched. A far cry from the calm model prisoner they'd dealt with since the retrieval. She leaned down as if to penetrate the closed concentration of his face. "The tech will be here in a minute," she explained carefully. "The med tech will help you."

Grant's eyes fluttered open. His fingers struggled for a better grip as he tried to rise, grasping the pockets on her uniformed leg. "No more surgery!"

The guard pushed him back down gently. "They'll do whatever they have to do. I'm sure it won't hurt. Just relax." She exchanged a quick glance of amused surprise with the second guard at this sudden display of cowardice from their infamous prisoner. Even more gently, she unpried his grasping fingers from her belt and folded his hand across his stomach.

Dagny slid her lower half over the side of the table and stood in one swift movement. She turned back to look at the tables on which her companions still lay. Pinpoints of red gleamed from her irises, uncloaking the darkness. She moved around the slab and approached the counter without hesitation. Her timed deactivation may have shut her system down so that she had no memory of the initial operations or the time since, and no sight or smell, but logic told her that what she sought would not be difficult to find.

The three units lay side by side in preparation for tomorrow's examination. She scooped up the three kernels and moved to the first table. Lifting Victor's arm, she returned the unit to the slot. It clicked in easily. Victor's eyes opened. She moved around the head of his table and lifted Dee-Dee's slender arm, clicking the tiny unit in with the same snap of her deft fingers. Almost as an afterthought, she reached an arm across her own body and inserted the last of the units. The action was unnecessary; the unit's function on her own body had already served its purpose — the shutdown timer had worked perfectly. The real control center elsewhere on her body had never been discovered.

"Won't you join us?" Jennifer's voice sounded strangely stilted to her own ears. It wasn't that she didn't mean it — she did. It was just that talking about Amelia was a lot easier than talking to her.

In a second everything had returned to normal. Valentine — the best of the elite Controllers — sitting cool and silent to her right; Amelia the Director, standing over them, surely intending only politeness while Jennifer's lack of proper protocol snagged the situation as it so often did . . .

Jennifer was relieved but not surprised when Amelia kindly sat.

The word *kindness* did not cross Valentine's mind.

Chuck managed his clothes with less difficulty than he expected. The injuries had been serious, yes; his lower back would have been burning without the pain-dulling medications applied earlier. He didn't

want to push himself — well, maybe a little . . .
determination was the only way he'd manage this —
but he had no intention of killing himself in the
process. Valentine would do that later.

Grant's eyes followed the closing of the door. The
guards would wait outside just as he had expected.
No doubt they wanted the privacy to smirk at his
overblown reaction to pain. The thought did not
bother him.

His glance took in the room cautiously, then more
quickly; it wasn't the room of earlier today, but it
was similar; and like that one, there were no security
monitors probing the interior. Just him and the
equipment, the sterilized aprons, tools, counters —
and a door leading elsewhere.

Giddily, he flexed his hand, his wrist and then
fingered the slim card that fell from his sleeve into
his palm. How many doors would it open? How long
before the guard missed it? A few minutes? Five?

An hour in Grant's world.

He twisted off the table in one fluid movement,
delivering himself to a crouch before the internal
door. It opened at a touch from the card.

"Clothes!" Dee-Dee pouted, arms covering her
bare breasts protectively. Dagny knelt before a cabinet
below the furthest counter to the right. She pushed
aside a broken fluoroscope, a dusty Ranger with a
cracked mirror, a bulky Meridian Washer Bowl with

grooves worn and dull. She reached into the dark recesses of the cabinet beyond the discarded and forgotten equipment and her fingers closed around fabric. Carefully, she pulled out the four neatly folded uniforms.

Grant moved stealthily through the dark laboratory, skirting a peculiar machine in the center, finding the door by the light filtering from the hall through the glass. It did not give. He used the card. Pulling the door back a fraction of an inch, he surveyed the corridor. His guards stood one door down. Quickly he closed the door again and studied the windowless door on the far wall. If it worked with the card it would open into an area in the opposite direction from the populated corridor. It could be only an internal storage room . . .

He moved toward it.

Jennifer sat silently, watching a couple dancing. Amelia, her arm resting on the table, sat watching the same couple.

Valentine watched Jennifer and Amelia.

No one saw him; at least, they gave him no notice. Chuck walked slowly at first, then, bolstered by the lack of discomfort, fell into his usual steady pace. When he stepped into the lobby, he met the hush of late night despite the people milling around. His Controller's uniform earned a curious glance or two, but his face meant nothing to the hospital personnel he passed.

Delighted, Grant stepped into a new hallway. Now where?

"He's in the Clinic area. They put him in Diag Three." The young woman swiveled on her stool restlessly. "A tech says he'll be here shortly. I don't need to call what's-her-name, do I?"

Claudia shook her head. "When did Griffin leave for dinner?"

The young woman glanced at her watch. "She won't be back for another fifteen minutes." Her voice held a note of expectation, her shoulders pressed forward as if ready for flight.

Claudia shrugged. "Go ahead. Go on. Bring me back a sandwich."

She glanced at the primary monitor dully. The Doctor slept soundly.

Jennifer leaned toward Amelia abruptly, motivated by a sudden gush of courage after minutes of struggle to find it. Her mouth came closer than she'd meant but she didn't pull back; her words so close to

248

Amelia's ear, their warmth burned her. "I remember," Jennifer breathed. "That was you, wasn't it? You hypnotized me, didn't you?" Her voice was low, excited, secretive.

Amelia tried to pull back, turned her head, found her face within inches of Jennifer's own. She froze, lips parted.

"I don't know how you did that," Jennifer whispered. "But I know you did. It hurt really bad before that — I was seeing stars!" She almost giggled; didn't. "As soon as I saw you there, I knew everything would be okay. I felt safe when I knew you were there. I knew you'd save me."

Amelia listened in confusion. Her secretary walked a line she did not seem to know existed. *I remember,* she'd said but there'd been no accusation, no sound of revelation. *You hypnotized me. I knew you'd save me . . . I felt safe.*

The voice was not loud enough to be overheard — even by Amelia's first officer. Amelia's thoughts clouded with confusion. What now/next/if, what should she say/do/say. Uncertainty crossed Jennifer's face.

She was making Jennifer uncomfortable with her silence. The need to correct that crashed into place as if no other priority had come into play, despite her sense only seconds before of being under siege.

"You're welcome," she said; the words from Jennifer, when combined, did constitute a thank you.

Jennifer's blue eyes sparkled. Amelia's own, still inches away, widened. Jennifer leaned forward. Amelia recoiled a millimeter, held her position.

Hot jealousy flooded into Valentine's face. The

249

sound escaped and she saw, horrified, Amelia glance in her direction, an eyebrow raising slightly in concern at the small no! of protest.

Not hearing, but encouraged by the unknown distraction, Jennifer's hand came up, touching Amelia's cheek, turning her face back toward her, as she leaned forward, pressing her mouth against the other woman's.

She held the kiss, her mouth full and soft against Amelia's. When Jennifer withdrew, Amelia felt a rush of cool air move over her face, felt an emptiness in the air, an odd gaping distance suddenly between herself and Jennifer, an instant sense of something lacking — as if the pressure of the mouth, the warmth of the face so close, the scent so tight against her that it still lingered, *belonged* to her instead of having been only a brief visit.

Valentine felt panicked. *She knew the look on Amelia's face. Had felt it on her own — when looking at the woman who was her superior.*

She rose without meaning to. Moved — only dimly aware that the tangle of legs from a chair prevented her from escaping — shoved the chair aside, the clatter lost in the din of the room.

"Thank you," Jennifer finished, oblivious to Valentine's departure in her return to shyness. She bit her lip, eyes downcast, not knowing how to make her own retreat, ecstatic and submissive now that her bravery was exhausted. "I won't keep you. I know you're busy."

Amelia turned carefully in her chair. Stood. She nodded, though Jennifer did not raise her head to receive the nod. When she walked away, she looked no more stiff than usual, her small form circling the edge of the room on her way out.

Grant shrugged into the tech coat he'd found. He walked unhurriedly. Luck was on his side. He didn't know where he was going. He didn't know what he was going to do; or rather, how he was going to do what he wanted to do. But luck had always been his best friend.

"How's she doing?" Chuck tried for all the officiousness he could muster. The woman in the Security Monitoring Room had certainly snapped up at his entrance. That was a good start.

"Uh. Fine." Claudia glanced at the monitor. "See, she's resting. She doesn't have much choice; the Director turned down her oxygen. It's life supporting, but she must be feeling pretty groggy."

"How many guards do you have on her?"

"Two." Claudia stood with her back to the monitor. "They'll be changing shortly. From the party — how come you're not there?"

He ignored her question. Watched as the door to the doctor's room opened and a female guard glanced in. Watched as the guard leaned down — what hair on that blonde! A pale cascading flow over her slender shoulders as she leaned over the prisoner, grasped a shoulder and pulled — *Pulled?*

"Were you with the group today? The ones that

got her?" Claudia was asking. Her gaze trailed over his slender frame, appreciated his blue eyes, the nice features. "What did you say your name was?"

"Chuck." He had to swallow hard to hide the guilty excitement racing through him. The other guard — another woman — had entered the room. Both women tugged at the limp body on the bed. A third person entered. A tall, narrow figure that Chuck recognized immediately. The androids! They were loose! They were in with the Doctor! He watched, breathing shallowly as Victor picked up the limp figure effortlessly and turned toward the open door, the two females in uniform already heading in that direction.

"You okay?" Claudia asked, noticing that his face had gone pale. She almost turned but was caught by his sudden grasp of her arm. "No!" he blurted out and then: "I shouldn't have come. Just wanted to make sure she was locked up." He leaned around her, his hand on the console, his body crowding hers, his head bowed. "I'm the one that was wounded today."

Claudia's arms went around him instantly. "You! What are you doing out of the hospital? My God!" She helped lower him into a chair. "You must be in terrible pain!" Her hands fluttered over him helplessly.

His glance flickered toward the monitor and the now empty cell.

Dee-Dee had to skip to keep up with Victor. Dagny walked briskly ahead of them, peering around corners, detouring them through stairwells, brushing her hands across door after door, passing each secured one, making her way downward via the mental blueprint she knew so well.

Grant was lost. He'd gone up and then down, passed through corridors and looked into empty rooms. Now he was encountering windows with sweet views of freedom, casual doors that passed into unsecured areas, tempting signs reading Cafeteria, Records, Processing, Dock, Officer's Club, Lounge, Lobby, Exit — tempting, tempting. Leaving now would be easy; nothing, in fact. He could walk out and away and vanish in minutes. They'd be pissed, yes — but not as pissed as if she were gone as well . . .

Using the card again, he let himself back through the main secured doors, retracing his steps.

Security. She was overdue to double-check security. Amelia knew this, thought it, but found herself outside, instead. The night air felt cool on her flesh. Not cool enough. She walked.

She looked up as she walked, an action unusual for her. She saw the stars not as stars but by their names and location. Knew which were satellites and which was a ship coming in low but far enough away that it appeared stationary at this distance.

She questioned the danger of what had happened to her. Found that each time she tried to examine it as a separate incident, no analysis came. The kiss and her response were outside of her experience — yet she recognized that beneath the warning of it being distracting to her purposes, it was not negative. That it had followed a sequence of which she herself had been a part. Her personality adaptation to Jennifer. Her concentration on Jennifer. How many times had she exploited such moments as the one only a few days before when she had picked up the pad of paper Jennifer had held — savoring the mist of memory it still held.

Valentine snapped her card into and out of the slot leading into Security. She was through with an impatient twist of her body and striding on, the sound of her booted feet echoing angrily behind her. Jennifer kissing Amelia was the last outrage on this miserable day. A girlish pass made under the guise of ignorance and gratitude. But to do it in front of another officer! To whisper in her ear! A civilian, a secretary, who the hell was *she*, an empty-headed frumpy subordinate whose world revolved around trivialities like dying cats . . .

As if it had been warned of her fury, the second door she encountered slid back quickly, silently as she neared it.

"I can walk!" The Doctor wriggled free, landing on the floor awkwardly. "I've got it." She smoothed her clothes, taking in the situation with the first cursory glance. "We're on second level. We've got two doors that require cards?" Her gaze sought Dagny's questioningly.

Dagny shook her head. Storing uniforms for the proverbial rainy day was one thing — an access card would have been missed.

"Damn. We'll never get out without a card." The Doctor made no attempt to move.

Dagny touched the Doctor's arm in alert only seconds before the sound of footsteps came from ahead. Almost simultaneously a heavy steel door somewhere behind them slammed.

Not that it was the kiss that bothered her. The woman — Jennifer — bothered her. The two of them together, even in thought — Jennifer and Amelia. The very idea was a joke, a mixing of the unmixable. It wasn't just officer and civilian, professional and non-professional, status and none. It was the contradiction, the differences, which should have been *opposition*. Valentine's stride slowed within a pace and stopped.

"Whoa!" Grant stopped short. "Surprise!"

The Doctor eyed him warily. "What're you doing loose?"

"I was just on my way to find you." Grant's smile seemed genuine. He held up the access card. "Think you could use one of these?"

* * * * *

"Oh no! *no-no-no* . . ." Claudia's protest became a moan. Her fingers clawed at clarity dials as if a shift in focus might repopulate the empty room on the screen. "Can't be. She cannot be gone . . . can*not* . . ."

"Damn," Chuck cleared his throat, his voice thick with guilt and excitement. "What're you going to do?"

She should get back to work. There was nothing else to do now. But Amelia continued to walk.
Vulnerabilities.

Why did the word hold such intrigue? *Because she had witnessed it in herself?* That seemed to be. Jennifer's vulnerability made her vulnerable. Jennifer's fragility made her fragile. Jennifer's existence mysteriously enriched her own. And if she had not recognized the vulnerabilities in Jennifer — would she have seen those in Valentine? *The learning never ends,* Amelia thought. *Only the teachers change.*

Even Jennifer's unpredictability triggered the same in Amelia. Like now — being here had no purpose. No responsibilities could be fulfilled here.

Still she walked.

Valentine scuffed the toe of her boot gently against the floor. She shook her head as she looked down. She could stand in this hallway replaying everything until dawn — the day, the week, her life — and it wouldn't make any more sense than the secretary worrying about the kinds of inconsequential things going wrong with her life that Valentine would never allow to go wrong in her own.

Grant slid the card in ceremoniously, withdrew it, stood back, gestured broadly as the door gave way to a rush of cool evening air. Vic, Dee-Dee, Dagny passed through, stopped, turned, waited; the Doctor turned to Grant. "You're the last person I'd want to owe," she stated firmly.

"I don't know that you do." His smile seemed genuine. "Can't remember when I've had this much fun."

Still, she hesitated. She looked to the open doorway, the three figures waiting for her. Motioned finally, a slight movement of her chin. "Go," she said quietly and then to Grant, "You, too. I've got something I have to do."

"I wouldn't think of deserting you." As far as he was concerned, she was his now. She'd been staked out, practically fitted for size.

"No . . . but if I could have the card —" They both froze as her words were sliced off by the nearby whoosh of a door; the booted footsteps that followed were unmistakable. A Controller was approaching.

Valentine stopped. She still didn't have a plan of action. Changes — was that what this was all about?

257

She needed to make some changes? She could do that. She could do anything.

What kind of changes though? *Let go . . . of what? The anger toward the woman who had given birth to her? But that was a part of her — an old and important part of her. Her own need to prove herself to such a degree that there was no alternative but for her to be the best? No matter what it took — or took from her.* Valentine frowned in confusion.

"Shit." The Doctor grabbed the card from Grant and pushed him toward the door. "Go." The shove was light, but it caught him off-guard. Grant tumbled through the open door and into Victor's arms. Dagny tossed the extra uniform packet to the Doctor, who caught it, turning, already in a race away from the approaching footsteps.

Valentine heard voices. A door.

Was her need — her ability — to excel, also holding her back? What was it about *Jennifer* that so appealed to Amelia? What was it that signified a strength of character, an individuality, a uniqueness to Amelia even in comparison to Valentine's own acknowledged skills and accomplishments? Was there an answer there? Could Valentine have overlooked something that large?

* * * * *

"Wait." Grant had no intention of losing his prize. From outside, he caught the door, preventing it from shutting. "I'm going with her! I'm coming with you!" he called, batting at Victor's hold.

The Doctor glanced back anxiously at the delay, her hand already reaching the corner of the corridor, ready to make the turn. She swung herself around it; did not look back again. Was gone.

And didn't her mother deserve the anger Valentine reserved for her? Even if that anger governed her own actions so many years later . . . The pointless shooting of the android . . . The fury against the doctor, the empty relationships and sterile beliefs that passed as her opinions along with her inability, time after time, to isolate her anger and prevent projection of it on to other subjects, situations, people . . .

Valentine felt the weakness of truth flood her legs with shocking speed, fluttering as it struggled up through the tightly wrapped coil that had nestled within her for as long as she could remember. She stepped toward the wall, touching, then leaning against it for support. Her head came back, against that wall, eyes closing as the weakness took over . . .

She had endangered herself. Fought herself. Held herself back. She had been playing out a script as programmed and rigid as one of those monsters for which she had stored so much hatred. She was as locked into her program as they were locked into theirs and the only thing she truly excelled at was denying its existence — at insisting she had written who she was instead of being able to see that it was what she feared being that really controlled her.

Grant shook off Victor's hand finally and lunged back into the hallway. Victor stepped back. The door swung shut, the androids out, Grant in. His eyes glittered with excitement. Perfect. Now she would have no one to protect her from him.

A chill of warning snapped through Valentine at the nearby slam of the heavy exterior door. Something just ahead in this section . . . How long had she been standing here since she'd heard the first sound?

Grant looked to his left and then to his right. Which way? Which way had the Doctor gone? Luck turned him toward what he believed to be that direction.

That luck turned the corner just before Grant did, bringing Valentine's weapon out of her holster a split-second before he arrived.

Epilogue

In three years I've had plenty of time to rethink the word "special."

You remember I called Amelia that. And you remember what else I said about her . . . Okay, I was a little younger then.

It's not that I'm changing my mind about Amelia — or Valentine. (She never did ask me out, by the way; I really thought she would. I guess I had her figured wrong. Actually, from what I hear she hasn't been seeing too many people lately — not like the old gossip always said she did, anyway. She seems a little different — not that I can put my finger on how. It's not like I see her much. She does seem to smile a little easier — but that could be my imagination.)

My point is — well I'm going to tell you a story, because I'm not very good at summing up things. There's some things I'd like to get across to you first.

This "change" business with the Controllers didn't mean as much as the President made it sound like it would. Not that I could see, anyway. They did start up these special squads on the police force — and those people were cadets from the Academies where they train Controllers. The public was no longer supposed to think of the Controllers strictly in terms of renegade androids, though I'll tell you something: that'll never stop completely. The name is synonymous with androids, you know?

I think in the long run, the issue that was the most talked about out of everything that happened in those couple of days — when there was trouble right here in the Commission building, and the President's son was kidnapped, and the Controllers were moved up as a Division, and Amelia was promoted as an individual, and the Doctor was captured along with all those other criminals — well, the subject of the most gossip was the escape. I know we all talked about it nonstop — all of us here at work — even though the President didn't and the media even played it down: how she got out along with her androids . . . though that guy named Grant was recaptured (by Valentine, no less) and is scheduled to stand trial for theft, kidnapping, a whole list of charges.

When you've got the President making an international big deal out of giving the Controllers, and Amelia in particular, more authority (in a world where authority means the kind of power money had in my great-grandparents' day), you wonder why a major screw-up — which had to be the least of what happened that night — could top off everything and get hardly more than a shrug. That's how it seemed to us, anyway.

We kept expecting to hear an investigation was underway, but nothing ever happened. Not that we could see anyway. Of course any investigation would have come from the office upstairs — that's right: Amelia's. The only thing that got underway was more rumors. People started connecting the incident with Agatha — if you recall that was the robot that took Amelia's assistant, I mean, secretary, hostage — but, how did that deranged robot from the laboratory go undetected? She was supposed to have been anchored (that means deprogramed, but left intact, so that they could study her malfunctions — but she couldn't act upon them. Don't ask me how they do that. Those guys down there are geniuses.) So here's a subject that was not only still extremely dangerous . . . but she's allowed to go up by herself to see the Director without any double-checking! That's weird. I know for a fact that those guys down there are real tight on procedure. You can't even get in without print checks, retina checks, and a new code every week.

I've gotta admit that I, too, thought that was strange.

There were almost as many questions going around as there was speculation as to what happened that night. How'd the Doctor's androids get reactivated? Who did that? How did the Doctor walk out of a sealed holding cell while a bunch of people from security were supposed to be watching her every move? And for that matter, how did Grant do it, too? Who had the access card and where'd they get it? What was Valentine doing back in the building — and how did she happen to capture just one of them — and where was Amelia during all of this? People said she left the party the same time as Valentine. But nobody knows where she went. The questions got stranger and stranger.

But not as strange as when I realized I had met the Doctor that night. Of course I didn't know it was the Doctor.

Let me tell you about it. (This is the story I said I was going to tell.)

I was working late. Several of us in the Decoding Department were. Things had been so hot, with the kidnapping and all, that a lot of other situations had been put on the back burner. So we were working late, running all the codes through to make sure everything would be ready for when the Controllers were ready to get back to business.

I like working at night. The building's never empty — some departments do most of their work at night, and I'm sure you've guessed by now that the Controllers are in and out of there twenty-four hours a day — still, the place feels different at night as a rule. Quieter, somehow. More relaxed. The supervisor was at that party over at the Hall, and as the Senior Decoder, I was more or less in charge, not that there was much to be in charge of.

We were doing our work and taking a few extra breaks; you know how it is in that kind of atmosphere. Especially when you know you could be at a party instead.

About 4:00 a.m., I went to the cafeteria. There were only a couple of people there. I didn't know any of them; there wasn't anything unusual about that. Like I said — night workers. Other departments. The Commission building is *very* large.

The food available at that hour is the kind where you use your ID card for retrieval as well as payment. I got some strawberry pancakes and a couple of slices of soybake and sat down at one of those little booths for two. Right away, a woman came up and asked if she could sit with me. She said she hated eating alone.

She was . . . well, this is how she looked to me: in her thirties, I guessed — forties, tops — and she had brownish hair and brown eyes and she was kind of cute. You know, personality cute, is what I mean. Even though I could tell she was older than me (she sure didn't look as ancient as they say the Doctor is though!), there wasn't a feeling of an age difference. She had a nice smile. A grin, actually. Kind of an impish little grin, as a matter of fact. The kind that makes you remember it most of all after you've met a person.

She wore a uniform. Not the kind like officers or

controllers or guards wear — just a blue uniform like half the people in the building do. A uniform that meant she belonged but who knew to what.

She seemed nice. Funny. One of those people who talk a lot, which I like — because I can be that way, too. We started in talking right away. About the kidnapping, the Doctor. Yeah. The Doctor. I said it gave me the creeps to know she was in the building. She said it gave her the creeps, too. And then we went on to other things. The usual. How the tanners in the bathroom keep getting left on until they burn up; how the vendos aren't filled often enough; how the Controllers had done it again. That kind of stuff. Like I've said before, the Controllers are *always* a big topic around here.

By the way — she did have a bandage on her left cheek, one of those little metal sets on her nose and bruises beneath her eyes. She said she'd been in a common-car accident. I didn't think twice about it. Then. You've gotta remember nobody knew she had escaped yet. The news didn't get out until the morning.

She ate two eggs over-easy while we were talking, and she drank a glass of milk. She asked me about Amelia. She seemed very interested in Amelia. I always enjoy talking about Amelia and my limited contact with her; the woman said she'd worked in the building for four years and had never even seen Amelia. That's the way it can happen. And the curiosity is always the same — which is what gets my ego going, I guess, and gets me talking about the encounters I've had.

Before I knew it, we were talking about the

Rumor. Was she or wasn't she? This is not the kind of thing you usually talk about with a stranger — even, or maybe especially, one who works in the Commission building — but it seemed natural with her. Neither of us was talking about it in a derogatory way; I guess that's what was obvious and what made the difference: we were just talking about it. She said she didn't think it could be true because that might mean Amelia was vulnerable to "that rascal the Doctor." (Her word, "rascal.") I said I didn't think it could be true either, because, even though they could probably build an android that couldn't be tampered with, the public — if they ever found out — would go crazy. They'd feel like they'd been tricked. I didn't think the President would chance that kind of controversy. Not to mention the Controllers. We had a good chuckle over that idea. Especially concerning Valentine. (She seemed pretty familiar with *her.*)

Have you ever sat and talked with someone, both of you completely agreed on everything, and yet you got the feeling that each of you was lying to the other one?

That's how that conversation felt. The part about Amelia. I thought it was because I knew I was holding back a lot of my opinions. I got the impression this woman was, too.

Aside from this lying bit — which was half me (and just a feeling), I didn't get anything else off this woman. She sure didn't strike me as psychotic or evil. I didn't feel any sense of being in danger, or of her being unpredictable. I mean we just talked — we *chatted.*

She seemed reasonably intelligent. She didn't strike me as being a super brain . . . She was nice and she was normal.

I didn't think anything more about it until I heard that the Doctor had escaped . . . Then I heard about the beating . . . and then I put the two together. I couldn't believe it. I kept going over it and over it. I just couldn't imagine that it had been her I'd been talking to. But I knew it had been.

I finally figured I'd better do something about it and I wrote it down.

It wasn't until after I read the report I'd made out, that I absolutely knew it was true. I had met her, all right.

Then I tore it up. I don't exactly know why. All I knew was — it didn't seem right to turn it in. Because, when I wrote that report, I tried to put in every single thing we talked about. (In decoding you learn quickly that the smallest fact can have great meaning.)

You remember some of the things I said we talked about? The tanners in the bathroom? The vendos? She knew about those things. She hadn't been lying when she'd said she worked in the building. She'd worked there. Or else she'd had access. Let me tell you, that was a jolt.

But so was remembering that brace thing on her nose. I knew by then why it was there. And a lot of other things started falling into place — or out of place.

It got me thinking, or maybe I should say rethinking, my opinion of Valentine — and that got me thinking about Amelia and the way Valentine acts about her; even a dimwit can see the sun rises and sets on that woman for Valentine. And then there's this other woman — the infamous Doctor — who's just about as serious a fugitive as you can get . . . and she got out. Who the hell let her out? And why was she having eggs-over-easy with me before she got her ass out of the building?

No wonder them catching her on that island had been a fluke. (Yeah, that particular rumor had gotten out.)

I could easily imagine all the possibilities this entailed. She could be tampering with the main banks, with Amelia's own computer, with private personnel files; she could be nosing in anywhere.

Which made me wonder why she'd chosen me to sit down with.

A couple of things kept going around and around in my head. That metal brace holding the Doctor's broken nose in place. Those puffy bruises beneath her eyes. Obviously that bothered me more than I can forget. A couple more smiles on Valentine's face these days doesn't change that. It's one thing to admire her because she's so impressive in that uniform; it's another to see a real person's face all bashed up by her. Kinda makes me take her more seriously than I wanted to. I felt like the Doctor had taken the time to deliver me a riddle — and though I was supposed to figure out the riddle, maybe I wasn't supposed to tell anyone else about it. Still I knew it wasn't just for me — but it felt like it was.

That's how I felt. So I didn't tell.

That's my story. It isn't just past history, mind you. I go over that conversation every day.

This may surprise you . . . but I don't feel traitorous by not having told, either. People have

269

always got to think for themselves, isn't that right? I have my feelings about Amelia, and I have my feelings about Valentine, despite that broken nose. And now I have my feelings about the Doctor, too. There's more there than meets the eye. Just like there is with Amelia. And with Valentine, too. If anybody can get in that far.

Even experienced Decoders . . . or top-of-the-line Controllers . . . can't always come up with the right answers to the riddles of life.

I have to say one more thing.

I know what you're thinking. You're wondering whether or not Amelia had something to do with the Doctor escaping. I bet you noticed that it was around that particular part of the conversation I chose to mention that I felt like the Doctor was telling me "sort-of" lies. The kind of lies I was telling. Like when you're protecting someone, or you think you are. I bet you're thinking, "Well, this Doctor person builds androids, right? — and it looks like Amelia might just be one — and if she is, she's got to be the best one ever built; and who else could have built her but the Doctor?"

And if you want to get really serious about these theories, you could start to question just why this kinda funny little woman (who has apparently never actually directly hurt anyone) is so damned wanted — as in, what if she knows and they want to keep her quiet? And why, after the Doctor was captured with so much hullabaloo, is the news of her escape treated like it's minor news? Who was protecting who? You remember who I said would have done the investigating about all of this?

Well, I don't know. If Amelia helped her to escape.

Was protecting her maker. Or other people. Or any of that stuff.

And I don't care.

And if you have to ask me why I don't care — I wouldn't know how to answer that. I just don't.

I'll tell you something else. I feel better because of it.

If I've learned nothing else in three years, maybe I've learned not to use such easy standards to judge people by. Android, human, beautiful, plain, obvious, subtle, good, bad — believe what you think you see or what you think you've heard — or feel it out for yourself. I have.

And it feels right.

And it leaves me feeling like I might just really be in love with Amelia in a way. Maybe for what she is.

Or isn't.

A few of the publications of
THE NAIAD PRESS, INC.
P.O. Box 10543 ● Tallahassee, Florida 32302
Phone (904) 539-5965
Mail orders welcome. Please include 15% postage.

PRIORITIES by Lynda Lyons 288 pp. Science fiction with a
twist.   ISBN 0-941483-66-5 $8.95

THEME FOR DIVERSE INSTRUMENTS by Jane Rule.
208 pp. Powerful romantic lesbian stories.   ISBN 0-941483-63-0   8.95

LESBIAN QUERIES by Hertz & Ertman. 112 pp. The questions
you were too embarrassed to ask.   ISBN 0-941483-67-3   8.95

CLUB 12 by Amanda Kyle Williams. 288 pp. Espionage thriller
featuring a lesbian agent!   ISBN 0-941483-64-9   8.95

DEATH DOWN UNDER by Claire McNab. 240 pp. 3rd Det.
Insp. Carol Ashton mystery.   ISBN 0-941483-39-8   8.95

MONTANA FEATHERS by Penny Hayes. 256 pp. Vivian and
Elizabeth find love in frontier Montana.   ISBN 0-941483-61-4   8.95

CHESAPEAKE PROJECT by Phyllis Horn. 304 pp. Jessie &
Meredith in perilous adventure.   ISBN 0-941483-58-4   8.95

LIFESTYLES by Jackie Calhoun. 224 pp. Contemporary Lesbian
lives and loves.   ISBN 0-941483-57-6   8.95

VIRAGO by Karen Marie Christa Minns. 208 pp. Darsen has
chosen Ginny.   ISBN 0-941483-56-8   8.95

WILDERNESS TREK by Dorothy Tell. 192 pp. Six women on
vacation learning "new" skills.   ISBN 0-941483-60-6   8.95

MURDER BY THE BOOK by Pat Welch. 256 pp. A Helen
Black Mystery. First in a series.   ISBN 0-941483-59-2   8.95

BERRIGAN by Vicki P. McConnell. 176 pp. Youthful Lesbian–
romantic, idealistic Berrigan.   ISBN 0-941483-55-X   8.95

LESBIANS IN GERMANY by Lillian Faderman & B. Eriksson.
128 pp. Fiction, poetry, essays.   ISBN 0-941483-62-2   8.95

THE BEVERLY MALIBU by Katherine V. Forrest. 288 pp. A
Kate Delafield Mystery. 3rd in a series.   ISBN 0-941483-47-9   16.95

THERE'S SOMETHING I'VE BEEN MEANING TO TELL
YOU Ed. by Loralee MacPike. 288 pp. Gay men and lesbians
coming out to their children.   ISBN 0-941483-44-4   9.95
                                         ISBN 0-941483-54-1   16.95

LIFTING BELLY by Gertrude Stein. Ed. by Rebecca Mark. 104
pp. Erotic poetry.   ISBN 0-941483-51-7   8.95
                                         ISBN 0-941483-53-3   14.95

ROSE PENSKI by Roz Perry. 192 pp. Adult lovers in a long-term
relationship.   ISBN 0-941483-37-1   8.95

AFTER THE FIRE by Jane Rule. 256 pp. Warm, human novel
by this incomparable author.   ISBN 0-941483-45-2   8.95

SUE SLATE, PRIVATE EYE by Lee Lynch. 176 pp. The gay
folk of Peacock Alley are *all* cats.   ISBN 0-941483-52-5   8.95

CHRIS by Randy Salem. 224 pp. Golden oldie. Handsome Chris
and her adventures.   ISBN 0-941483-42-8   8.95

THREE WOMEN by March Hastings. 232 pp. Golden oldie. A
triangle among wealthy sophisticates.   ISBN 0-941483-43-6   8.95

RICE AND BEANS by Valeria Taylor. 232 pp. Love and
romance on poverty row.   ISBN 0-941483-41-X   8.95

PLEASURES by Robbi Sommers. 204 pp. Unprecedented
eroticism.   ISBN 0-941483-49-5   8.95

EDGEWISE by Camarin Grae. 372 pp. Spellbinding
adventure.   ISBN 0-941483-19-3   9.95

FATAL REUNION by Claire McNab. 216 pp. 2nd Det. Inspec.
Carol Ashton mystery.   ISBN 0-941483-40-1   8.95

KEEP TO ME STRANGER by Sarah Aldridge. 372 pp. Romance
set in a department store dynasty.   ISBN 0-941483-38-X   9.95

HEARTSCAPE by Sue Gambill. 204 pp. American lesbian in
Portugal.   ISBN 0-941483-33-9   8.95

IN THE BLOOD by Lauren Wright Douglas. 252 pp. Lesbian
science fiction adventure fantasy   ISBN 0-941483-22-3   8.95

THE BEE'S KISS by Shirley Verel. 216 pp. Delicate, delicious
romance.   ISBN 0-941483-36-3   8.95

RAGING MOTHER MOUNTAIN by Pat Emmerson. 264 pp.
Furosa Firechild's adventures in Wonderland. ISBN 0-941483-35-5   8.95

IN EVERY PORT by Karin Kallmaker. 228 pp. Jessica's sexy,
adventuresome travels.   ISBN 0-941483-37-7   8.95

OF LOVE AND GLORY by Evelyn Kennedy. 192 pp. Exciting
WWII romance.   ISBN 0-941483-32-0   8.95

CLICKING STONES by Nancy Tyler Glenn. 288 pp. Love
transcending time.   ISBN 0-941483-31-2   8.95

SURVIVING SISTERS by Gail Pass. 252 pp. Powerful love
story.   ISBN 0-941483-16-9   8.95

SOUTH OF THE LINE by Catherine Ennis. 216 pp. Civil War
adventure.   ISBN 0-941483-29-0   8.95

WOMAN PLUS WOMAN by Dolores Klaich. 300 pp. Supurb
Lesbian overview.   ISBN 0-941483-28-2   9.95

SLOW DANCING AT MISS POLLY'S by Sheila Ortiz Taylor.
96 pp. Lesbian Poetry   ISBN 0-941483-30-4   7.95

DOUBLE DAUGHTER by Vicki P. McConnell. 216 pp. A Nyla
Wade Mystery, third in the series. ISBN 0-941483-26-6   8.95

HEAVY GILT by Delores Klaich. 192 pp. Lesbian detective/
disappearing homophobes/upper class gay society.
ISBN 0-941483-25-8   8.95

THE FINER GRAIN by Denise Ohio. 216 pp. Brilliant young
college lesbian novel. ISBN 0-941483-11-8   8.95

THE AMAZON TRAIL by Lee Lynch. 216 pp. Life, travel & lore
of famous lesbian author. ISBN 0-941483-27-4   8.95

HIGH CONTRAST by Jessie Lattimore. 264 pp. Women of the
Crystal Palace. ISBN 0-941483-17-7   8.95

OCTOBER OBSESSION by Meredith More. Josie's rich, secret
Lesbian life. ISBN 0-941483-18-5   8.95

LESBIAN CROSSROADS by Ruth Baetz. 276 pp. Contemporary
Lesbian lives. ISBN 0-941483-21-5   9.95

BEFORE STONEWALL: THE MAKING OF A GAY AND
LESBIAN COMMUNITY by Andrea Weiss & Greta Schiller.
96 pp., 25 illus. ISBN 0-941483-20-7   7.95

WE WALK THE BACK OF THE TIGER by Patricia A. Murphy.
192 pp. Romantic Lesbian novel/beginning women's movement.
ISBN 0-941483-13-4   8.95

SUNDAY'S CHILD by Joyce Bright. 216 pp. Lesbian athletics, at
last the novel about sports. ISBN 0-941483-12-6   8.95

OSTEN'S BAY by Zenobia N. Vole. 204 pp. Sizzling adventure
romance set on Bonaire. ISBN 0-941483-15-0   8.95

LESSONS IN MURDER by Claire McNab. 216 pp. 1st Det. Inspec.
Carol Ashton mystery — erotic tension!. ISBN 0-941483-14-2   8.95

YELLOWTHROAT by Penny Hayes. 240 pp. Margarita, bandit,
kidnaps Julia. ISBN 0-941483-10-X   8.95

SAPPHISTRY: THE BOOK OF LESBIAN SEXUALITY by
Pat Califia. 3d edition, revised. 208 pp. ISBN 0-941483-24-X   8.95

CHERISHED LOVE by Evelyn Kennedy. 192 pp. Erotic
Lesbian love story. ISBN 0-941483-08-8   8.95

LAST SEPTEMBER by Helen R. Hull. 208 pp. Six stories & a
glorious novella. ISBN 0-941483-09-6   8.95

THE SECRET IN THE BIRD by Camarin Grae. 312 pp. Striking,
psychological suspense novel. ISBN 0-941483-05-3   8.95

TO THE LIGHTNING by Catherine Ennis. 208 pp. Romantic
Lesbian 'Robinson Crusoe' adventure. ISBN 0-941483-06-1   8.95

THE OTHER SIDE OF VENUS by Shirley Verel. 224 pp.
Luminous, romantic love story. ISBN 0-941483-07-X   8.95

EACH HAND A MAP by Anita Skeen. 112 pp. Real-life poems
that touch us all. ISBN 0-930044-82-7   6.95

SURPLUS by Sylvia Stevenson. 342 pp. A classic early Lesbian
novel. ISBN 0-930044-78-9   7.95

PEMBROKE PARK by Michelle Martin. 256 pp. Derring-do
and daring romance in Regency England. ISBN 0-930044-77-0   7.95

THE LONG TRAIL by Penny Hayes. 248 pp. Vivid adventures
of two women in love in the old west. ISBN 0-930044-76-2   8.95

HORIZON OF THE HEART by Shelley Smith. 192 pp. Hot
romance in summertime New England. ISBN 0-930044-75-4   7.95

AN EMERGENCE OF GREEN by Katherine V. Forrest. 288
pp. Powerful novel of sexual discovery. ISBN 0-930044-69-X   8.95

THE LESBIAN PERIODICALS INDEX edited by Claire
Potter. 432 pp. Author & subject index. ISBN 0-930044-74-6   29.95

DESERT OF THE HEART by Jane Rule. 224 pp. A classic;
basis for the movie *Desert Hearts*. ISBN 0-930044-73-8   7.95

SPRING FORWARD/FALL BACK by Sheila Ortiz Taylor.
288 pp. Literary novel of timeless love. ISBN 0-930044-70-3   7.95

FOR KEEPS by Elisabeth Nonas. 144 pp. Contemporary novel
about losing and finding love. ISBN 0-930044-71-1   7.95

TORCHLIGHT TO VALHALLA by Gale Wilhelm. 128 pp.
Classic novel by a great Lesbian writer. ISBN 0-930044-68-1   7.95

LESBIAN NUNS: BREAKING SILENCE edited by Rosemary
Curb and Nancy Manahan. 432 pp. Unprecedented autobiographies
of religious life. ISBN 0-930044-62-2   9.95

THE SWASHBUCKLER by Lee Lynch. 288 pp. Colorful novel
set in Greenwich Village in the sixties. ISBN 0-930044-66-5   8.95

MISFORTUNE'S FRIEND by Sarah Aldridge. 320 pp. Historical Lesbian novel set on two continents. ISBN 0-930044-67-3   7.95

A STUDIO OF ONE'S OWN by Ann Stokes. Edited by
Dolores Klaich. 128 pp. Autobiography. ISBN 0-930044-64-9   7.95

SEX VARIANT WOMEN IN LITERATURE by Jeannette
Howard Foster. 448 pp. Literary history. ISBN 0-930044-65-7   8.95

A HOT-EYED MODERATE by Jane Rule. 252 pp. Hard-hitting
essays on gay life; writing; art. ISBN 0-930044-57-6   7.95

INLAND PASSAGE AND OTHER STORIES by Jane Rule.
288 pp. Wide-ranging new collection. ISBN 0-930044-56-8   7.95

WE TOO ARE DRIFTING by Gale Wilhelm. 128 pp. Timeless
Lesbian novel, a masterpiece. ISBN 0-930044-61-4   6.95

AMATEUR CITY by Katherine V. Forrest. 224 pp. A Kate
Delafield mystery. First in a series. ISBN 0-930044-55-X   8.95

THE SOPHIE HOROWITZ STORY by Sarah Schulman. 176
pp. Engaging novel of madcap intrigue.   ISBN 0-930044-54-1   7.95

THE BURNTON WIDOWS by Vickie P. McConnell. 272 pp. A
Nyla Wade mystery, second in the series.   ISBN 0-930044-52-5   7.95

OLD DYKE TALES by Lee Lynch. 224 pp. Extraordinary
stories of our diverse Lesbian lives.   ISBN 0-930044-51-7   8.95

DAUGHTERS OF A CORAL DAWN by Katherine V. Forrest.
240 pp. Novel set in a Lesbian new world.   ISBN 0-930044-50-9   8.95

THE PRICE OF SALT by Claire Morgan. 288 pp. A milestone
novel, a beloved classic.   ISBN 0-930044-49-5   8.95

AGAINST THE SEASON by Jane Rule. 224 pp. Luminous,
complex novel of interrelationships.   ISBN 0-930044-48-7   8.95

LOVERS IN THE PRESENT AFTERNOON by Kathleen
Fleming. 288 pp. A novel about recovery and growth.
                                          ISBN 0-930044-46-0   8.95

TOOTHPICK HOUSE by Lee Lynch. 264 pp. Love between
two Lesbians of different classes.   ISBN 0-930044-45-2   7.95

MADAME AURORA by Sarah Aldridge. 256 pp. Historical
novel featuring a charismatic "seer."   ISBN 0-930044-44-4   7.95

CURIOUS WINE by Katherine V. Forrest. 176 pp. Passionate
Lesbian love story, a best-seller.   ISBN 0-930044-43-6   8.95

BLACK LESBIAN IN WHITE AMERICA by Anita Cornwell.
141 pp. Stories, essays, autobiography.   ISBN 0-930044-41-X   7.95

CONTRACT WITH THE WORLD by Jane Rule. 340 pp.
Powerful, panoramic novel of gay life.   ISBN 0-930044-28-2   9.95

MRS. PORTER'S LETTER by Vicki P. McConnell. 224 pp.
The first Nyla Wade mystery.   ISBN 0-930044-29-0   7.95

TO THE CLEVELAND STATION by Carol Anne Douglas.
192 pp. Interracial Lesbian love story.   ISBN 0-930044-27-4   6.95

THE NESTING PLACE by Sarah Aldridge. 224 pp. A
three-woman triangle—love conquers all!   ISBN 0-930044-26-6   7.95

THIS IS NOT FOR YOU by Jane Rule. 284 pp. A letter to a
beloved is also an intricate novel.   ISBN 0-930044-25-8   8.95

FAULTLINE by Sheila Ortiz Taylor. 140 pp. Warm, funny,
literate story of a startling family.   ISBN 0-930044-24-X   6.95

THE LESBIAN IN LITERATURE by Barbara Grier. 3d ed.
Foreword by Maida Tilchen. 240 pp. Comprehensive bibliography.
Literary ratings; rare photos.   ISBN 0-930044-23-1   7.95

ANNA'S COUNTRY by Elizabeth Lang. 208 pp. A woman
finds her Lesbian identity.   ISBN 0-930044-19-3   6.95

PRISM by Valerie Taylor. 158 pp. A love affair between two
women in their sixties.   ISBN 0-930044-18-5   6.95

BLACK LESBIANS: AN ANNOTATED BIBLIOGRAPHY
compiled by J. R. Roberts. Foreword by Barbara Smith. 112 pp.
Award-winning bibliography.   ISBN 0-930044-21-5   5.95

THE MARQUISE AND THE NOVICE by Victoria Ramstetter.
108 pp. A Lesbian Gothic novel.   ISBN 0-930044-16-9   6.95

OUTLANDER by Jane Rule. 207 pp. Short stories and essays
by one of our finest writers.   ISBN 0-930044-17-7   8.95

ALL TRUE LOVERS by Sarah Aldridge. 292 pp. Romantic
novel set in the 1930s and 1940s.   ISBN 0-930044-10-X   7.95

A WOMAN APPEARED TO ME by Renee Vivien. 65 pp. A
classic; translated by Jeannette H. Foster.   ISBN 0-930044-06-1   5.00

CYTHEREA'S BREATH by Sarah Aldridge. 240 pp. Romantic
novel about women's entrance into medicine.
                                       ISBN 0-930044-02-9   6.95

TOTTIE by Sarah Aldridge. 181 pp. Lesbian romance in the
turmoil of the sixties.   ISBN 0-930044-01-0   6.95

THE LATECOMER by Sarah Aldridge. 107 pp. A delicate love
story.   ISBN 0-930044-00-2   6.95

ODD GIRL OUT by Ann Bannon.   ISBN 0-930044-83-5   5.95

I AM A WOMAN by Ann Bannon.   ISBN 0-930044-84-3   5.95

WOMEN IN THE SHADOWS by Ann Bannon.
                                       ISBN 0-930044-85-1   5.95

JOURNEY TO A WOMAN by Ann Bannon.
                                       ISBN 0-930044-86-X   5.95

BEEBO BRINKER by Ann Bannon.   ISBN 0-930044-87-8   5.95
        Legendary novels written in the fifties and sixties,
               set in the gay mecca of Greenwich Village.

VOLUTE BOOKS

JOURNEY TO FULFILLMENT   Early classics by Valerie   3.95

A WORLD WITHOUT MEN   Taylor: The Erika Frohmann   3.95

RETURN TO LESBOS   series.   3.95

These are just a few of the many Naiad Press titles — we are the oldest and
largest lesbian/feminist publishing company in the world. Please request a
complete catalog. We offer personal service; we encourage and welcome
direct mail orders from individuals who have limited access to bookstores
carrying our publications.